LONDON

By the Author

McCall

London

Innis Harbor

The First Kiss

Wild Wales

Laying of Hands

Return to McCall

Visit us at www.boldstrokesbooks.com

LONDON

by
Patricia Evans

2024

LONDON
© 2024 By Patricia Evans. All Rights Reserved.

ISBN 13: 978-1-63679-778-6

This Trade Paperback Original Is Published By
Bold Strokes Books, Inc.
P.O. Box 249
Valley Falls, NY 12185

First Edition: November 2024

THIS IS A WORK OF FICTION. NAMES, CHARACTERS, PLACES, AND INCIDENTS ARE THE PRODUCT OF THE AUTHOR'S IMAGINATION OR ARE USED FICTITIOUSLY. ANY RESEMBLANCE TO ACTUAL PERSONS, LIVING OR DEAD, BUSINESS ESTABLISHMENTS, EVENTS, OR LOCALES IS ENTIRELY COINCIDENTAL.

THIS BOOK, OR PARTS THEREOF, MAY NOT BE REPRODUCED IN ANY FORM WITHOUT PERMISSION.

Credits
Editor: Stacia Seaman
Production Design: Stacia Seaman
Cover Design by Tammy Seidick

LONDON

Chapter One

She knew who it was before Victoria had even finished rocketing her name across the men's department of Selfridges.

"Jacqui Bailey...Is that you?"

Jaq had a feeling when she'd tipped her triple espresso into her lap that morning that something bad was going to happen, and so far, that spill had been the best part of the day. She'd just ducked into Selfridges on her lunch break to buy another pair of pants, and of course, at that exact moment, Victoria Barton was searching through the silk ties.

"I can't believe it. I haven't seen you since graduation!" She paused, giving Jaq a full sweep with her eyes. "Still shopping in the men's section, I see."

"Good morning, Victoria," Jaq said, leaning into Victoria's trademark double air-kiss. "Lovely to see you."

"What are you doing back in London?" she said, looking Jaq up and down. "I thought you went back to Oklahoma or Kansas or something."

"Texas. Austin, Texas."

"Still looking as dashing as ever," she said, standing an inch too close and dropping her voice to a whisper. "Now, why is it that we never got together in school?"

"I can't remember," Jaq said with a slow smile, "but it was obviously my loss."

"Well," she said, flicking her hair over her shoulder, "you've lost your chance now. I'm getting married on Saturday." She stopped, then cranked the volume up several notches. "Wait, Jacqui, you simply must be there!"

She handed Jaq her purse to hold and dug around in the pockets of her coat for her cell phone.

"Okay," she said, leaving her holding the large, very pink bag. "Now, where can I send the invitation? I'll have it couriered so it arrives this very afternoon."

"You can send it to my office. I'm in the Curtis Green Building, Victoria Embankment. The courier can just leave it at the front desk, they'll get it to me."

Victoria typed at lightning speed and dropped her phone back into her bag, finally taking it from Jaq and pushing it back onto her shoulder. "Promise me you'll come?" She pulled Jaq into an air-kiss goodbye and squeezed her shoulder. "Now that I know you're back in London, it simply wouldn't be the same if you weren't there."

Her heels clicked a steady rhythm down the tile floor, then stopped. Jaq turned back around.

"You know Bronwyn Charles is coming, of course." Victoria paused long enough to get the reaction she was hoping for, then turned the corner and clicked out of sight.

Later that afternoon, Jaq leaned back in her chair and looked at the invitation that had just landed on her desk like the explosive device it was.

Bronwyn Charles.

Even at twenty-nine, she still had nightmares about that night. Waking up to the key turning in the lock of their dorm room, blinding flashlights shining in their eyes, Bronwyn's mother shouting, and then feeling Bronwyn's warm body ripped from her arms.

Jaq shook her head and picked up the invitation.

Great, she muttered, *it's in Northumberland.*

Northumberland was nearly seven hours away, closer to Scotland than Jaq was to the sandwich cart downstairs. The location effectively turned the hour-long wedding she'd agreed to into a weekend-long affair. Wait, scratch that, it was a bank holiday weekend, so possibly even longer. Fabulous.

❖

"You're not wearing that, Bronwyn. You'll embarrass your father."

Elizabeth Charles, Bronwyn's mother, was standing in the mahogany and mirror-lined dressing area reserved for Selfridges clients working with personal shoppers. She sank into the ivory velvet chaise along the wall and pointed at the mirror.

"You look like a poof, darling, it's shameful." She fanned her face with a brochure from the side table and looked at her daughter with a raised eyebrow. "Although maybe that's what you're going for. I wouldn't know."

"Seriously, Mother," Bronwyn said, whipping her head around to look directly at her. "I don't remotely resemble a gay man, although I might look better if I did." Bronwyn paused to lower her voice and take a deep breath. "And you cannot refer to anyone as a 'poof.' I've told you that a thousand times."

Bronwyn looked in the mirror again at the dove gray and charcoal suit. The shape was masculine, but it was a Stella McCartney design and cut for a woman. But it wasn't quite right. It needed something more than just the black stilettos she planned to wear with it.

Her personal shopper, Andrew, swept back into the dressing area just then and stood behind Bronwyn, looking with her into the three-way mirror.

"It's not doing you justice, is it?"

"Quite right," Bronwyn said in her soft West London accent, still staring with him into the mirror. "But I can't work out what it is."

Andrew stepped to the side of the mirror and looked again. "It's the shirt."

"Well, thank God," her mum said, rolling her eyes as if to ask for strength from the patron saint of homophobic mothers. "Finally someone has the good sense to put you in a decent silk blouse."

"Actually," Andrew said with a wink at Bronwyn in the mirror, "lose the shirt completely and put the stilettos on. Let's pin the legs all the way down to pull in the fit and see what that does."

Bronwyn took the blouse off in the dressing room and slid the jacket back over her bare shoulders.

"Andrew?" she said from behind the door. "Bra or no bra?"

"No bra, darling. This is no time to ruin the line of that gorgeous suit with unnecessary layers."

"Bronwyn, this is your mother." Elizabeth spat out the words at a startlingly high volume, as if Bronwyn was suddenly hearing impaired and might have forgotten who was on the other side of the door. "You are wearing a decent blouse to that wedding. And I've had enough of this nonsense. I'll be at the bar on the fourth floor. Have someone fetch me when you're finished."

Bronwyn waited until she heard the door shut behind her to step out of the dressing room and onto the platform in front of the mirrors. The stilettos changed the entire look, giving her legs a clean, long line, and the jacket now came together in a deep V shape that showed the perfect amount of skin.

"Wow," she said, turning slightly to either side in the mirror. "You're a genius. This is perfect."

Andrew folded and pinned the extra fabric all the way down her legs to the hem, then nipped in two inches off the waist. Bronwyn tilted her head in the mirror and looked at herself from the side.

"You don't think that smaller waist is going to make it look too girly?"

"Not at all," Andrew said with pins in his mouth, motioning for her to turn her back around. "You've always had that sexy androgynous thing going for you. We're just playing up those angles and giving it a little edge."

Bronwyn turned and kissed Andrew on the cheek. She'd been lucky enough to meet him a few years prior and hadn't shopped without him since. Her mother was always pushing her to wear more feminine clothes, which she did for the most part, but occasionally, she wore something she liked, and this was one of those times.

Andrew was always telling her she needed to forget everyone else and wear what she loved. Perhaps he was right.

"Thanks, love," she said, starting to unbutton the jacket. "I may actually survive this wedding thanks to you."

Andrew laughed and added one more pin to the hem of her trousers. "Well, maybe me and a large vodka tonic. Stay far away from your mum and tell me all about the sexy butches at the reception next time I see you."

"Not that there's ever any of those," she said, smiling. "But if there are, you'll be the first one to know it."

Bronwyn stepped back into the dressing room and handed her suit out to Andrew for tailoring, then sat down on the overstuffed bench next to the mirror, twisting the diamond band on her finger. Something about this wedding had her unsettled, which was not a good sign when her own was only three months away.

❖

Jaq shoved her bag onto the luggage rails and settled into the only empty double seat on the train to Northumberland, hopeful that no one would need the seat next to her. She wasn't in the mood to make small talk, not that she ever had been. Even as a kid, she stayed in her room with the door shut as much as possible. Her mother waitressed at a truck stop down the highway most nights, and by the time Jaq left for school in the morning, she was usually already asleep on the couch, the trailer door still ajar, and her purse limp on the floor beside her.

Jaq always looked around for her as she left for school because if her mom was in her room with the door closed, that meant she had company. And that meant they'd probably still be there when she got home in the afternoon. The trailer always smelled different when there was someone else there. Cigarette smoke, sweat, and forgotten ash crowded every breath of air when she opened the door. After a few years, she'd learned just to crawl through her window at the back of the trailer if her mom had someone over. She still had a

• 13 •

scar on the heel of her hand from where she'd sliced it on the sharp aluminum windowsill when she was ten.

Everything changed the summer she turned fourteen. Her school had started summer classes for kids who needed extra help, and since Jaq didn't have anywhere to be, she asked one of the teachers, Miss Stowe, if she could sit in with the math class she was teaching. Technically, there was supposed to be a charge for the summer classes, but Jaq didn't mention it, and Miss Stowe didn't either.

The first day was slow, but it was better than being at home. Miss Stowe wrote a single problem on the chalkboard and everyone was supposed to solve it. Numbers were the only thing Jaq had ever understood, so she solved it right away, then broke it down into other, more complex combinations. She painted them into equations to match the ones in her head, like an artist left alone in a room with a blank canvas. By the end of the class, the new spiral notebook Miss Stowe had let her borrow that morning was more than half filled, the pages crumpled and stiff with the density of the penciled equations.

As the class ended and everyone shuffled out, Jaq realized she'd used way more paper than Miss Stowe had probably wanted to lend her. Everyone else had only used two or three pages at the most, and Jaq had used up half of a new spiral notebook. The only option she had at that point was to give it back to Miss Stowe and offer to bring her a new one, although that wasn't an option at all, really. School supplies weren't high on her mom's priority list.

She handed it back to Miss Stowe after everyone else left the room.

"Sorry about your notebook," Jaq said, not quite meeting her eyes. "I'll bring paper next time."

She took it and flipped through the pages slowly, which made Jaq nervous, and she glanced at the door, but she knew it would be rude to leave before Miss Stowe said something. She stood there while Miss Stowe flipped through several more pages, then started to thumb through the rest, the paper creating a breeze that moved a delicate lock of blond hair across her forehead.

"Do you have any other books with you?" Miss Stowe said, looking behind Jaq at the surface of her desk. It was empty; she'd only brought a pencil, and that was in her pocket. "Or a cell phone?"

Jaq shook her head. "I don't have a cell phone."

The industrial clock on the wall ticked off the seconds through an invisible megaphone.

Miss Stowe looked up and locked eyes with Jaq. "How do you know how to do all this?"

Jaq dropped her eyes; she'd asked the question but didn't seem like she expected an answer, so Jaq didn't give her one. She started to walk toward the door but the teacher stopped her, closing the notebook and looking at Jaq again for a few seconds before she spoke.

"Jacqueline, can you come to class early tomorrow? About a half hour?"

She just said yes and closed the door behind her. The walk back to the trailer would take more than an hour, and it was time to get home.

❖

"Mum, I know you hate to drive with Daddy," Bronwyn said, trying to finish her packing both quickly and silently since she'd just told her mother she'd already driven halfway up the northern countryside on the way to the wedding. "But just make sure he doesn't have any sandwiches with him and you'll be fine."

Bertrand Charles loved to enjoy a sandwich or three on a long drive, almost always dropping pickles and assorted relishes in his lap, mostly because it annoyed his ex-wife. He'd offered to give Bronwyn's mum a ride to Northumberland, and she'd accepted against her better judgment.

"No." Bronwyn sighed. "I cannot turn around and come get you. It's a seven-hour drive and we'd be driving all night."

Bronwyn carefully hung the suit she'd wear to the wedding the next day in a garment bag and draped it over her arm, lugging the suitcase as quietly as possible down the stairs and into her front hall.

• 15 •

"I do have to go now, Mum, traffic is dreadful. I'll see you at the wedding tomorrow."

Bronwyn clicked her phone off before her mother could protest and picked up her purse from the hall table, pulling the door shut behind her. She tossed everything into her blue Citroën and paused to look in the rearview mirror before she backed out. Truth be told, she looked a mess, but thankfully she wouldn't see anyone tonight anyway; it would be half seven before she even arrived. A glance into the rearview mirror reminded her she'd need to go straight to her room and avoid the hotel bar completely, where everyone she knew from school would be holding martinis aloft and shredding each other into ribbons with the gossip they hid under their breath. Her dark hair was defiantly shedding its ponytail, and because of the rush, her pale skin was flushed a ridiculous pink. She'd stopped wearing much makeup after high school but still wore a soft, imperfect smudge of dark gray liner and inky mascara that brought out her light green eyes. Jaq had told her once, as they were lying in bed, that they were the color of the forest floor shot through with sunlight.

Bronwyn shook her head as if to clear the image of Jaq from her mind. There was no use thinking about that now—she needed to get on with things. She should be missing Ian, her fiancé, not wasting her time pining for the girl who had forgotten her years before. After the night her mother burst into their dorm room in the middle of the night and pulled her out of Jaq's arms, she'd insisted that Bronwyn pack her things and had taken her out of Stratford Academy the next day. They'd just wedged the last of her bags into her mother's car when she saw Jaq striding across the parking lot toward her. Jaq's eyes were intense, locked onto hers, and as she got closer, Bronwyn felt the rest of the world cracking and falling away, leaving just her and the girl she loved. When she reached the car, Jaq slid her hand strong around the back of Bronwyn's neck and pulled her into a kiss that lasted until her mother's threats reached an alarming pitch. Jaq's hands were warm against her cheeks as she pressed her forehead to Bronwyn's and took a breath. Then she was gone.

Bronwyn completed the last half of the term at home, and Jaq had graduated by the time she returned to Stratford. Her heart still ached when she remembered the endless nights she'd spent pouring her heart out into the letters she'd sent every day until the term ended. She'd waited every afternoon for the post to come through the door until the last few weeks, when she knew in her heart nothing would be there and it was just too painful to be right.

Just as the London skyline disappeared behind her, her mobile rang. She tossed it into the passenger's seat and let it go to voicemail. Ian refused to come to the wedding, so why couldn't he just let her get on with it? He'd started to get possessive the instant he'd slid the diamond on her finger; suddenly, she'd become one of his investments and he was aggressively protecting his interests. His behavior aside, the truth was, she was avoiding his calls because she knew he was going to ask about the wedding dress fitting she'd canceled at the last minute that morning. She didn't know why she'd done it. But she knew she didn't want to talk about it.

Their relationship wasn't bad. In fact, it was quite good in all the ways one could see from the outside. He was in banking, corporate investments, and had a bright future with one of the top London firms. He was tall, with beautiful blue eyes and great hair. And perhaps more importantly, all of her friends were already married, most having children, yet she was somehow an old maid at twenty-eight. Well, perhaps that was a bit harsh. Her mother could have meant something else entirely when she reminded her twice last week that her chances of actually keeping anyone interested were decreasing by the day.

Bronwyn shook the thought out of her head, rattled around in the glove compartment until she found a protein bar, and ripped it open with her teeth. Ian was perfect on paper. But she couldn't shake the dread constantly in the center of her chest. The instant she opened her eyes in the morning it settled over her, smothering her, stealing her breath. It must just be the wedding. She was running out of time to figure it out and needed this weekend away to get her head around it. His constant presence was doing her head in. She'd never been head over heels in love with him, but this sense of unshakeable dread didn't make sense, even to Bronwyn. Things had happened, but everyone had their faults. He had a temper, but they'd been together for three years, he was perfect husband material, and the sex wasn't terrible. It wasn't anything she thought about the next day or even remembered the day after that, but that's just real life, isn't it? Sex in a long-term relationship isn't fireworks. It just isn't.

    Bronwyn rolled down her window to clear her head with the fresh, late September air. She'd always loved the drive into the northern countryside. The green rolling hills looked like velvet against the bright blue sky, and a smattering of trees in fiery shades of orange and scarlet unfurled like a ribbon between them. As she rolled up her window, she amused herself with the thought of how horrified her mother would be if she knew Bronwyn had just unhooked her bra, pulled it out through the sleeve of her shirt, and tossed it in the back seat.

❖

    Jaq slipped out of the trailer before dawn the next morning and walked toward the highway. She'd found a stack of old papers at the back of the TV console the night before and spent an hour sifting through them, looking for the ones with the printing on just one side. She'd stapled them together to make a notebook for class so that she didn't have to borrow one from Miss Stowe. It actually looked pretty decent in the end, or at least decent enough, which was the same thing.

    She walked along the side of the highway with a hoodie pulled up to cover her face and a coat over that. She took long, aggressive steps and kept her eyes in front of her. She'd learned a long time ago that if you looked like a girl, the wrong people would pull their cars over to the side of the road.

    The morning was bright yellow by the time she got to the school, so she let herself in and walked down the wide, shiny hall to Miss Stowe's classroom. The door scraped the floor as she opened it and she froze in the doorway, the door falling heavy against her back. There were three people in the room. One was Miss Stowe;

the other two she'd never seen, but they dressed as if they were important.

"Jacqueline," Miss Stowe said, smiling and waving her over to one of the groups of student desks where they were all sitting. "This is Dr. Benson and Dr. Carver. They both teach at universities here in Austin, and I've asked them here to find out a little more about what you're doing with your numbers."

Jaq nodded and slipped into one of the student desks. The man got up and started writing on the board.

"I'm going to put a problem here on the chalkboard, Jacqueline, and then you can try and solve it." He smiled at her over his shoulder, and the strangeness of all this began to settle in her stomach. "If you can't solve it, no big deal, just tackle the parts of it that you recognize."

He put the chalk down and sat back down in one of the student desks. Jaq walked up to the board and studied it for a few seconds, then erased the problem and started to rewrite it in the far upper left corner of the chalkboard.

"If that one was too much to start with," she heard the man's voice behind her, "I can give you a different one."

There wasn't anything to say, so she didn't. He'd just taken up too much room on the board. She started writing, and solving, and shattering the equation like cold glass before she pieced it back together into something different. She manipulated the numbers until they became what she wanted, then spun them quickly into an unexpected direction, following them around the perimeter of the board. It took her less than five minutes to fill almost every inch of the available space. Suddenly she was aware again that there were other people in the room and finished quickly in the tiny blank borders she'd left around the edges of the chalkboard. Jaq turned around when she ran out of room, unsure whether to sit or stay standing. She put the chalk down and dug her fingernails into the palm of her other hand, waiting. The adults were all looking at each other but no one was talking. Finally, someone cleared their throat and spoke.

The next few months were a blur. Jaq was given a full scholarship to a prestigious secondary school in England, the Stratford Academy in London, which turned out to be Dr. Benson's alma mater. When she stepped off the plane into Gatwick Airport, her life changed in an instant. She had most of the same classes as the other students but started to work with math professors at the university level and beyond just days after she arrived. In three months, she'd completed university physics and maintained both her regular classes and an increasing number of Oxford University courses over the rest of the year. For the first few months, she woke up desperate every day to soak it all in before someone snatched it away. Then slowly, as months turned into years, she started to relax. Until life exploded again into a million shimmering pieces the day she met the girl with eyes like the forest.

Chapter Two

Rain pelted Bronwyn's windshield from every direction and traffic slowed to a crawl. The wedding wasn't actually until the next day, Saturday afternoon, but she'd hoped to be in her suite at the hotel by now, chin deep in a hot bath. She should have been in Northumberland by six, but she was miles away, and it was half seven already. The rain was still coming down in angry gray sheets, and finally Bronwyn just took one of the exits outside of town, hoping to find a way to circumvent the bumper-to-bumper traffic moving slower by the minute. Unfortunately, every dark road looked the same, and streetlights were few and far between. They all seemed to end at yet another pasture, and except for a few pubs and family homes, she couldn't see anything that even gave her an idea where she was. She tossed her phone back into her bag and pulled over to the side of the road to decide what to do. Thoughts of a hot bath and a brandy were fading fast.

Not long ago, she'd passed a country pub and wondered now if she should just pack it in and see if they rented rooms as well. The rain started to pelt her window from a different direction and a sudden crack of thunder that sounded as if it was in the back seat jolted her into a decision. She'd drive back to the pub and see if they had any rooms going spare. At least she'd get to have a decent meal, and she was close enough to the city to drive in early tomorrow and get settled into her hotel for the rest of the weekend.

Bronwyn turned the key and shifted into first, then second. The car went nowhere, and Bronwyn leaned back in her seat and slowly rubbed her temples. She didn't need to get out of the car to know that her wheels were spinning, but a brief look out the door confirmed her fate. Pulling over to the side of the road must have sunk the tires into the mud, then she'd spun herself deeper trying to get out of the ruts. She opened her door again and stepped out, instantly drenched by the cold rain. The crescent moon was just visible through the treetops, and a spotted owl swooped overhead and disappeared into the darkness. She'd freeze if she kept standing out here in the storm like an idiot, and the only other option was down the road, so she gathered her bags and locked up the car. She trailed the suitcase behind her as she walked down the center of the road, slicked black with rain. Thankfully, she wasn't far from the pub she'd seen earlier, The Dog and Gun, and it soon came into view as she crested the hill. By the time she got there, she was soaking wet and chilled through, and the warmth of the pub as she opened the door felt like heaven. It was a proper country pub, with crackling fireplaces and laughter from every corner. There was a beautiful antique bar with a mirrored wall behind it, which seemed like the place to inquire about accommodation.

"Pardon me," she said when she caught the barmaid's eye, suddenly very aware she was dragging her soaked luggage behind her. "Would you have any vacancies for tonight?"

She went to check with the owner, so Bronwyn stepped over to the closest fireplace to shake some of the water out of her hair and warm her hands. She'd worn jeans and fussy flats for the drive, but underneath she had only a silk shirt, and she was still shivering under her wet wool coat. The scent of roasted meat warmed the air, and Bronwyn spotted a gentleman in the corner tucking into an undeniably beautiful dish of bangers and mash, which reminded her that aside from what she'd found in the glove box, she hadn't eaten all day.

The barmaid walked over to the fire, carrying a small glass of brandy.

"I'm afraid we're fully booked for this evening," she said, handing her the glass, "but you're welcome to stay here by the fire for as long as you'd like."

Bronwyn tried to pay her for the brandy, but she kindly refused, telling her again to linger as long as she wanted. Bronwyn thanked her and sank down in the chair closest to the fire, running a hand through the damp length of her hair.

"You're welcome to share my table if you'd like."

The voice was low, husky as if the edges of it had been charred and splintered. Bronwyn's stomach dropped as she turned around to see Jaq Bailey getting up from the small oak booth in the corner. Jaq was taller than she remembered, slender, with broad shoulders and sharper angles to her face. Her dark hair was short now, cut close in the back with longer layers in front that she ran her hand through as she walked over to Bronwyn.

"Oh my God," Bronwyn said, as if she was speaking to herself. "I can't believe it's you."

Jaq laughed and pushed up the sleeves of her gray plaid shirt, the muscles in her forearms flexing as she picked up Bronwyn's bags.

"Care to join me?"

Bronwyn just nodded, following her to the booth and sinking down opposite Jaq. She slid her coat off her shoulders and remembered too late that her bra was in the back seat of her car and her silk blouse was still damp and very sheer.

"Why don't you go up to my room and dry off," Jaq said, pulling the key from the pocket of her jeans and sliding it across the table to Bronwyn. "There's a wool sweater on the bed that might help you get warmed up."

Bronwyn took it and got up from the table, still in shock. The barmaid pointed to the stairs, and she soon found Jaq's room and let herself in. She took the sweater off the bed and locked herself in the bathroom. She'd finally seen Jaq again, and she looked like a drowning victim pulled from the Thames. Of course. Her one consolation was that she'd had the sense to take her purse, so at the very least she had a brush and some makeup with her.

Five minutes later, she'd blown her hair dry with the dryer she found attached to the wall, washed her face, and applied a touch of mascara and some charcoal liner around her eyes. Jaq's green wool

• 23 •

sweater was at least two sizes too big for her, but she rolled the sleeves up on her way back down the stairs. When she got back to the table, Jaq had ordered her a Guinness.

"I didn't know what you'd like to eat, so I just ordered you what I'm having."

"What are you having?"

"Steak pie with a side of mash."

"Thank God," Bronwyn said, leaning back against the wooden wall of the booth. "That sounds like heaven."

Jaq took her in for a moment, then met Bronwyn's eyes. Her voice was softer when she finally spoke.

"It's good to see you. You look beautiful."

Bronwyn looked down at Jaq's hands. They'd always been bigger than Bronwyn's, square, with long, masculine fingers. Bronwyn had always loved them, even before she knew why. She looked up at Jaq and held her eyes for a second too long. The words fell out of her mouth and scattered across the table before she could catch them.

"And you look sexy as hell."

Jaq laughed at that, her eyes sparkling as she glanced down. "Who's the lucky person?" she nodded toward her engagement ring.

Bronwyn glanced down at it as if seeing it for the first time, then slid her hand under the table. "His name is Ian Norton. He's an investment banker."

Jaq waited for her to go on, but she didn't. "When's the wedding?"

Bronwyn found it hard not to melt at the sound of that slow Texas accent. *Get yourself together, Bronwyn. You're a grown woman.*

"Wait...please tell me you didn't come all the way back to England for Victoria's wedding," she said, hoping to change the subject.

"Hell no, are you kidding?" Jaq raised an eyebrow as she took a sip of her Guinness. "I didn't want to go to the wedding at all. She cornered me in Selfridges and made me promise to come."

"That sounds about right," Bronwyn said. "She came to my

house with the invitation in her hand and wouldn't leave unless I promised to be there. I said yes out of self-preservation."

The Guinness was beginning to warm her from the inside out, and by the time their pies came, the long years between them had started to ease away.

"So what do you do?" Bronwyn held a forkful of mash aloft.

"I haven't been back in the country long, about eight months." Jaq nodded and held up two fingers when the barmaid caught her eye. "I'm in London, still working with numbers." She smiled, spearing steak with her fork. "I know—it's a shock."

"I heard you went on to Oxford," Bronwyn said, as two more pints of Guinness appeared on the table between them. "And then stayed there for graduate school?"

"I did," Jaq said. "I finished my PhD there last December and tried to go back to the States, but it didn't take, apparently."

Thank God, Bronwyn thought, then stopped herself. What the hell was she thinking? She was getting married. Soon.

"What about you?" Jaq looked up just in time to catch the knife Bronwyn dropped, then handed it back to her.

"I went to Wellesley in the States, then back to London for graduate school."

"I've heard Wellesley is packed with lesbians," Jaq said, trying not to smile. "How the hell did you come out of there with a man?"

Bronwyn knew as it was coming out of her mouth she was playing with fire. "You were a tough act to follow, I guess."

Jaq smiled and looked at Bronwyn's glass. "One more comment like that and I'm confiscating your pint." She took a breath and pushed her hair back with her hand. "So what do you do these days? I see you're still painting."

"How did you know I'm painting?"

"You have a drop of green paint on your left thigh."

Bronwyn looked down to check and raised an eyebrow. "Maybe you should be the one losing your pint."

"Yeah," Jaq said, holding her eyes. "Maybe I should."

The check appeared, and Jaq laid her card on it before Bronwyn could protest.

• 25 •

"I shouldn't let you do that, but thank you," Bronwyn said. "This has been the most fun I've had in ages."

"So, I never asked you what happened tonight," Jaq said, as she signed the check and took the receipt. "Did your car break down?"

"No, the rain got so bad I pulled over to figure out where I was and got stuck in the mud."

"I can get that out for you tomorrow before the wedding." Jaq paused as if choosing her words carefully. "Why don't you stay here tonight?"

"Oh, I asked," Bronwyn said, looking toward the bar. "They're fully booked."

"No," Jaq said. "I meant stay with me."

Bronwyn hesitated, taking her words in. "You were already nice enough to buy me dinner. I don't want to impose. I'm just going to call a taxi and go into the city. I have a hotel booked for tonight. I just never made it."

"A beautiful woman in my bed is not usually an imposition," Jaq said with a slow smile. "I'll sleep on the couch, I promise."

"Actually," Bronwyn said, folding her napkin and setting it on the table, "I might take you up on that if you're sure?"

Jaq nodded, and they stood, edging out of the booth.

Bronwyn looked her up and down. "How tall are you? I don't remember you being this much taller than me."

Jaq shrugged. "I'm five eleven or something. I grew two inches when I turned eighteen, I have no idea why."

She leaned down and picked up Bronwyn's luggage.

"I can get that," Bronwyn said, reaching for the bags. "You don't have to carry it all the way upstairs."

Jaq smiled and turned toward the stairs. "I think I can manage."

❖

After a hot shower and some dry clothes, Bronwyn was starting to feel almost normal again. She walked out of the bathroom and sank down on the bed, suddenly more tired than she'd realized.

Jaq handed her a glass of tawny port from the in-room bar. "Are you trying to kill me?"

"What?" Bronwyn looked up, confused.

Jaq raised an eyebrow and nodded at her black silk shorts and sheer white tank.

"It's what I wear to bed," Bronwyn said, reaching over and pulling Jaq's sweater back on over the top, leaving her legs bare, with just a hint of black lace at the top of her thigh. "Does that make it better?"

"Jesus." Jaq averted her eyes and tried not to smile. "No, actually," she said. "That makes it even worse."

Bronwyn settled back on the bed and took a sip of the port. "You, by the way, do not look like you push numbers around for a living. I'm not sure I believe you." She leaned back into the pillows and watched as Jaq reached up to slide her bag onto the top shelf in the wardrobe. "No one gets abs like that from math."

"I'll take that as a compliment." Jaq smiled over her shoulder and sat on the other end of the bed with her port. "You never told me what you do for a living." She paused. "Besides making it torture to sleep in the same room as you, of course."

Bronwyn laughed and threw a pillow in her direction. "I teach chemistry at Stratford, but I'm taking this semester off to paint."

The lights suddenly flickered and went dark, lightning flashing a blue streak across the night sky outside the window.

"Wait, isn't Victoria's wedding supposed to be outside?" Jaq asked, getting up to pull a curtain aside.

Bronwyn didn't try to hide her excitement. "What if it's canceled?"

"Don't tease me." Jaq lay back on the bed and looked at the ceiling. "I can't believe I agreed to hold a champagne flute all day and talk to people I didn't even like at school."

There was a knock at the door then, and Jaq went to answer it. It was one of the pub employees with a box of emergency candles.

"Great," Jaq said, stepping back and closing the door with her foot. She set the box of candles on the dresser as if they were already on fire. "Candlelight. This is all I need."

• 27 •

Bronwyn came over to look and lit one of the candles with the matches she found in the box. "Do you remember when we got locked in the attic because the girls' dean decided to do that unscheduled campus tour for the parents?"

"Yeah," Jaq said, lighting another candle and putting it on the nightstand next to the bed. "We'd only gone up there to be alone for a minute, then we were trapped for hours."

"The candles you found were beautiful." Bronwyn lit the last ivory candle and put it on the mantel, standing beside the fireplace grate, thankful for the space between them. "And you made that bed for us on the floor out of the drama department costumes."

Jaq sat on the bed across from the fireplace, her eyes locked onto Bronwyn. She watched her for a moment before she spoke. "And what else do you remember?"

"That it was our first time. Well, my first time, anyway."

Jaq laughed and looked down, shaking her head. "Other than kissing one of our teachers, at that point, you were all I knew. I'd never been with anyone either."

"You kissed one of our teachers?"

"What can I say," Jaq said, smiling. "She liked bad bois."

Bronwyn walked from the mantel to where Jaq was sitting on the edge of the bed. It mattered, what she chose to do now, what she made happen. Bronwyn stepped between Jaq's knees and rested her hands on her shoulders. Jaq closed her eyes and paused, then slid her hands slowly up the back of Bronwyn's thighs.

A loud knock at the door shattered the silence, and the same employee popped in with an apology and a spare box of matches. He closed the door, and Bronwyn stepped back, covering her face with her hands.

"Fuck," she said, rubbing her forehead. "What the hell am I doing?"

"First I'm going to lock that door, then you're going to bed," Jaq said. "And you're going to try your best not to look gorgeous while you do it."

Bronwyn slid under the covers. "Jaq," she whispered, as if it was a secret, "will you sleep in the bed with me?"

Jaq looked at her for a moment and ran her hand through her hair. Blowing out the candles, she slipped under the covers, still dressed, pulling Bronwyn into her arms and breathing in the still-familiar scent of her hair. Her fingers found the natural silver streak of her hair near the top of her head, a birthmark she'd had since she was a child. In school, Jaq would run her fingers through it while Bronwyn slept. It was a slightly different texture than the rest of her hair, a touchstone. If she found it in the dark, then Bronwyn was in her arms, and that's all that ever mattered to her.

Outside the rain pelted softly against the window and slid down in dark rivulets, reflecting every flash of lightning in intricate patterns across the wall.

Bronwyn whispered into the dark. "I never forgot you."

Jaq brought Bronwyn's hand to her heart and covered it with her own.

Chapter Three

The next morning, Bronwyn woke up to the sun beaming through the window and onto her face. The birds were singing outside, a charming reminder she was in the countryside, but the volume seemed unnecessarily loud. A pillow over her head afforded her another twenty minutes of sleep, but the sun was relentless in its golden prodding after that, so she gave up and sat on the bed. Jaq wasn't there, and the bathroom door was open, so she saw it was empty. Bronwyn looked around for a note, but there was none. Her heart dropped.

She looked over at the desk by the fireplace then and saw Jaq's wallet and phone. She wouldn't have gone too far without them, but Bronwyn was surprised at how panicked she'd felt.

She dug through her bag and found the black underwear she'd brought for the suit she was wearing to the wedding and went to turn on the hot water in the shower.

"You're not sixteen years old, Bronwyn." She looked at herself in the mirror while it heated up and the steam started to rise around her like translucent clouds. "And for fuck's sake, you're getting married in three months. Get a grip."

The hot shower relaxed her, and a plan started to take shape in her head. She'd go to the wedding with Jaq, have a lovely time, then go home. That was it. If she just stuck to the plan, it was a foolproof way to keep from wrecking her own life. She turned the water off and wrapped herself in a fluffy white towel. If she let herself have feelings for some high school crush because she had wedding jitters, it presented an enormous new set of problems, and Bronwyn had no desire to start navigating those. Her life was settled, and she was marrying a decent man. End of story.

She walked back into the room just as Jaq was coming through the door. She took her jacket off and sat down at the desk across from the bed.

Bronwyn pulled the towel a bit tighter around her, suddenly aware her sheer black underwear was all she had on underneath. "Where have you been? And did you pass coffee on the way? In that order, please."

"I called someone early this morning to tow your car out of the mud, so I went down and met them there." She pulled a mud-splattered small black box out of her pocket and set it down on the desk. "Do you have any idea who put a device under your car to track where you are?"

Bronwyn came closer and looked at it. "What do you mean, track?"

Jaq tapped her thumb on the desk, looking at the muddy black square. "As your car came out of the mud, I was standing to the side of it and saw this underneath the front driver's side. Whoever put this under your car is virtually tracking its location from their computer." She paused, looking up at Bronwyn. "And if you don't know who did it, there's a reason it's hidden."

Distracted, Bronwyn reached for the box to look at it. Unfortunately, she did that with the hand that was holding up her towel. Jaq didn't even try not to stare.

"Jesus," Bronwyn said, catching the towel at her waist and quickly wrapping it back around her. "Pretend you didn't see that."

"I'll do no such thing. That might have been the best moment of my life."

Jaq was teasing her, and it was hard not to be charmed by her, even in the midst of the drama. She picked up the box and looked at it.

"I've never seen this before," she said. "I didn't even know it was possible to do that."

• 31 •

"Well, I've disabled it now, so whoever has access to it is shit out of luck." Jaq set it back on the desk and looked toward the door. "Now, I believe you said something about coffee?"

Jaq showered and dressed fairly quickly. Her clothes for the wedding were simple and straightforward: gray G-Star jeans, polished wingtips, white button-up shirt, and a cropped navy jacket that Bronwyn noted walked the line between masculine and sexy as fuck.

Jaq went down to have a drink in the pub while Bronwyn finished her makeup and got dressed. It occurred to her as she took the suit off the hanger that she'd not tried it on after the alterations, and the start of panic fluttered in her stomach as she slipped it on. But as usual, Andrew was spot-on, and the lines of the fabric perfectly followed the lines of her body.

She buttoned the jacket and looked in the mirror. She'd always had a lean frame and high cheekbones, the clash of feminine and androgyny, but over the years, she'd altered her style to fit what Ian preferred. Classically feminine clothes crowded her pastel closet at home, which was fine for teaching, but it wasn't until she saw herself in the suit Andrew had tailored to her body that she realized how far from herself she'd strayed.

Her face was bare except for intense smoky eyeshadow, and she'd pulled her hair up into a loose, imperfect twist, loosening sections to soften it. "More bedroom than ballerina," as her best friend Moira liked to say. The soft curve of her breasts was the perfect contrast to the crisp lines of the suit, and the jacket buttoned just low enough to show a hint of curve from the side. She slid on her black stilettos and a cream cashmere scarf on the way out the door.

On the way down, she realized the wedding was supposed to start in twenty minutes. Jaq was sitting at the bar with a rocks glass of whisky, swirling it slowly around the sides. She looked up as Bronwyn entered the room, and didn't breathe again until she spoke.

"Christ, Bronwyn."

Jaq swept her eyes slowly over Bronwyn's body, then ran her hand through her hair, her eyes following her as she slid onto the barstool beside her, her hand warm on Jaq's thigh. The bartender strained a drink out of a shaker into a frosted martini glass and set it down in front of her.

"Pardon," Bronwyn said as he turned to leave. "What is this?"

"Bombay Sapphire martini, ma'am."

Bronwyn thanked him and turned to Jaq. "How do you know I love gin?"

Jaq smiled. "Do you remember that night we snuck out onto the roof?"

Bronwyn nodded. "And we talked until the sun came up and we both went to class looking shattered."

"Exactly," Jaq said, her eyes soft with the memory. "You told me that night you used to drink the rest of your father's martinis after he'd gone to bed."

"I remember," Bronwyn said, then paused. "I just can't believe you do."

Jaq dropped her eyes and finished the rest of the whiskey in her glass. "I remember everything."

Bronwyn sipped from the icy surface of her martini. The plan was not working. Already. It didn't help that Jaq somehow looked like a grown-up version of the bad boi she fell in love with. Her dark hair looked like she'd just woken up and run her hand through it, and her silvery blue eyes were dark with thought. Bronwyn realized she still had her hand on Jaq's thigh and made herself remove it.

"So," she said, "I had a thought while I was getting dressed."

"About the box?"

"Kind of," she said. "Maybe. I don't know."

"I'm listening."

"A few months ago, I was on the way to the shops and realized my phone was dead on the way out the door. I plugged it in and set it on the hall table next to the front door and went upstairs to my studio to clean my brushes."

Jaq slid a hand behind her neck and leaned back on her stool, listening.

"I got distracted and worked on one of my canvases, so it was about an hour before I came back downstairs. But when I got there, it was gone."

"Okay," Jaq said. "Who has a key to your house?"

Bronwyn thought for a moment. "My mum, of course, my best mate Moira, and Ian. But I'm almost sure it wasn't locked. I usually only lock it when I leave the house, so I assumed it was stolen. Although my purse was there as well and it hadn't been touched."

"Did you ever find it?"

"That's the strange part," Bronwyn said. "When I came back from the shops it was sitting in the same place on the hall table, plugged into the charger."

Jaq tapped her keys on the bar. "Is it the same phone you have now?"

Bronwyn nodded.

"Do me a favor?" Jaq said. "Leave your phone in the room until we get back. Let me think on it, and we'll figure it out tonight." She looked at her watch and got up from the stool, holding her hand out for Bronwyn. "Our taxi is probably out there now. If we're lucky, we'll miss the ceremony completely."

❖

The wedding was at the Staffordshire Abbey, a few miles outside the city in Northumberland. The actual abbey was just stone walls and freestanding gothic entryways—it dated from the sixteenth century, and the roof had long since succumbed to the elements. The late afternoon light was fading already, the sun low and golden beyond the ruins. A long, winding path led to the abbey, and another wound down to the stone great hall built in the same style just beyond it, covered in ivy.

"Two roads diverged in a wood..." Bronwyn looked over at Jaq.

Jaq raised an eyebrow. "Please tell me you're thinking about skipping the wedding completely and just making an appearance at the reception."

"Victoria is lucky I'm attending at all," she said, as they turned down the path leading away from the abbey and toward the great hall. "She and her best mate Amber made my life hell when I came back to Stratford. They heard the rumor about you and me and wouldn't let it go. All her little friends whispered about it for the rest of the year."

"I wish I'd been there. She wouldn't have gotten the chance to even open her mouth."

The great hall looked like a medieval manor in the setting sun. Light spilled out of the windows from three levels, and in the front were massive wooden double doors that looked to be hundreds of years old, with hand-forged iron hinges and handles. As they got closer, they realized the staff was still setting up inside, so Bronwyn took Jaq's hand and led her over the crest of the hill to the stone steps beyond it. The steps descended into lush gardens, velvety green even in early autumn, then to a maze made of hedges set at the edge of the woods. A symphony of evening sounds started to surround them, led by the sudden swoop of bats weaving an invisible pattern above their heads.

"Isn't the maze mysterious?" Bronwyn said. "I was here once, years ago, and I wanted to go into it so badly but it was already dark, and I knew I'd get lost."

"Well then," Jaq said, "I'd say it's high time we got in there, don't you?"

Jaq led her down to the maze, and it took a little under thirty seconds before Bronwyn was lost. She crinkled up her forehead and turned one way, then another, until she finally just sat down on one of the stone benches. "See?" she said. "This thing could be on fire, and I'd have no idea how to get out."

Jaq laughed and sat down beside her. "We've only taken three turns," she said, looking back where they'd started. "How can you be lost already?"

"My dad has always told me I was his favorite child..."

"Wait," said Jaq, "aren't you an only child?"

Bronwyn nodded. "But that I needed constant supervision. I always thought he was just teasing me, but it isn't very far from the truth. I tend to get into trouble if left to my own devices."

"I always liked him," Jaq said, pulling a leaf off the hedge and folding it like paper. "Although he can't have been happy I got you pulled out of school."

"Actually," Bronwyn said, smiling at the memory, "when we got home from school the day I left, Mom went straight into his office at the house, and I heard her telling him about you kissing me by the car."

"Oh wow," Jaq said. "Really?"

"I think she'd expected him to back her up, but he just laughed and told her it took some balls to do what you did. And that's a quote." Bronwyn smiled. "She was not happy."

"I can imagine," Jaq said. "How are your parents these days?"

Bronwyn started to answer, then paused. "Have you ever seen a reality show called *Romance Island*?"

"I'm not sure I've ever seen any reality show, but someone in the office next to mine at work is obsessed with it. I think she's watched every single episode."

"Everyone watches it. The latest season ended in August. It's the number one show in Britain during the summer," Bronwyn said. "Anyway, Dad is the producer for the show, and he left Mom last year for Catherine Flack, the host."

"Ouch." Jaq shook her head. "Let me guess. She's about twenty-two?"

"No," she said, laughing. "She's actually in her early forties and surprisingly likable."

Music and laughter started to float over the hedges. In a few more minutes, the gardens would be dark, and walking out of them with someone other than Ian could make her life difficult if anyone noticed.

"I guess we'd better make an appearance at the reception?" Jaq said.

Bronwyn's voice was heavy with dread. "Fine. But only because we'll freeze if we stay here."

"You can always use those self-defense moves I taught you."

"Oh my God, I forgot all about that! That's one of the first things we ever did together. I still remember them."

"They were actually legit, but I only offered to teach you so I'd have an excuse to touch you."

Jaq smiled and took her hand, squeezing it then letting her go when they emerged from the maze.

They strolled back to the great hall, which now looked gorgeous with the sparkling fairy lights strung from tree to tree surrounding it against the night sky. Large windows facing the gardens framed the golden chandeliers hanging high from the rafters.

They'd barely walked in the door before a very thin, very loud woman ran up and kissed Bronwyn, nearly splashing red wine on her suit in the process.

"Bronwyn, dear God, you look like an Italian model!" She kissed both her cheeks and paused, staring at Jaq. "I could swear Ian was not nearly this good-looking last time I saw him."

Her eyes swept Jaq's body, and she leaned in to whisper loudly into her ear. "I don't know if you've heard, but there was a rumor in our school that Bronwyn here has been known to like the ladies."

"Jaq," Bronwyn said, the muscles in her jaw visibly tense, "This is Amber Norton. She was a few years behind you at Stratford, so you two may not have met."

"No," Jaq said, extending her hand, "I don't believe we have."

"Your reputation precedes you, but I hadn't heard you were American," Amber said, keeping her eyes locked on Jaq and ignoring her hand. "So that begs the question…however did *you* get into Stratford?" She tilted her head and waited for Jaq to answer.

Jaq paused, then turned to Bronwyn. "Drink?"

"God yes. Two, if possible."

Jaq squeezed her hand as she walked away, and Bronwyn was left with Amber.

"So," she said, as soon as Jaq was out of earshot. "Ian is suddenly out of the picture, and you're fucking an American dyke. How the hell did that happen?"

Tact had never been one of Amber's attributes, probably because she didn't need to mince words in her social circle. After Stratford, she'd married very well and once told Bronwyn at a boozy Christmas party that her husband was richer than God.

"First of all, Ian is not out of the picture. And I'm not fucking Jaq Bailey." Bronwyn fought to keep her voice even.

"Pumpkin!"

Bronwyn heard her dad behind her before she turned around, and as she kissed him hello, Catherine Flack walked up as well and hugged Bronwyn with genuine affection.

Finally, Bronwyn thought, *someone else for Amber to focus on.*

"Where's Mum?" Bronwyn knew her dad had offered her a ride to the wedding since Catherine had been filming and was going to meet him at the church.

"She got a migraine at the last minute and said she'd changed her mind."

Jaq returned and handed Bronwyn a martini as Angus Charles extended his hand.

"Good to see you, Jaq," he said, smiling. "A buddy of mine works at the Yard and told me they'd finally gotten you back to London."

"Yes, sir," Jaq said. "They seem to have finally gotten me locked down."

"Well," Bronwyn's dad said, clinking his glass of whiskey to Jaq's, "London is the better for it."

Jaq smiled. "Thank you, sir."

Bronwyn watched them. She couldn't quite put her finger on the undercurrent there, but perhaps that was because Amber was carrying on a conversation with Catherine at an ear-splitting pitch.

"I'm sure you know my husband. He's an executive at ITV2." She paused to wave at someone over Catherine's shoulder. "Isn't that the television network that owns your little reality show?" Catherine started to respond, but Amber's attention had already drifted.

"I hate to interrupt, dear," she said, interrupting Bronwyn's conversation with her father, "but where the hell is Ian?" Amber was starting to slur her words ever so slightly.

Bronwyn took a deep breath. "Unfortunately he couldn't attend, he had other commitments."

"Well," Amber said, shaking her head, "I wouldn't let my Martin get away with that. But mind you, it takes some work. They don't come out of the box that way. If you want them to behave, you have to train them." She drained the last of the wine in her glass. "Treat them mean, keep them keen." She raised her eyebrow at Bronwyn and started to go on.

Catherine cut her off. "Amber," she said, "Isn't that Martin over there?"

Amber followed Catherine's gaze across the reception hall.

"He's to the left of the bar," Catherine said. "I believe he's the one with his hand on that bridesmaid's ass."

Amber finally spotted him and scurried away, her face a flaming red.

"Thank Christ," Bronwyn said, rubbing her temple with the pads of her fingers as Catherine put her arm around her shoulder and squeezed her. "Cheers, I love you for that."

The bell announcing dinner sounded, and everyone was directed first toward the board showing the seating arrangements, and then on to the dining room. Jaq and Bronwyn were seated together, along with her father and Catherine, Moira and her husband James, and Amber and Martin Norton. Of course.

Moira and James were already at the table, and she jumped up to hug Bronwyn the second she saw her. They'd been friends since primary school. Before she let her go, she whispered, "Oh my God, is that who I think it is?"

"Yes," Bronwyn whispered, glancing over at Jaq. "I might be losing my mind. I'll fill you in later."

Bronwyn introduced her to Jaq briefly, then Moira moved on to hug Bronwyn's father. She tried her best not to seem star-struck when he then introduced her to Catherine.

"I just want you to know," she said, leaning in and touching her arm, "I watched *Romance Island* every night this season." Moira was from Liverpool in Northern England, but even seven years at a posh school in London hadn't put a dent in that sharp Scouse accent.

"I'm flattered, thank you," Catherine said, clinking her glass to Moira's. "I'll have to catch you up later on what's going on behind the scenes." She dropped her voice to a whisper. "All is not as it seems. I'll give you the scoop."

The speeches commenced, and after what seemed to be a thousand lengthy toasts to the happy couple, dinner was served. Amber had made a noisy entrance at some point between the speeches and was now picking at the prime rib and Yorkshire pudding on her plate. Martin was still nowhere to be seen.

"So, Jacqueline," Amber said finally, sitting back in her chair with her wine glass dangling precariously from two fingers. "We all know what Bronwyn's Ian does for a living." She paused for effect. "What is it that you do?"

"Well, I've always worked with numbers in some capacity," Jaq said. "I was back in the States for a few months after school, but it looks like I'm settled now in London."

"Ah," Amber said, peering over her glass at Jaq and nodding slowly as if all was becoming clear. "You're looking for work."

"Not at the moment, no," Jaq said, glancing at Bronwyn.

"Well, not that it's my place to say it," Amber ignored the sharp elbow Moira was nudging her with, "but I'd imagine that your *look* has a little something to do with you being unable to progress in a career."

That was enough for Jaq. She set her scotch down and held Amber's eyes. The table fell silent, and Bronwyn caught her dad smiling out of the corner of her eye.

"Actually," Jaq said, "I have a PhD in Linear Analysis and Numerical Theory from Oxford. I was recruited last year by Scotland Yard as a detective sergeant to head up their forensic accounting division in London."

Amber launched into a shrill laugh, then stopped and dropped her voice when she realized Jaq was serious. "Really?"

Jaq held her eyes, unflinching. "Yes, really."

Catherine tried not to laugh, but the situation was just too delicious to ignore, and the laugh came out anyway as more of a stifled snort.

"Well," she said, her eyes sparkling, "that cleared it up nicely. Wouldn't you say, Amber?"

Mr. Charles stood up. "On that note, I'm headed outside for

some air." He pushed his chair away from the table and dug his cigarettes out of his jacket pocket. "Jaq, care to join me?" When they left, it was suddenly all too much for Moira.

"You're an idiot, you know that?" she said, turning to Amber. "Why in the world would you say that?"

"All I'm saying is that obviously Ian is the perfect man for Bronwyn." She cleared her throat. "Emphasis on *man*."

She was too drunk to argue with. Catherine rolled her eyes, scooted her chair closer to Bronwyn and Moira, and launched into all the juicy details on what happened with the cast on *Romance Island*. Moira was delighted, and even Bronwyn was drawn in after a few minutes. Jaq and Mr. Charles reappeared while the band was testing the sound system for the dancing to come.

"Okay," Amber slurred with a look in Jaq's direction as they sat down. "Just one more question."

Bronwyn glared at her and started to say something, but Jaq stopped her.

"No, it's fine," she said, her hand touching Bronwyn's briefly. "Let her go ahead."

"What I want to know is," Amber shifted her gaze to Bronwyn, "Which one of you is the man in the bedroom?"

Catherine didn't give Jaq time to answer, just leaned forward over the table to Amber. "Isn't that funny?" she said. "We were just wondering the same thing about you and Martin."

❖

It was late by the time Bronwyn and Jaq finally escaped the reception and returned to the pub, and the bar was locked up tight. They climbed the steps to the room, and Bronwyn turned suddenly to Jaq.

"I just assumed you'd let me stay the night again," she said, suddenly hesitant. "I should have asked."

"Oh," Jaq said, taking her hand and leading her to the door. "That's cute. You thought I'd let you stay somewhere else?" She smiled down at Bronwyn, far shorter than she was again now that she was carrying her stilettos. "Not a chance."

Bronwyn smiled and started unbuttoning her jacket the second she got through the door, digging a pair of silk pajama bottoms out of her suitcase.

"Ah, now I see," Jaq said, looking at the navy blue silk pile in her hand. "So you were torturing me last night. You didn't have to wear tiny lace shorts to bed. You just wanted to make me suffer."

Bronwyn stepped closer to her, fingers holding the last button on her suit jacket. The silence fell dense between them.

"If I wanted to torture you, Jaq…you'd know it."

She released the last button on the jacket, and it fell open to the waist, barely covering her breasts.

"Christ, Bronwyn," Jaq said, the words coming out in a rough whisper.

Her eyes took in every inch of Bronwyn's skin. Finally, she reached out and touched a finger to Bronwyn's bottom lip, then slid it slowly down between her breasts to her waistband.

"You have to put some clothes on, Bella," Jaq said, using her nickname for Bronwyn when they were at school. "I can't be trusted when you're naked like this."

Bronwyn stepped away and went into the bathroom, closing the door behind her. She sat on the tub, thinking, trying to remember the last time she felt like this. In truth, she'd forgotten what it even felt like. Most nights, she went home alone, and on the rare nights Ian slept over, she'd tried to get into making love with him, but really just counted the minutes until he finished. It wasn't that he was a bad lover, not really, but sometimes she wasn't sure it even mattered to him that it was her there, and not someone else.

She took her suit off and hung it up on the back of the door, slipping on her pajama bottoms and a white tank top. She brushed out her hair and took off her makeup, then opened the door. Jaq was sitting on the hearth, coaxing flames up from tinder to the logs. Her hair looked like she'd just run her hands through it, standing it on end, and she'd changed into jeans and a wool sweater.

Bronwyn sank down on the sofa across from the fire, tucking her feet underneath her. "So, Detective Sargent," she said, her eyes teasing. "Why didn't you tell me about Scotland Yard?"

Jaq smiled and put another log on the fire, sending a spray of red and gold sparks up the chimney. "It's not that I didn't want to tell you. I just don't really bring it up unless I have to."

"Well, you picked the perfect moment. I've been waiting for someone to shut Amber up since Stratford." Bronwyn beamed, leaning back and basking in the memory. "And that was beautifully done."

"I never thought about what you had to come back to the next year after I graduated." Jaq looked up from the fire. "Did everyone know?"

Bronwyn nodded. "Everyone knew. And some of the parents even pulled their daughters out of my dorm, like I was going to convert them or something," she said, pulling at a thread on the hem of her shirt. "It was a huge scandal."

"I'm so sorry," Jaq said. "I had no idea."

"It's not your fault. We did nothing wrong. They just saw an opportunity to freeze me out, and they did. I heard myself called 'that dyke' so many times I forgot I had a name."

Jaq looked up and saw the tears she was trying to hide. She walked over and pulled Bronwyn into her arms.

"It was a long time ago," Bronwyn said, wiping her eyes. "I don't know why I'm crying about it now."

"Because it was shitty." Jaq pulled her closer and kissed the top of her head. "And you had to deal with it all by yourself."

"But it wasn't all bad," Bronwyn said, catching a tear on her chin with her hand. "Moira heard what was happening and convinced the dean to let her transfer to my dorm, then switched rooms with my neighbor, so she had the room next to mine. The first thing she did was march into Amber's room and call her an evil cow."

Jaq laughed, and Bronwyn caught the last tear on her cheek and wiped it away.

"We were friends before, but I've never forgotten how she

defended me when it wasn't easy and she didn't have to do it. We've been close ever since."

"I knew she was a badass when I met her at the wedding." Jaq smiled. "Those Liverpool girls don't take any shit."

They watched a log crumble into glowing red pieces in the coals, Jaq slowly trailing her fingertips back and forth across Bronwyn's back.

"Did you ever tell your parents about it?"

Bronwyn looked up at Jaq as she said it, but she just stared into the fire. Bronwyn knew enough to wait until she spoke.

"After school, I went home to Texas for a month before I started Oxford. I hadn't had the money to fly home for years, and Mom didn't have any other family, so there was no one to keep me updated on anything."

Jaq paused for a long moment, then cleared her throat and went on.

"When I finally got back to Austin, her trailer was there but strangers were living in it. I asked at the bar and they told me she'd died the year before. Drank herself to death, apparently."

Bronwyn turned around, pulled Jaq into her arms, and hugged her hard.

Sometimes there's just nothing to say.

"It's okay," Jaq said after a minute, wiping her eyes with the heel of her hand. "It was a long time ago."

Bronwyn got up after a few minutes and poured her a scotch from the bar.

"I definitely should not drink that," Jaq said when she came back to the sofa and tried to hand it to her.

"Why?"

"You've looked in the mirror tonight, right?" Jaq kept her eyes on Bronwyn. When she spoke again, her voice was low and ragged around the edges. "It's taking everything I've got not to pick you up right now and lay you down on that bed."

Bronwyn didn't speak, just sat down next to her and slowly handed her the glass.

Jaq closed her eyes. When she spoke, her voice sounded like the raw scrape of metal against rock. "Fuck, Bronwyn." The muscles in her jaw tensed as she spoke. "You have no idea what you do to me."

Bronwyn took the drink out of her hand, took a long sip, then handed it back to her. "I think I have a pretty good idea."

The fire sparked and flared as the last log collapsed into the coals. Jaq got up and put another log on top of it, waiting until it caught and the flames threw shadows onto the walls before she came back to the couch. When she did, she drank half of the scotch, then put the glass down and took an ice cube out of her mouth. Bronwyn watched, holding her breath as Jaq reached out and touched her with it. Her shirt clung to her skin where Jaq held it against her, her nipple tight and hard under the rough edge of the ice. Jaq's voice startled her.

"Close your eyes."

Jaq moved the ice slowly around her other nipple. Bronwyn's breath deepened and her hand found Jaq's thigh. She felt Jaq lean in, then the slow warmth of her breath on wet skin, and finally the lightest scrape of Jaq's teeth against her nipple. As she opened her eyes, Jaq tossed the ice into the fire where it hissed and steamed in the flames.

Jaq's eyes shone as she stared into the firelight. "Have a better idea now?"

Bronwyn took Jaq's hand, still cold from the ice, and ran her tongue lightly across her palm before she pulled one of her fingers into the warmth of her mouth, circling and stroking it with her tongue.

Jaq closed her eyes and let out a low growl. "Fucking hell," she said. "I surrender."

"What was that?" Bronwyn held Jaq's fingertips to her mouth as she spoke. "I didn't hear you." Jaq pulled her over onto her lap and paused, dropping her eyes to her mouth.

"I want to kiss you more than I've ever wanted to kiss anyone," Jaq said, tracing the outline of her bottom lip with her thumb. "But I can't."

"Why not?"

Jaq pressed her forehead against Bronwyn's. "Because I want you, Bella." She whispered, "Not just this."

It was hours before Bronwyn fell asleep that night. For the first time in a long time, she remembered what it was like to be in love. And exactly how it felt to hear her heart crack into jagged edges and break wide open when Jaq disappeared.

Chapter Four

The next morning, Bronwyn opened her eyes to see Jaq, already showered and dressed, sitting at the desk, taking the back off her phone with a tiny screwdriver.

"Good morning," Jaq said, without turning around. "I apologize for this. I should have asked, but I didn't want to wake you." She looked back at Bronwyn. "I'm trying to see if there's a tracking device on this or if there's just the one in your car."

She lifted the back off the phone and held it up to the light, turning it in every direction.

"Don't apologize," Bronwyn said. "I must have a hundred calls from him since I left London. Before I went to bed last night, I saw he'd called incessantly while we were at the wedding."

"Do I have your permission to connect it to my laptop so I can scan it with my software?"

Bronwyn nodded and stretched, climbing onto the top of the duvet, sweeping her hair up into a bun. She glanced over at Jaq. "Will you toss me that pencil on the desk?" She held one hand out and caught it, then stuck the pencil through the twist of hair at the nape of her neck to secure it.

Jaq watched, the phone forgotten. "That might be the cutest thing I've ever seen."

Bronwyn laughed and nodded toward the desk. "Wait, isn't it a crime to distract a detective sergeant on the job?"

"Too late." Jaq smiled, turning back to the phone and screwing the pieces back together. "And the shirt isn't helping."

❖

An hour later, Bronwyn had showered and dressed in jeans and her gray suede boots she left unlaced at the top.

"You do realize I'm taking this home with me, right?" she said, pulling Jaq's green sweater over her silk camisole and rolling up the sleeves.

Jaq smiled, clicking through screens on her computer, Bronwyn's phone still hooked up by a cable on the side.

"When do you have to be back to work, by the way?"

Jaq paused. "Not till Wednesday. It's a bank holiday, so we're off tomorrow, then there's a series of internal meetings I don't have to attend on Tuesday." She stopped scrolling and leaned into her computer screen.

"I found it."

"Found what?"

"The spyware app hidden in your phone. Whoever did it knew what they were doing. After it installed, any trace of the app or installation process was buried underneath mountains of code."

"I have no idea what that even means," Bronwyn said, peering over her shoulder at her naked phone.

"It's the internal series of numbers that tells the computer in your phone what to do," Jaq said, screwing the cover back onto her phone. "And in your case, there's no way to completely remove what was put into it."

"What do I do?"

"Get another phone," Jaq said, handing it back to her. "It's powered off now, but I suggest you leave it in a public trash in town before we head back."

"I've been thinking about getting a new one," said Bronwyn. "I haven't replaced my phone since the dark ages anyway."

She stood on tiptoe and slid her arms around Jaq's neck. "Thank you for trying to keep me safe."

Jaq pulled her closer, breathing in the scent of her skin. "I've wanted to keep you safe since I left you in that parking lot." Her hands slid down the curve of Bronwyn's back.

"Well," Bronwyn said, "You've done an amazing job of it this weekend."

The air between them was heavy with the fact they were leaving in just a few minutes and heading back to London. Jaq finally let her go and packed up her bag, while Bronwyn blew her hair dry and touched up her eyes in the bathroom. After a last look around, Jaq left the key on the desk and pulled the door shut behind them in the hall.

"I may starve before we get to your car," Jaq said. "I meant to eat something this morning but forgot until it was too late."

"If I remember right, you love a proper fry-up," Bronwyn said, "And I know exactly where to take you."

❖

Twenty minutes later, they were tucked into a corner booth at McCleary's, a tiny café hidden down a back cobblestone alley in the heart of the city. As they walked in, the older gentleman behind the grill raised his eyebrow, and Bronwyn held up two fingers. A precarious stack of brightly colored teapots occupied a corner with an odd collection of crocheted tea cozies dotting the wall behind it. Jaq chose the booth while Bronwyn filled one of the pots with boiling water and three teabags.

"Did you choose the rose print pot just for me?"

"No," Bronwyn said, "I chose this dainty pink teacup and saucer for you. Look at the cute little rosebud in the very bottom!"

"Fantastic," Jaq said, dumping sugar into her cup and stirring it with the tiny silver spoon on the table. "I happen to love tiny pink teacups with gold handles."

Bronwyn laughed and poured tea into her cup, noticing the laugh lines at the corner of Jaq's eyes. Jaq had always been sexy, but now as an adult, she had a smoldering edge to her.

"So," Jaq said, "you weren't kidding about Ian calling you

constantly. He called three times this morning before I shut down your phone."

"He's not always that bad." Bronwyn looked into her cup, trying to think of how to explain it. "He just likes to know where I am." She picked up the spoon to stir her tea, then did nothing with it. "It does stress me out, though. I hate making him angry, but if I don't answer or let him know what I'm doing, he gets annoyed pretty quickly."

Jaq looked at her, and waited until Bronwyn met her eyes to speak. "Are you scared of him?"

"Not really," Bronwyn said. "I just wish he'd let me have a bit more space sometimes."

The older gentleman they'd seen as they walked in set two plates in front of them, piled with beans, tomatoes, rashers, black pudding, eggs, and sausages.

"Thanks," Bronwyn said, as she stood to kiss his cheek. "Jaq, this is my uncle, Rothesay Charles, my dad's older brother."

Jaq stood and extended her hand, and he shook it, looking her over before he turned back to Bronwyn.

"Still marrying that Ian fellow, are you?" Rothesay did not look pleased as he waited for an answer.

"I know you and Dad don't like him, but I swear—"

Roth guessed the rest of her answer and turned to Jaq before she finished. "See if you can talk some sense into our girl." He lowered his voice slightly and looked Jaq in the eye. "Trust me, that Ian's a right prick."

Bronwyn just dropped her face into her hands. There was no stopping him once he got an idea in his head. Luckily, someone rang the bell at the counter and he stepped away.

"Sorry about that," she said, picking her fork and knife back up. "They got off on the wrong foot. It wasn't that big a deal."

Jaq just looked at her, waiting.

She picked up her toast, then set it back down on the edge of her plate. "We were here last year. Ian was upset about something and grabbed my wrist across the table. He didn't know Rothesay was my uncle. Anyway, he saw it just at the wrong time. It looked like something it wasn't, and of course now he hates Ian."

"Smart man," Jaq said slowly, her eyes intense, leaning back in the booth. "Ian's on my shit list now too."

"No, it wasn't like that. It looked much worse than it was," Bronwyn said, dropping her eyes to her plate and cutting into her fried tomato. "Ian was just trying to make a point, but Uncle Roth never forgot it."

"Did he tell your father?"

"I'm sure he called him before we even left the table."

Jaq poured more tea into Bronwyn's cup and spooned in two sugars. "Okay," Jaq said, "I'm going to ask you something, and I want you to answer me honestly."

Bronwyn hesitated.

"Has he," she said, making Bronwyn meet her eyes, "and it doesn't matter what the reason is, ever left marks on you? Like bruises?"

Bronwyn shoved a bite of bacon in her mouth to buy herself time. She'd completely lost her appetite at that point.

"He had a huge issue at work about a year ago and almost lost his job," Bronwyn said, finally. "I said the wrong thing and he got upset."

Jaq put her fork and knife down and waited for her to go on. She didn't. After a while, Bronwyn realized Jaq wasn't going to let her off the hook and she had to say something.

"It's not an issue anymore. He never did it again and he apologized for days."

Jaq held her eyes and let out a slow breath. "What did he do?"

"Is it okay if we don't talk about it? I don't want to get upset." Bronwyn looked over at her uncle, who was still taking an order at the counter.

"Will you tell me when you're ready?"

Bronwyn nodded.

"And by when you're ready," Jaq said, "I mean today."

That made her laugh, and she swatted at Jaq with her toast.

• 51 •

Jaq held her cup between them. "Hey, I don't think it's fair that you get to wield that toast and all I have to defend myself with is this dainty little teacup."

Bronwyn knew Jaq was trying to cheer her up, and she appreciated it. Actually, she'd never told anyone about what happened, mostly because it made sense when he explained it later. He was right; she had been pressing his buttons. Either way, though, she just wanted to pretend it never happened.

They finished their breakfast and Bronwyn went to the restroom while Jaq tried to pay the bill.

Bronwyn's uncle was having none of it.

"My brother spoke to me about you years ago," he said, waving her wallet away. "We were both sorry that happened to you kids." He cleared his throat, looking toward the restroom for Bronwyn. "Look after her for me, will you? I don't trust that Ian."

Jaq nodded. "I'll do my best, sir."

They shook hands just as Bronwyn was coming out of the hall toward the counter. She stepped behind it to give her uncle a kiss on the cheek.

"Thanks for the breakfast, Uncle Roth."

"Lovely to see you, Petunia," he said, handing her a couple of sandwiches wrapped in paper for the road and nodding in Jaq's direction. "Bring this one back anytime."

The bell on the door clanged against the glass on the way out, and Jaq took her hand as they walked down the cobblestones toward the car.

❖

"Wait," Jaq said a few hours later, holding up her phone, "I think we might have gotten off track. This says we've turned off toward Blackpool, not London."

Bronwyn looked over at her and took the next exit. "You probably don't remember this, but my family went to Blackpool during school holidays one year."

"I do. I'd just turned seventeen the week before."

"Exactly. When I came back, I was trying to tell you about it, but you said you'd never been on an ocean pier, like the one at Blackpool seaside, so you couldn't picture it."

Jaq looked over at her. "I still haven't."

"I figured. That's why I asked you this morning where you'd been since you came back to England. I've booked us a place to stay there tonight, and I'm taking you for fish and chips on the pier for dinner."

Jaq stared out the window, then lowered it a few inches to let in the salt air.

"But we don't have to…" Bronwyn faltered, suddenly aware she might have something, or someone, else to return to London for. "I should have asked."

"I've wanted to come here since I was a kid, my first year at Stratford," Jaq said, still looking out her window. "I can't believe you remembered."

Bronwyn turned into town, taking a narrow road behind the Blackpool Tower to the right and up a winding hill.

"Wait," Jaq said, "how did you do it? We left your phone in the room."

"I didn't," she said, slowing and looking along the row of houses to her left. "While you weren't looking, I had the owner of the pub do it for me and write down the details. I already knew where I wanted us to stay."

Bronwyn slowed to a stop in front of a church, half covered in verdant moss and wild vines, complete with church bells in the belfry towering above the roof. Bronwyn took an envelope off the door and looked around for Jaq, who had walked to the side and stopped, peering down at Blackpool below.

"Look," Jaq said, pointing, her eyes scanning the length of the beach. "You can see the ocean from here. And is that a Ferris wheel on the pier?"

An enormous Ferris wheel sat in the center of Blackpool's central pier, so tall it looked as if the low, misty clouds that obscured the view had sliced off the top. Blinking gold and blue lights lit up the ocean skyline, and the pier seemed to go on endlessly, the waves crashing beneath it where it suddenly dropped off into the swirling gray sea.

"I can't believe you brought me here."

"You're easily impressed, thank God." Bronwyn smiled. "We can walk down there for dinner later. You haven't had British fish and chips until you've eaten them at the seaside in a newspaper cone."

She started to walk back up to the church entrance, but Jaq was still staring down into the lights of Blackpool.

"Did you know there are three separate piers down there?"

Bronwyn smiled. "I did."

She watched Jaq scanning the shoreline and taking it all in, as if it might suddenly disappear if she looked away. She walked back up to the car and hadn't gotten to the door when Jaq called out to her, still looking out over the sea.

"Don't touch those bags, Bronwyn."

Jaq turned around then and ran back up the slope, picking Bronwyn up and wrapping her legs around her waist at the car. Her words were warm as she whispered them into her neck. "Thank you for this."

Jaq grabbed their bags out of the car and brought them to the Gothic doorframe of the church, while Bronwyn opened the envelope and pulled out an old brass skeleton key. She tried to turn it in the lock but it wouldn't budge. She took it out and reinserted it, turning it both ways. Jaq took it and knelt down at the keyhole to compare it with the key itself.

"Well," Jaq said, "I think they may have left you the wrong key. This one won't even insert fully."

Bronwyn turned the key over in her hand, her brows furrowed with sudden worry. "I can try to contact the owner. I think I must have the paper they gave me somewhere."

She started to walk back to the car but Jaq touched her arm and pulled her back. She pulled a Swiss Army knife out of her pocket and crouched down so the keyhole was eye level. Three seconds later, there was a click and Jaq turned the door handle.

"Bloody hell," Bronwyn said. "How did you know how to do that?"

"You don't want to know," Jaq said, opening the door and stepping aside. "Let's just say it's a childhood skill that's remained useful."

The inside of the church was bright and unexpectedly beautiful. Enormous stained glass windows circled the room, and the light shining through them fell in tinted beams onto the wide plank oak floors. A bed was placed on the platform where the pulpit once stood, piled with a fluffy white duvet and layers of navy and white pillows. A fireplace was set into the wall to the left, with a bright yellow overstuffed couch with a long coffee table crafted from an antique door. Another larger sitting area was to the right, with a small kitchen behind it.

"Wow," Jaq said, setting the bags down where she stood.

She kicked off her shoes and ran toward the bed, taking an impressive leap and landing in the center of the enormous pile of pillows. Bronwyn watched for a second then did the same, Jaq ducking out of the way just in time.

"This bed is amazing," Bronwyn said, lying on her back and looking up into the belfry.

Jaq settled beside her, folding a pillow under her head and looking up. "If things were different," she said, her voice low and soft, "I'd never let you out of it. Even for fish and chips."

Bronwyn rolled over on her elbow, facing Jaq. "Do you ever wonder if it would be different after all these years?"

"What?" Jaq said, her eyes dropping slowly to Bronwyn's mouth. "Sleeping together?"

Bronwyn nodded.

Jaq laughed, running a hand through her hair. "I don't have to wonder, I know it would be." She tucked a stray lock of hair back behind Bronwyn's ear. "What about you?"

"I've thought about it." Bronwyn smiled, the diamond on her left hand catching the light. She resisted an urge to throw it across the room. "Why are you so sure it would be different?" She caught the hem of Jaq's T-shirt and pulled it up just an inch, running her fingertips over the soft blond hairs across her stomach.

"Well," Jaq said, raising her arms and putting them behind her head, "I know what the hell I'm doing now, for starters."

"What, you were just guessing back then?"

"I knew I wanted you like I'd never wanted anything in my life," Jaq said, "but no, I had no idea what I was doing."

"Well," Bronwyn said, tucking her hair behind her ear, "then you're a good guesser."

"Now look who's easily impressed." Jaq smiled, catching Bronwyn's hand and holding it when she started tracing the button on Jaq's jeans with her finger.

Bronwyn looked at Jaq's hand covering hers and arched an eyebrow.

"I can only take so much, Bella," Jaq said, her eyes intense as she brought Bronwyn's hand to her mouth, her breath warm against her palm, "and it's getting harder not to touch you."

❖

Later, the seagulls soared overhead as they sat on the edge of the pier at the very end, each holding a portion of fish and chips wrapped in newspaper, complete with a tiny wooden fork. The water shimmered with the last of the afternoon sun, and the waves crashing beneath them drowned out everyone's voices but theirs.

"Can I ask you something?" Bronwyn squinted into the sun and pulled her jacket tighter around her. The wind was sweeping into shore over the water, and even with the golden autumn sun, it had a bite to it.

"Of course."

"I've always wondered this," Bronwyn said. "But now that you're here and I can ask you, I'm not sure I want to know the answer."

"So what is it?" Jaq said, looking over at her. Bronwyn watched the wind running its fingers through Jaq's hair, standing it on end. Jaq's eyes were intense, dark, and locked onto hers.

Bronwyn crumpled up her newspaper cone and set it beside her on the pier. "Why did you never write me back after Mum took me out of school? I wrote you every day until the term ended, but you never responded." Her eyes started to burn with ancient tears, and she paused. "Did you even open them?"

"What? I wrote you every day too." Jaq just looked at her for a moment, confused. "I never got one letter from you, I swear."

Bronwyn looked up and Jaq wiped a tear from her cheek with her thumb.

"That's why I never came to find you after school. I thought maybe your mother had finally convinced you I wasn't good enough for you."

Bronwyn stood and tried to put the pieces together so they made sense. "How is that possible? I wrote you every single night and posted it the next day."

Jaq stood too, tossing her paper cone into the trash. "I swear I never got them. Not one."

"Wait," Bronwyn said slowly. "Wasn't the girls' dean the one who always passed out the mail in the dorm?"

Jaq nodded, the pieces beginning to come together. "And all the outgoing post was dropped off with her secretary at the front desk."

They looked at each other for a moment before Bronwyn spoke. "Either it was her idea or my mum convinced her to do it, but someone intercepted our mail."

The wind picked up suddenly and blew Bronwyn's hair around them like a curtain. Jaq held her face gently and kissed her, pulling every inch of Bronwyn's body against hers. She kissed her like love, like forever, like she'd thought about doing every day since she'd forced herself to walk away.

Chapter Five

"Bronwyn," Jaq said, still kissing her, hands slipping under Bronwyn's jacket, then under her shirt to the warm, bare skin of her waist. "We've got to get off this pier before we get arrested."

Bronwyn laughed, the wind whipping around them, and nodded. "That might be a good idea."

Jaq led her back down the pier. The lights of Blackpool were beginning to sparkle, and seagulls glided above, chattering and swooping above the crowds. The Promenade, the busy main street that separated the sea from the town, was already packed with bank holiday visitors, and bar and pub patrons spilled out of doors to sit at tiny bistro tables set up outside. As they started up the winding hill to where they were staying, Jaq stopped at the shop on the corner to buy a bottle of wine. As she stood at the counter, she watched Bronwyn standing just outside, the last of the evening sun reflecting off the Irish Sea. She ran her fingers through the dark layers of her hair, the light filtering through them like a flash of gold underwater.

"That's twenty-nine pounds, seventeen pence, please, sir."

The shopkeeper's voice broke the spell, and Jaq pulled out her wallet.

"Of course, thank you," she said, handing the woman her card and turning once more to look at Bronwyn.

❖

After they'd gotten inside the church, Bronwyn opened the wine and poured them each a glass, then she took it over to the hearth where Jaq was trying to sweet-talk the fire. She was staring at the rapidly dying flames she'd managed to coax briefly into existence, only to see them disappear into ash right in front of her.

"I don't know why, but I've never been able to build a decent fire." She sighed and balled up several pages of the *London Times* beside her on the hearth to start again. "You should definitely avoid being lost in some massive English forest with me at any point in the future because we'd be shit out of luck."

Bronwyn smiled and handed her a wine glass. Jaq looked up at her as she settled in on the couch. "Listen, I know this is all sudden. You're with someone else now." Jaq broke kindling into smaller pieces and stacked it in a haphazard grid across the iron fireplace grate. "I know it can't go past the weekend."

Bronwyn took a sip of her wine, wrapping the glass in her hands and tilting it so the light filtering through the stained glass windows sifted silently through the garnet layers.

"I think I started dating him because I couldn't take having my heart broken again."

She took a sip of the wine and set it on the coffee table, pulling her legs up underneath her on the couch. Since the fire was unsurprisingly oblivious to her charms, Jaq gave up and sat on the hearth, listening.

"I just told myself I was better off avoiding the whole love issue and just settling down. He grew on me, I guess."

"And now?"

Suddenly the reluctant tinder caught fire and quickly took over the logs, engulfing them in blue heat and flashes of gold.

Bronwyn smiled, raising her eyebrow in the direction of the flames. "Now it's complicated."

Jaq walked over to the couch and sat, as Bronwyn lay back and rested her head on her leg.

"So what about you?" she said. "Breaking any hearts at Scotland Yard?"

"Well, after that thing I had this summer with Victoria..."

• 59 •

"What?" Bronwyn propped herself up on one elbow and looked at Jaq. "I'm going to assume you're joking. She's got a face like a smacked ass."

"Easy now," Jaq said, laughing. "I've dated, but I've been so busy since I came back, I haven't even thought about asking anyone out."

"I have a hard time believing that you can walk around looking like you do and not turn any heads at Scotland Yard," Bronwyn said, settling her eyes on Jaq's mouth. "I'd be willing to bet there are more than a few lesbians at London headquarters."

"True," Jaq said, slipping her hand under Bronwyn's sweater and across the soft skin of her stomach. "But I think you're more their type than I am, to say the least."

She glanced up at Jaq. "So what is your type?"

Jaq studied her face for a moment. "Girls with eyes like the forest and a bit of an edge to them." Jaq smiled, and her eyes settled on Bronwyn's mouth. "You've always been braver than people give you credit for."

"I have to admit," Bronwyn said, "before this weekend, I would have assumed you'd be more likely to go for a perfect Essex blonde in a tight skirt and stockings."

"God, no," Jaq said. "I like a smart girl in glasses who can pull off a suit with nothing underneath it."

Jaq tilted the last of the wine in her glass and looked into the fire. The wind rushed around the outside corners of the church and scraped against the windows. The rain that had started as they were walking back from the beach pelted the roof with a dense, staccato urgency. When she finally spoke, her voice was softer, as if she was holding the memory in her hand, slowly studying the shape of it.

"When you stepped up to me last night and unbuttoned your jacket," she paused, her eyes still on the fire, "it was the most turned on I've been in my entire life."

Bronwyn paused for a moment, then moved onto Jaq's lap, facing her. Jaq leaned her forehead into Bronwyn's chest, breathing her in before she lifted her sweater over her head, letting it fall onto the couch, Bronwyn's thighs tensing against hers. She ran her hands under the silk camisole she'd found under the sweater, letting it slip through her fingers like water as she dropped it to the floor too, leaving Bronwyn bare to the waist. The raw denim of her jeans was a rough contrast to her skin, and Jaq drank her in, then slid her hands from Bronwyn's hips to her ass, pulling her close.

Bronwyn's body had always been lean and sculpted, but there was a soft fullness to her breasts now, her nipples a tawny pink that Jaq longed to watch flush and harden, then tremble as an orgasm swept through her body. She traced the outside curve of Bronwyn's breast with her tongue, feeling her breath catch and hold as she got nearer to the center. She stopped and laid her hand over Bronwyn's heart, the warmth of her palm soft over the center of her chest.

"Take a breath, baby," she whispered.

Bronwyn closed her eyes and breathed, her heart racing under Jaq's hand. Jaq looked into her eyes when she finally opened them, her words soft. "We don't have to do this."

Bronwyn shook her head, her hair falling over her shoulder and around her face. "I want it. It's just surreal."

Jaq slid her hand gently across the back of Bronwyn's neck and pulled her close until she felt the warmth of her breath. Jaq bit her bottom lip softly, then tipped her chin up, keeping it there with her thumb while she ran her tongue down her neck and between her breasts. She paused over Bronwyn's nipple, her breath warm and still on her skin. She circled it with her tongue, stopping just short of pulling it into her mouth. She knew how sensitive her nipples were; she'd watched Bronwyn have her first orgasm in her bed the night she'd touched them the first time.

"Jaq," Bronwyn whispered, "please."

Jaq held her hand against the small of Bronwyn's back to steady her, then just touched her mouth to Bronwyn's nipple, so lightly it was more breath than skin. She held Bronwyn's eyes as she drew it into her mouth, stroking it with her tongue. Bronwyn took a sharp breath, tightening her hands on Jaq's shoulders. Her breath deepened, and she raked her fingers through her hair. Jaq leaned back and ran the back of her hands over both of her nipples, the texture a rough contrast to the slick warmth of her mouth, using just enough pressure to catch and turn them slightly as she moved her hands across them.

"Oh my God," Bronwyn said, the words soft and lost in breath.

Jaq turned one hand over and worked that nipple with her fingers, then pulled the other hard into the heat of her mouth. Bronwyn shuddered, her breathing quick and shallow, her hips moving against Jaq's. Her fingers tangled hard into Jaq's hair as Jaq worked Bronwyn's nipple with her tongue, creating almost enough intensity to push her over the edge. Almost.

Finally, she stood, Bronwyn's legs around her waist, and walked over to lay her down on the bed. Dusk had turned to dark, the fire the only light in the room, close enough to paint shadows onto Bronwyn's skin. Jaq leaned down to kiss her, standing as she trailed a fingertip down to the button of Bronwyn's jeans.

"Don't move."

Jaq pulled a Zippo out of her pocket while she walked away and lit the ivory candles dotted around the room, then placed them on the windowsill under the tall stained glass panes. The flames cast shapeshifting shadows onto the rough stone walls beside them as Bronwyn watched from the bed. Jaq looked thoughtful, unbuttoning her shirt as she walked, then laid it on the back of the sofa before she picked up their wine glasses. There was something rough about Jaq if you didn't know her: the definition in her arms and broad shoulders, her husky voice like the scrape of gravel, and her steadfast tendency toward silence. But Bronwyn did know her. Knew the way her eyes fell when she thought, and the gentleness of her hands as she touched her, as if she was made of the thinnest sheets of glass, fingertips moving like seawater over her skin.

She handed Bronwyn her wine glass and sat back against the headboard, made from the inner panel of an old confessional. Both of them wore only jeans, the angles and softness of their bodies more contrast than reflection. The wine shimmered with the undulating light of the candles on every side of them, and Jaq ran her hand through her hair, leaning back, her eyes moving slowly over Bronwyn's body. The storm blue of them had deepened, like pools of dark water on a cobblestone alley.

Bronwyn moved toward her, and Jaq's hands wrapped strong around her back as she laid her down on the bed underneath her. Bronwyn felt her breath, then the barest scrape of her teeth across her shoulder as Jaq brought both of her hands above her head and held them with one of hers. She lowered her mouth to the curve of her breast, just brushing it with her lips, then moved down to the sensitive skin just above the button of her jeans. Her touch was warm and insistent, and she held Bronwyn's eyes as she unfastened each button, then followed her fingertips with her tongue. After the last, she paused, then sat back and watched Bronwyn slide the jeans down her hips and push them off the edge of the bed.

Bronwyn closed her eyes as she raised her hips to let Jaq slip her panties off, then listened to her take off her own clothes and drop them to the floor. After what felt like forever, Jaq's hands moved slowly down the inside of her thighs, but she stopped after just a few seconds. Bronwyn didn't realize she was trembling until Jaq already had her arms around her, leaning back into the headboard and pulling Bronwyn close.

She whispered into her ear, her hand stroking Bronwyn's hair. "I don't want this unless you do."

Bronwyn shook her head. "I do," she said, her cheek warm against Jaq's bare chest. "It's just...intense." Bronwyn paused, unsure of how to describe it. "You were the last girl I was ever with. I missed you so much I made myself forget how it feels."

"I know," Jaq said, her thumb tracing the outline of Bronwyn's lip. Bronwyn felt the rise and fall of her breath several times before she answered.

"I did the same thing with my heart."

Jaq turned Bronwyn's face toward hers and looked into her eyes, searching for any sign of hesitation, then held her face as she kissed her, sinking down onto the length of her body and pulling Bronwyn's knee up beside her. She ran her tongue over the base of her neck and across Bronwyn's shoulders, stopping every few seconds to return to her mouth, as if it was the only way she could draw a breath. Bronwyn closed her eyes, soft moans replacing words, her fingers tightening on Jaq's shoulders. Jaq's hand moved down between their bodies as she slid her mouth down to bite the soft skin between Bronwyn's breasts, circling her nipples, then drawing them deep into her mouth, feeling them tighten against her tongue. Bronwyn's hips pressed harder against Jaq, her breath raw.

She found Jaq's wrist and pulled it close, then held her breath as she felt Jaq's fingertips slide across her clit. Then time stopped as Jaq's fingers slid slowly into the liquid heat of her body. Bronwyn arched, her breath deep and quick. Jaq's knee held Bronwyn's thighs open as she moved her fingers inside her while sliding the slick heel of her hand gently over the tight bud of her clit.

"You're so wet," Jaq whispered, bringing her fingers to her mouth. Bronwyn watched as she drew them into her mouth, then slid them slowly back inside her.

Bronwyn arched as Jaq slowly stroked both inside her and across her clit. Just as her orgasm threatened to spill over the edge, Jaq paused, holding her eyes as she slid deeper inside. Bronwyn's walls tightened around her fingers. Jaq's other hand held Bronwyn lightly against the bed at the base of her neck as her eyes swept across Bronwyn's body. An uneven flush had bloomed across her chest, and her breath was sharp and ragged, as if she'd been underwater too long and just broken the surface. She closed her eyes, begging with her breath, desperate to feel more of Jaq inside her.

As her climax started, she fell silent, then arched her back harder and moaned deep, hands tangled in Jaq's hair, her hips meeting every thrust of Jaq's hand. Each wave of her orgasm was stronger than the last until she tightened her thighs around Jaq's wrist, breathless and hoarse.

"Jaq, I can't," she said, "I can't take any more."

Jaq stilled her hand until Bronwyn started to relax, then moved up her body and pulled her into her arms.

"Bella," she said, her voice a rough whisper, hands smoothing her hair away from her damp forehead. "Tell me I didn't hurt you."

"God no," Bronwyn said, finally catching her breath somewhat and looking up at Jaq. "I just forgot. I forgot how you make me feel."

Jaq brought the duvet around their bodies and held Bronwyn in her arms, her face soft against Jaq's chest, her breathing slow and deep as she fell into a dark sleep. Someday she'd tell her that for the first time in her entire life, she knew what it felt like to be home.

Chapter Six

When Bronwyn woke the next morning, vivid images of the night before washed over her. Jaq Bailey undressing her, watching her mouth slide down the inside of her thigh, feeling her deep inside as she came so hard she forgot to breathe. She didn't remember falling asleep, but as the sun streamed in through the stained glass windows, Jaq was already gone, her side of the bed cold to the touch.

The enormity of it all started to settle like an anchor onto her chest, and she pulled the sheet back up around her as she stared at the belfry above the bed. Ian would be livid by now. She'd stopped answering her phone before the wedding, so the fact he hadn't been able to reach her since then would have driven him insane. Being so at ease with Jaq, not having to watch every word that came out of her mouth, feeling safe in her arms…everything reminded her of how tense things had gotten with Ian since the engagement. She couldn't imagine kissing him, telling him some massive lie about where she'd been since the wedding, then going back to her wedding plans as if nothing in her life had changed. But she would. She had to. The last few days with Jaq already felt like a dream, but she wasn't a kid anymore. Real life was complicated, and she'd already made her choices.

Jaq came through the door just then with takeaway coffee cups in both hands and kicked the door shut with her foot. She wore black jeans pulled low on her hips with a leather belt, an undershirt under an unbuttoned plaid flannel shirt, with black high top Converse unlaced at the ankles. She put the bag down in the kitchen and walked to the bed, handing Bronwyn her coffee as she sat up and pulled the sheet up around her.

"Morning." Jaq leaned in and kissed her. Her eyes were soft, and she tucked a lock of hair behind Bronwyn's ear as she kissed her again. She looked at her for a moment, her eyes sweeping the length of her body. "How did I forget how beautiful you are in the morning?"

Bronwyn smiled and opened the lid of her coffee cup. "What is this?"

"Triple espresso with one sugar."

"How did you know to get me espresso?" She looked up at Jaq. "I don't think we've ever even had coffee together."

Jaq smiled, kicking off her shoes and sitting against the headboard. "Lucky guess. You look like an espresso girl. But I got a latte to trade you in case I was way off base."

Her hair was still damp from the shower, and Bronwyn leaned into her neck to smell her skin. She smelled the same as she had in school: American Ivory soap and something like bay rum. She'd always sworn she didn't wear a scent, but Bronwyn had never believed her. She still didn't.

"How did you get a shower without waking me?" Bronwyn leaned back and blew gently on the black surface of the coffee to cool it, the steam rising and disappearing into the air. "What time is it?"

"It's almost ten."

"Is town already packed? Everyone floods Blackpool on bank holiday Mondays. I should have gotten up earlier."

"I went for a run before my shower, and the streets were already crowded before nine, so it wouldn't have made a difference." She looked over at Bronwyn and winked. "We never stood a chance."

Jaq pulled six sugar packets out of her shirt pocket and ripped the tops off all of them at the same time, then tipped them all into her cup, swirling it gently before she put the top back on.

"Do you need to go home today?" She sipped her coffee as she spoke, running her hand through her hair and looking over at Bronwyn.

"Not if I can borrow your phone." Bronwyn dropped her eyes to her coffee. "Ian will be going mad."

"Of course," Jaq said, pulling it out of her back pocket and handing it to Bronwyn. "I need to get something out of the car anyway, so take as long as you need."

She set her coffee on the bedside table and pulled on her shoes. She leaned over to Bronwyn, tipped her chin up with her finger to kiss her, then left, closing the front door behind her. Bronwyn took a deep breath, irrationally angry that she had to worry about what Ian would do if she didn't get in touch. She dialed his number then erased it, typing in a new number that picked up on the second ring.

"This better be you, B," Moira said, without waiting to see who was on the line. "I'm sick to death of Ian calling me at all hours of the day and night."

"It is," Bronwyn said, her stomach sinking at the thought of Ian calling everyone they knew. "I'm fine. I just called to let you know so that maybe you can call my mum for me. I know it's a big ask, but if you call her, she'll tell Ian, and maybe he won't be quite so pissed off by the time I get home."

"Of course I will." Moira let out a long breath and whispered into the phone, "Where the fuck are you, anyway?"

"I'm in Blackpool."

"With Jaq?"

Bronwyn looked over at the door she'd just walked through. "Yes," she said. "With Jaq."

"Okay, Bron," she said, "You know I think Ian's a dickhead, so I'm not judging, but what the holy fuck is going on? How did you two even get back in touch?"

"I'll tell you all about it when I get back tomorrow night. I have no idea what I'm doing, but all I know is I have to be with her right now." She squeezed her eyes shut, holding the phone to her ear, trying to put words together to explain what even she didn't understand. "I can't not do this."

"I understand, honey." Moira's voice was soft. "Are you thinking about staying with her?"

There was a long silence on the other end of the line, and when Bronwyn finally spoke, there were tears in her voice.

"How can I? I have a life with Ian. I can't do that to him."

Moira paused. "I know. And I can't imagine what your mum would say if you left Ian for Jaq. I genuinely think she'd lose her mind." Moira hesitated, as if she wanted to say something else but decided against it.

"What are you going to tell them about why I'm still here?"

"I'll tell them that you had car trouble and it took them forever to fix it because of the bank holiday." She paused. "And that somehow you lost your phone in the process."

"That will work."

Jaq came back through the door and shrugged off her jacket, going over to the fireplace to dump an armload of logs onto the hearth.

"Maybe. I don't know. Has my mum called you?"

"Yesterday, but I covered for you. She was mainly pissed about some wedding appointment you missed." Moira paused. "Just a heads up, though, it's not her you have to worry about, it's Ian. He's pissed as hell, which makes me like him even less. Brace yourself."

"Jesus." Bronwyn let out a long breath that lofted a piece of hair that had fallen against her face. "Okay. I'll deal with that tomorrow."

"Can I just tell you one more thing before you go?"

"Of course." Bronwyn tensed and closed her eyes, steeling herself for further reports of Ian's behavior.

"I know this doesn't make anything easier, but Jaq looks fucking hot." Moira cleared her throat, and Bronwyn could hear her smile. "She grew up, to say the least."

"You're not wrong there." Bronwyn looked over at Jaq. "And you don't know the half of it."

Moira squealed so loud Bronwyn pressed the phone closer to her face to keep Jaq from hearing her.

"I want details the second you get your ass back here!"

• 69 •

She sighed loudly as Bronwyn heard an insistent beep on the line. "Ian's calling again, I have to go so I can tell him to fuck off. But you and me at the pub Wednesday night?"

"Deal."

Bronwyn clicked off the phone and put it down on the bed. Jaq turned to look at her.

"You okay?" She walked over to the bed and sat down, kicking off her shoes. "I'll understand if you need to go home."

"No, it's not that," Bronwyn said, not quite meeting her eyes. "Ian has been calling my mum and Moira for days."

"Seriously?" Jaq paused and steadied her voice. "You weren't even supposed to be home until last night, right?"

"Yes, but I haven't been answering my phone." Bronwyn sank back down into the pillows and set her cup on the night table. "I can understand that he'd be worried, but Moira says he's beyond angry."

"Is she going to tell him you're fine?" Jaq's brow was creased, and the muscles in her jaw were tense and flexed.

"Yes, along with a few choice words, I'm sure."

"Are you sure you're okay going home to him when he's like that?"

"I'll be fine." Bronwyn shook her head as if to clear the thought from it. "He'll calm down eventually. He just doesn't like to be out of the loop."

Jaq stared straight ahead, her hand moving slowly through her hair to grip the back of her neck.

"He's a big talker," Bronwyn said, letting the sheet fall off her body as she straddled Jaq and leaned in to kiss her neck. "Don't worry."

Jaq held her face and kissed her, more softly than she expected. "I do worry, and I'll kill him if he lays a hand on you."

Jaq's hands moved around her hips to her bare ass. Bronwyn's breath caught as Jaq pulled her closer and flipped her onto the bed underneath her with one smooth motion.

"This doesn't seem fair. I'm the only one naked." Bronwyn raised an eyebrow.

Jaq smiled down at her and shrugged off her flannel, and had reached to pull her undershirt over her head when the phone rang. Jaq reached for it then held it up so she could see the number. Bronwyn took it and clicked the answer button and the speaker.

"I just spoke to him, so don't worry, I've got it under control." Moira paused, then whispered so close to the phone it was almost louder than her regular voice. "And just so you know, I told Catherine about you and Jaq after the wedding and she said it was a shame Jaq's obviously in love with you because she'd switch teams in a second for someone that hot."

Jaq rolled off Bronwyn and laughed out loud.

"Speakerphone, Moira." Bronwyn tried not to laugh but couldn't quite manage it. "You're on speakerphone."

"In that case, I'm late for something," Moira said, with not a hint of shame. "See you Wednesday!"

The phone clicked, and Bronwyn pulled the sheet up over her head.

❖

After Bronwyn showered, she wrapped herself in a towel and crouched by her bag, looking at every piece of clothing then tossing it back. Jaq watched from the bed, sipping the rest of her coffee.

"I can get out of here if you need some privacy to get dressed."

"No," Bronwyn said, picking up a black lace bra and underwear and balling them up into her fist. "It's not that."

Jaq just waited. She had an idea what the problem was, but it wasn't for her to talk about. She'd learned a long time ago that wrapping your own words around someone else's experience meant they'd never find their own.

Bronwyn zipped up her bag, then sat down on the stone floor and pushed it away with her foot. "I don't know how to describe it," she said, still looking at the bag as if it might decide to edge itself closer. "Sometimes I feel like I've disappeared. I haven't thought about it in years, but nothing I wear ever feels like it belongs to me."

"Why do you wear it?"

"I don't know. I guess people see me as a specific type, you know?"

Her damp hair fell into her face, and she pushed it back with her hand. She tucked the towel around her chest and wrapped her arms around her knees, her bare feet pale against the polished mahogany floorboards.

"After what happened with us, I learned pretty quickly that the only way to make Mum happy was to look like it never happened. Remember those black leather boots I used to wear with my uniform?"

Jaq nodded.

"She hated those and binned them the second I got home. She hated everything I loved."

She stopped, and Jaq looked down at the red marks Bronwyn's nails had left on her palm as she uncurled the fist she didn't realize she'd made. Jaq leaned back against the headboard and sat in the silence with her, letting it settle around them.

"After I left school, she took it personally if I didn't fit into her version of what a girl should look like, even in the smallest ways, like I'd failed her somehow. I just buried myself, I guess. After a while, I didn't have the energy to push back."

"What did your dad say about it?"

"I don't even think he realized what was happening." She stared out through a clear panel in the stained glass window beside her. "He was out filming on location so much."

Jaq took the last sip of her coffee and set it on the nightstand. "I remember your style." She rolled her sleeves up as she talked. "There was always a defiant little contrast to it. I remember walking into our dorm room one morning while you were getting dressed and you were standing there in those tough black boots and some delicate ivory bra and underwear. Your hair was all wild, and you were looking everywhere for your glasses. You didn't even realize I was there."

Bronwyn looked up at her, the start of a smile starting around her mouth.

"That's still the sexiest thing I've ever seen." Jaq looked up at her, holding her eyes. "You had no idea how beautiful you were. And still don't."

Bronwyn held up the black lace bra in her hand. "Well, the lingerie obsession is still the same. I still love it."

Jaq walked over to the couch and grabbed her bag, setting it down in front of Bronwyn on the floor.

"Let's see what you do with that."

Bronwyn laughed and started to toss the bag back to Jaq on the bed.

Jaq shook her head. "No, I'm serious. Just humor me."

Bronwyn set it down slowly and unzipped it, then stood to pull on her bra and underwear. The black lace bra was cut low and straight across her breasts, straps set wide at her shoulders, and so sheer Jaq could see her nipples from the bed. She rolled her eyes and threw a pillow in Bronwyn's direction.

"I can't believe I managed to stay on the bed while you did that." She smiled, nodding at the bag. "Put some clothes on. I can't promise how much longer I can hold out."

Bronwyn smiled and pulled out the gray G-Star jeans Jaq had worn to the wedding. She stepped into them and zipped them up.

"Come here," Jaq said, reaching for her. She held the denim on both sides of Bronwyn's body and tugged it down low on her hips. "You have an amazing body. You can wear these like a guy would and pull it off."

Jaq nodded toward the full-length mirror on the wall. "Go look."

"Wow." Bronwyn looked in the mirror for a long time, her eyes moving from the delicate bra to the raw, unfinished denim sitting on her hips. "Now what?"

Jaq laughed and leaned back against the headboard. "No way, I'm not directing this. You are."

She pulled out a hoodie and looked at it, then put it back, finally tugging a long-sleeved shirt out of the bottom of the bag.

"Let's see it." Jaq watched her from the bed, but Bronwyn was lost in her own thoughts as she pulled it on and buttoned it up.

"I like the shirt, but it looks awful on me," she said into the mirror, staring as if she was trying to read something written in a different language.

Jaq got up from the bed and stood behind her at the mirror.

"Sometimes it's not what you're wearing but how you're wearing it that makes the difference." Jaq turned Bronwyn around to face her and unbuttoned the top three buttons of the shirt. Bronwyn had buttoned it almost to her neck, but losing three of the buttons made the shirt come together just above the center of her chest, making it somehow look both more masculine and feminine at the same time. Jaq rolled the sleeves up to her elbows and tucked just the front of her shirt into her jeans, leaving the back out. Then she turned Bronwyn back to face the mirror and watched.

She didn't say anything for what seemed like forever, just stared into the mirror until Jaq saw her swipe at a tear with the heel of her hand.

"I wish I was this person."

"Well," Jaq said, wrapping her arms around her from behind, "You're in luck because you always have been."

❖

After Bronwyn finished getting ready, they walked into town, the sharp breeze a contrast to the bright sunshine that dappled the beach and lit up the surface of the water. Bronwyn looked up at Jaq with an excited smile.

"Can I take you somewhere?"

She didn't wait for an answer, just laced her fingers into Jaq's, leading her down the sidewalk toward the west end of town until Jaq stopped suddenly and pulled Bronwyn into an alley, people streaming past on both sides until they rounded the corner. She pressed her up against a brick wall under a stairwell, slipping her hands under her shirt and up the bare warmth of her back. Bronwyn's breath caught as Jaq pinned her to the wall with her mouth, covering every inch of bare skin. Jaq had always been tender with her, but now, as an adult, an edge paired with that tenderness, a wordless confidence in how she handled her body.

After a few minutes, Jaq paused to look down the alley, but Bronwyn pulled her back. Jaq growled into her neck and pressed her hips hard into Bronwyn's, the brick wall scraping the hands she'd braced on either side of Bronwyn's shoulders. She slipped one thigh between Bronwyn's legs and pressed it hard against her.

"Fuck," Bronwyn whispered as she closed her eyes and leaned her head back against the wall.

Jaq held her hips tight and moved Bronwyn against her thigh, running her tongue over the bare skin of her chest and up the side of her neck.

"We have to stop," Bronwyn whispered, her voice rough with desire. "Someone is going to see us."

"I know," Jaq said, dipping her head to pull Bronwyn's nipple into her mouth and work it with her tongue until she heard her breath turn to a moan. "And it won't look great for either of us if we get arrested."

Bronwyn hesitated, then slowly unbuttoned her jeans, taking Jaq's hand and guiding it inside her. Jaq bit Bronwyn's lip gently and tensed, fighting the sudden feeling that she might come just touching her. Bronwyn was beyond wet and felt like silk, her G-spot already swollen and tight under her fingertips. Jaq leaned into her body, sinking as deep inside her as possible, listening to her moan and feeling her tighten around her fingers, moving Bronwyn's hips with her own. Bronwyn sank against her after just a few seconds and started to come against Jaq's hand, instantly slicking it to the wrist. She was still coming hard when Jaq bit Bronwyn's shoulder to keep from crying out as her own orgasm ricocheted through her body, stealing her breath with its intensity.

Jaq finally pushed herself slowly away from the wall. Bronwyn's cheeks were still flushed, and damp strands of hair stuck to her skin until Jaq kissed her gently and pushed them away. Jaq closed her eyes and leaned her forehead into Bronwyn's, her voice deep and raw.

"Holy fuck. That was insane."

She ran her thumb over Bronwyn's lower lip, then kissed her softly, sliding her hand around the back of her neck.

"I had no idea it was even possible to come like that," Bronwyn whispered, eyes still closed.

Jaq stood, running a hand through the damp layers of her hair as she looked around. "I can't believe I'm saying this, but I don't think anyone saw us."

"Which is fortunate because it wouldn't have mattered if they had," Bronwyn said, smiling and tucking the front of her shirt back into her jeans.

Jaq pulled her into another kiss, then took her hand and led her back to the street and into the crowds of people.

"Weren't you going to show me something?"

"Well, it will be anticlimactic after that," Bronwyn said, flashing her a smile and leading her through the crowd, "But yes, I want to show you the place I was in love with as a kid."

Ten minutes later, they'd walked down the Promenade to Blackpool Tower, then up the stairs into the ornate lobby of the Empress Ballroom. Bronwyn ran to the window in the ballroom doors, but her face had fallen when she turned back around.

"I got to go inside once when I was a kid, but it's only open for a few hours a day, and both times I've been back to Blackpool I've missed it. I took ballroom dancing for years just in case I got to see it again."

Jaq looked through the window at the ballroom, which looked like the inside of a palace, with golden balconies balanced under a beautiful Victorian lofted ceiling, also gleaming with gold leaf and antique painted murals. A massive oak dance floor was the central feature, with a few dozen tables and red velvet chairs to each side. Crystal chandeliers scattered amber light across the dance floor, and a lofted stage sat at the end of the room, with ivory organ pipes rising from the floor on either side.

"It's quite a sight if you've never seen it."

They turned around and saw an older woman in a staff uniform, wearing a red velvet blazer. She was searching for something behind the ticket counter and eventually found it, folding a piece of paper into her coat pocket.

Bronwyn turned back around and looked through the window one last time. "I was here when I was little, and I thought it must be what heaven looks like."

"We're closed for an event this evening, I'm afraid," she said, "But perhaps you'll come back to see us."

Jaq nodded and kissed Bronwyn's cheek, looking through the window and trying to memorize it. It was a nice thought, but they both knew they wouldn't be back together. As they turned to leave, the woman stopped them, drawing a heavy set of keys out of her coat pocket and unlocking three separate locks, one by one, on the door. As she stepped in and motioned for them to follow, Bronwyn looked as if she might die from happiness and walked quickly ahead, spinning around with her arms stretched out the second she stepped onto the floor.

"We don't want to put you out," Jaq said, taking note of the tiny rainbow pin on the collar of her jacket as she spoke.

"Nonsense," she said. "We're done cleaning, and we won't need to set up for hours. Take your time."

"Thank you," Jaq said, shaking her hand. "We don't have much time together. This means a lot to us."

They both looked over at Bronwyn, standing in the center of the dance floor and gazing up at the ornate ceiling paintings.

"My wife took me here on our first date, and it's still one of our best memories." She squeezed Jaq's shoulder as she left and told her she'd be back in an hour or so.

Bronwyn looked over at Jaq as she stepped onto the floor, then behind her toward the door.

"Where did she go?"

Jaq walked toward her, hands in her pockets, thinking that Bronwyn had never looked more beautiful.

"It looks like I may have met your fairy godmother," Jaq said. "We have the place to ourselves for an hour."

Just as the words were out of her mouth, the music started, as clear and rich as if it were coming from the orchestra pit beyond the stage. The first song was an orchestral version of "Come Away with Me," by Norah Jones.

"This is surreal," Bronwyn said, her eyes shining. "I can't believe it's happening."

Jaq held out her hand. "Dance with me?"

Bronwyn looked at her, hesitant, then took her hand. Jaq pulled her close and kissed her, then swept her into a classic waltz, gliding across the floor with Bronwyn in her arms, her steps sure and light. Bronwyn looked into her eyes as if she'd never quite seen her before.

"You can dance?"

Jaq spun her smoothly out to the edge of the dance floor, their steps perfectly together as if they'd been dancing together all their lives. She smiled down at Bronwyn. "Looks like it."

They danced to every song that played for the next hour. Most were ballroom dances set to music by modern artists like Michael Bublé, Sting, and even Loreena McKennitt, but Bronwyn paused when she heard the start of an Argentine tango.

"I'm not sure about this one," Bronwyn said, looking up at Jaq and biting her lip. "I don't think I know enough of the steps to be able to move well."

"You don't have to, Bella," Jaq whispered, her fingers soft at the back of her neck. "I'll move you."

Jaq placed one foot between hers and ran her hand down the back of Bronwyn's thigh, lifting it to rest against her hip. She held her eyes as she bent her back, pulling Bronwyn's hips tight into hers and bringing her back up slowly, every inch of her body unfolding onto Jaq's until they were face-to-face, lips almost touching.

"Wow," Bronwyn whispered, breathless before the first step.

Jaq led her through a perfect Argentine tango, the Gipsy Kings playing in the background, lifting her so her feet were just above the floor during the most difficult steps, then shaping her body beautifully around her own for the slower, more sensual moves. As the song ended, Jaq spun Bronwyn into her body and held her there, their faces an inch apart. She kissed her as the music faded, and the staff they hadn't noticed watching clapped and whistled.

Bronwyn blushed, and they took a quick bow as Jaq led her off the dance floor toward the exit. She looked around for the woman who had let them into the ballroom, finally spotting her watching from the balcony with another butch woman sitting next to her, arm around her shoulders. Bronwyn stopped and blew them a kiss, which only amped up the applause they could still hear as they left the building and stepped back onto the street.

Chapter Seven

Bronwyn made herself wait until they had chosen an out-of-the-way pub and tucked themselves into a dark corner booth with pints of Guinness.

"Okay, Bailey," she said, locking her eyes on Jaq, "spill it."

Jaq laughed and looked down at her pint. "There's not much to tell."

Bronwyn smiled and sat across from her with her arms folded. "Let's start with how a tomboy from a Texas trailer park learned how to dance like that. And I'm not leaving until you tell me."

Jaq ran her hand through her hair and leaned back in the booth. "It's not that exciting. It just kind of happened."

Bronwyn raised an eyebrow.

"My mom used to bartend at the American Legion Club quite a bit, and I sometimes went with her and waited until closing so I could help her clean up." Jaq took a long swig of her pint and tapped her fingers slowly on the side of her glass before she went on. "At first it was fine, but then she started drinking earlier and earlier while she was serving, so by the time they closed she was usually wasted. I had to restock the bar and wait until she was sober enough to drive us home."

"That's awful." Bronwyn leaned across the table and brushed Jaq's hand with hers. "I'm so sorry."

"Don't be," Jaq said. "I didn't know any different at the time, so I was just used to it."

"What was the American Legion?"

"It was a social club that other organizations rented out for events, and they hired Mom to work the bar sometimes. One of the ballroom dancing studios in Austin started using it for extra dance space that summer, and I'd sit at the bar all night watching them." She paused as if seeing them again in her mind. "I'd never seen anything so beautiful."

"How old were you?"

"Twelve. But by that time I was already five-nine, with an attitude and a guy's haircut, so I looked a lot older." She swirled her Guinness around the bottom of her glass and drank the last of it. "The instructor, Greg, noticed one night that Mom was sitting at the end of the bar passed out, and he asked me if I needed a ride home. I turned him down and told him I hadn't restocked the beer cases yet. The next night he asked me if I wanted to learn how to waltz."

"What did you say?"

"Well, I was drinking a Coke, and I remember I laughed so hard it came out my nose."

Bronwyn laughed, thanking the waitress as she brought their food and silverware. She pushed Jaq's burger toward her, but she didn't even look at it.

"He said no one watches like I did if they didn't want to learn, so he made a deal with me that he'd help me restock the bar after close if I let him try to teach me to dance. I didn't realize it then, but he was gay. We never talked about it, but I think he knew I was queer too."

"What was your first lesson like?"

"Awkward." Jaq looked around and signaled the waitress for another Guinness. "By that time, I'd been watching for months, so I knew what position to start in, but he just shook his head, switched places with me, and said he was going to teach me to lead."

Bronwyn smiled. "Yep, he knew you were gay."

"After the first lesson, I started practicing at home. I even looked up the steps and memorized them before he had a chance to teach me."

"Did you start taking more lessons?"

"He let me clean his dance studio in town for free lessons, and

• 81 •

I went every day. When I got good enough, I helped him with the classes."

"Did he ever ask you how old you were?"

Jaq shook her head. "He never asked me anything. I think he wasn't sure if I was even a girl for a long time, but I don't think it mattered to him either way."

"How long did you study with him?"

"Almost two years. After the first year, he bought me a pair of dance shoes and paid me to teach, and then eventually trained me to enter one of the Austin ballroom dance competitions with one of his other female dancers. At first, I was so nervous I screwed it up, but by the third competition, I hit my stride, and we started winning. I got to the national championships the year I turned fourteen as a junior dancer with a female partner."

"You competed as a boy?"

Jaq nodded. "No one ever questioned it."

The waitress brought the pint, and Jaq was quiet for a few minutes, just looking down at the top of the glass.

"So what happened after that?"

"We won the junior ballroom national title." Jaq ran her hand through her hair and looked past Bronwyn toward the wall, her face set. "Then later that night, two guys from my school came to my trailer while my Mom was at work and beat me up. Evidently, one of them had a sister in the competition who recognized me and told them I was a girl."

"Oh my God." Bronwyn covered her mouth with her hand.

"It wasn't that bad." Jaq cleared her throat and took a sip of her beer. "But when Greg saw it, he made me tell him what happened. He pulled me out of competition, but two weeks later, I was on my way to Stratford, so it didn't matter anyway."

"What did he say?"

"He didn't say much, but I remember him hugging me when he saw the bruises on my face, and when he let me go, there were tears in his eyes. I never forgot him. I still keep in touch with him and his husband, and I worked my way through university giving dance lessons in East London. I could never have done that without them."

Bronwyn pushed Jaq's plate toward her until Jaq picked up her burger, then sat back in the booth. "I guess I've never thought about what it must have been like to look queer when you were so young."

"It never caused me problems after that." Jaq took a bite of her burger and smiled. "Well, until your mom found out I was sleeping with her daughter."

Bronwyn set her knife and fork on her plate and pushed it away.

"Mum always told me they expelled me and said that's why she was taking me home." She looked up at Jaq. "But it never made sense to me because you stayed in school for the rest of that year. Do you think she was lying?"

Jaq nodded. "She was just desperate to get you away from me. They wouldn't have expelled you—or your dad's money." She scraped a chip across a lake of HP Sauce on her plate. "They named the new lacrosse pitch after him the year after it happened, for fuck's sake."

Bronwyn watched as she stacked chips across her burger and replaced the bun.

"Actually, they wanted to expel me until he stepped in."

"What?" Bronwyn leaned forward over the table. "What are you talking about?"

Jaq wiped her mouth with her napkin and set it down beside her plate. "The day after you left, he just showed up at the dorm and told me to get in his car."

"That doesn't sound like him." Bronwyn looked puzzled. "He always liked you, as far as I know."

"I thought it was going to be a repeat of what happened after the dance competition, but he was just there to take me to lunch. We went to the Copper Pig pub in London, and he bought me my first pint. I had no idea what was going on."

"What did he say?"

"He asked me right away how I felt about you."

"What did you say?"

"I told him I was in love with you."

Bronwyn smiled. "You never said that to me."

"Let's just say I gave that information out on a need-to-know basis." Jaq smiled, reaching over and tucking a stray lock of hair behind her ear. "And I figured your dad needed to know."

"What else did he say?"

"That he'd spent the morning in the dean's office making it clear that if I was expelled, his money went with me."

Bronwyn smacked her palm down onto the tabletop. "I knew there was something about that whole situation he wasn't telling me. I could tell at the wedding."

Jaq smiled. "He called me every year or so after that just to check in, and I think he may have even had a hand in getting me an interview at Scotland Yard. I don't know how they would have known about me otherwise, and no one there will tell me."

"That makes sense," Bronwyn said. "His college roommate is fairly high up there." She looked at Jaq, her eyes moving down to her mouth. "So after all this time, when I thought I'd never see you again, my dad was keeping tabs on you."

"You could say that." Jaq smiled. "It was great to see him at the wedding."

Bronwyn just shook her head and stole the pickle off the edge of Jaq's plate.

❖

By the time they made it out of the pub, it was late afternoon, and the warm autumn sun was sparkling on the navy blue surface of the sea. Jaq led Bronwyn down to the beach, still crowded with kids in rolled-up jeans trying to outrun the waves crashing into the sand. Navy and white striped deckchairs dotted along the shore from pier to pier like late summer garland. The rides on the main pier rocketed around their tracks, adding to the backdrop of children's laughter, waves bringing the incoming tide, and carnival music tinkling down from the ice cream stands at the edge of the promenade.

"So when is the wedding?" Jaq turned toward her as they walked along the shoreline, squinting into the late afternoon sun.

"It's in three months." Bronwyn's voice was suddenly soft, almost swept away by the wind.

They walked in silence for a while, Jaq tucking Bronwyn's smaller hand inside hers to shield it from the cold salt air. There was nothing to say. Jaq knew they hadn't talked about the possibility of staying together because it didn't exist.

"Dad told me a while ago that he'll be there to support me, but he says he can't give me away if I marry Ian."

"Wow," Jaq said, looking over at Bronwyn and squeezing her hand. "What made him dislike Ian so much?"

"Remember when I told you that Ian had that crisis at work a year ago?" She smoothed the sand with her foot. "Well, he got really drunk one night and left some marks on me…"

"What kind of marks?"

"It doesn't matter," Bronwyn said, avoiding Jaq's eyes. "They weren't that bad, honestly, but I went home to Mum and Dad's for a few days afterward, and somehow Dad saw them."

"Did you tell him what happened?"

"No." Bronwyn slowed, then sat on the beach and took off her shoes, rolling up the hem of her jeans. "I didn't lie to him, but I didn't tell him what Ian did, either." She dug her toes into the cold sand and looked up at Jaq. "Then after my uncle told him what he'd seen Ian do in his cafe, Dad was so angry that I worried he'd go after him or something."

"Did he?"

"No," Bronwyn said, watching a seagull glide smoothly over their heads and out toward the water. "I made him promise he wouldn't."

Jaq picked up a shell and threw it as far as she could into the waves. "Has Ian ever done anything like that since?"

"No, not since then." She looked out over the sea. "He's a good guy, he just has a temper."

Jaq looked out over the undulating surface of the sea, the sun dipping lower toward the horizon at the edge of the dark water. When she finally spoke, her voice was low and rougher than Bronwyn knew it could be.

"That'll be the least of his worries if he ever puts his hands on you again."

Bronwyn looked over at Jaq, still staring out over the waves. Her jaw was tense. She rubbed her forehead and ran both hands through her hair before she spoke.

"If he ever does anything like that again, Bella, please come find me and let me protect you. I can't let you go tomorrow unless you promise me you will."

Bronwyn nodded. "I promise."

Jaq looked at the last of the sunlight casting flecks of gold into Bronwyn's eyes. She wanted to say a thousand things, but she just held her face in her hands, pulled her close, and kissed her.

❖

On the way home, they bought some ingredients at the market for dinner, and as they climbed the hill, the stars were just starting to sparkle in the velvet black sky over the piers below. Jaq opened the door for Bronwyn and went to put the groceries on the counter. She looked thoughtful for a moment, then tore off a piece of the paper bag and wrote something down.

"What's this?" Bronwyn looked at it as she handed it to her.

"I just realized we don't even have each other's phone numbers."

"That's true, although I may have a different one after I get a new phone tomorrow." Bronwyn tore another strip of paper off the bag and wrote down her address. "This is my address in Notting Hill, and I'll text you my number tomorrow."

"Notting Hill?" Jaq raised an eyebrow. "That's so posh even I recognize it."

"Don't be impressed, I didn't buy it. Dad gave me the house after I finished grad school. It was his grandmother's. It's a three-story semi-detached across from the park."

Bronwyn opened the bottle of sauvignon blanc they'd gotten at the wine shop in town and poured a glass for each of them. "Cheers," she said, clinking her glass to Jaq's.

After she'd gotten everything out of the bags, she tossed Jaq a hunk of parmesan and dug a grater out of the drawer.

"Any chance you can grate this for me while I start the pasta? Suddenly I'm starving for some reason."

"If you'd like, I can remind you why that might be," Jaq said, brushing Bronwyn's nipple with the back of her hand as she took the grater.

Bronwyn looked at her and smiled. "You're torturing me. You know that, right?"

"That has not been proven, Ms. Charles. I think it's the other way around." Jaq took a sip of her wine and pulled herself up to sit on the counter.

Bronwyn put the pasta on to boil while she put together a simple white wine and cream sauce. By the time it was done, Jaq had managed to coax a fire out of the logs she'd brought in earlier and they settled in on the couch to eat.

"Wow," Jaq said, coming up for air after a few bites of pasta, "this is seriously good."

"Don't be impressed. There's like four ingredients, and one of them is pasta."

Jaq leaned over and refilled her wine glass. "By the way, I saw a painting last week that reminded me of you," Jaq said. "Well, not a painting really, but a mural. It was on the side of an overpass near one of the council estates."

"Did you like it?"

"I loved it, but it was just unexpected. I've driven by that area for years when I was in grad school, and it's always been just concrete and council houses, typical low-income housing. Not too much different from the same kind of neighborhood in the States." Jaq poured more wine into Bronwyn's glass and handed it back to her. "I know it sounds dramatic, but it really did make everything around it look better."

Bronwyn took a last bite and put her bowl back on the coffee table. "Which one was your favorite?"

"The one of a waterfall near Camden...but how did you know there's more than one?" Jaq looked at her for a moment and put her fork down. "You painted them, didn't you?"

Bronwyn shook her head. "No, not at all." She tucked her bare

• 87 •

feet under Jaq's legs on the couch. "I've been working with the council on them for the last two years as a community project. I plan the murals, map them out in sections, and families from the neighborhood each take one. It's a little like paint by numbers, and I work with them to try to keep the sections looking consistent. By the time it's done, the community feels like they've done something great together." She smiled up at Jaq. "Or that's the idea, at least."

Jaq leaned back on the arm of the couch and pulled Bronwyn's feet into her lap. "That's amazing, but I can't say I'm surprised. It sounds like something you'd do."

Bronwyn crawled over to Jaq and settled into her arms.

Jaq smoothed the hair off her forehead and slipped her hand under her shirt to run her fingertips across Bronwyn's back. "How am I supposed to forget you when your paintings are all over London?"

Bronwyn kissed Jaq's chest, so soft it felt like breath. "I don't want you to forget me."

Jaq brought her face up and kissed her, slowly unbuttoning her shirt at the same time. She whispered into her neck, "Then let me see you again."

It was a long time before Bronwyn answered, and when she did, her voice broke. "I can't."

Jaq saw the shimmer of tears in her eyes before she turned her head to hide them. She'd been in love with Bronwyn since she was seventeen, but Bronwyn belonged to someone else now. It might have been different if they'd known the truth all those years ago, but there was no way to go back, and it wasn't fair to ask.

"I know, Bella," Jaq said, tipping her face up and kissing the tears away. "Don't think about it now."

Jaq kissed her with the intensity of every moment she'd never have, every morning they'd never wake to, every kiss she'd lost years ago and now had lost again. She slipped her shirt off her shoulders, brushing her lips over the pink buds of Bronwyn's breasts, watching them harden under her touch, then held her eyes as she sank to her knees in front of the couch. She unbuttoned Bronwyn's jeans and eased them down her hips, following every inch with her tongue.

She took her time, memorizing her slowly, trying not to think that it might be the last time she'd ever see her. Bronwyn's breath was soft and deep as she leaned back on the couch, watching as Jaq picked up her hand and drew her finger into her mouth, swirling it with her tongue, the silky warmth of her mouth making her ache. Jaq slipped her hand under the edge of her panties, leaving Bronwyn to feel the last heat of the dying fire touch her inner thighs as Jaq slid her thumb slowly over her wet clit.

"What do you want, baby?" Jaq said as she slid her tongue up Bronwyn's thigh.

Bronwyn leaned back and closed her eyes as Jaq leaned in closer, hands on her hips, dragging the tip of her tongue over her clit and down the length of her soft inner lips, then back again.

Bronwyn tangled her fingers in Jaq's hair, pulling her closer. Her breath was ragged and left little room for words. "God, Jaq, you're torturing me. I can't take this."

She opened her eyes and Jaq saw how flushed her cheeks already were, her hands closed tight around Jaq's shoulders, pulling her closer.

"Bella," Jaq whispered, smiling, her hand warm across Bronwyn's stomach. "I haven't even started with you yet."

Bronwyn ran her hands through her hair and moaned as Jaq drew her clit lightly into her mouth, brushing it achingly slowly with her tongue. She slid the tip slowly around the most sensitive parts, lightening her touch when Bronwyn's breath quickened, then suddenly giving her the pressure she needed until Bronwyn started to moan. When she did, Jaq leaned back, slowly, letting just the heat of her mouth hover over her clit.

She moved back up Bronwyn's body to kiss her, working the fine mist of sweat gathered on her chest into her skin, then drawing her nipples hard into her mouth before letting them go with a soft scrape of her teeth. Hands tightened into Jaq's hair as she moved back down between Bronwyn's thighs, kissing the sensitive skin of her stomach before dragging her tongue back over her clit.

"Christ." Bronwyn's hips begged, but Jaq stopped again just before she went over the edge and just kept her there, patient and silent. She sat back finally, looking into Bronwyn's eyes as she slid two fingers inside and stroked her, listening to Bronwyn's breath as she closed her eyes and moved her hips with Jaq inside her.

"Do you want more, baby?"

"I don't know." The fine mist of sweat on her chest had gathered now on her hips and thighs, shimmering in the last of the firelight. "I don't know what I can take anymore."

Bronwyn arched her back as Jaq slid one more finger inside her. Her moans were soft and wordlessly pleading, then sharply intense as Jaq slicked her tongue back over her clit while she continued to stroke her inside. This time she didn't stop when Bronwyn started to go over the edge, just slid her fingers deeper as she trapped Bronwyn's hard clit under her tongue.

"Jaq," Bronwyn whispered, "God, don't stop..."

Her thighs trembled as her orgasm started to take over, her clit pulsing and hot in Jaq's mouth. She cried out, her arms above her head, gripping the back of the couch as she shuddered to an orgasm that shook her with blinding power until she was breathless and trembling. As it finally faded, Jaq pulled Bronwyn to her chest, holding her there, smoothing damp hair away from her face until she finally caught her breath. When she finally heard her breathing calm and turn toward sleep, she got up slowly and offered Bronwyn her hand. Bronwyn looked doubtful—her thighs were still trembling—but she stood and followed her to bed, climbing in and watching Jaq undress in the dying firelight.

"I'm so sorry about your shirt," she said, looking back at where it lay on the couch and pulling the duvet up around her. "I don't know how I got it so wet."

Jaq smiled, running a hand through her hair. "I know, Bella. That's why I put it underneath you."

Jaq climbed into bed, her naked body pressed to Bronwyn's, listening to the last sparks of fire settle into ash in the fireplace.

"How did you know how to do that to me?" She whispered it into Jaq's ear, not sure she could say it if she looked in her eyes.

Jaq smiled, running her fingers through Bronwyn's hair. "This isn't exactly my freshman year with the whole lesbian sex thing."

Bronwyn was quiet, trailing her fingertips low across Jaq's abs. "I want to know how to make you come like that."

Jaq raised up on her elbow and kissed her, pulling away with a soft bite at Bronwyn's lip.

Bronwyn held her eyes, still and intense. "Teach me."

Jaq's gaze swept her naked body, then she turned over on her back, pulling Bronwyn over to sit across her hips. Bronwyn's hair was wild and falling around her shoulders, her breasts still flushed, her nipples pink and tender. Jaq stopped to take in every inch of her, memorizing the sound of every breath. The silence was intense as her hands slid from Bronwyn's hips to the familiar curves of her ass, pulling her tighter against her body. Bronwyn ran her palms over Jaq's nipples, watching them tighten, then leaned forward and drew them slowly into her mouth, closing her eyes and delicately working each with her tongue. Jaq groaned, surprised at how much it affected her. Bronwyn was bolder now than when they were younger. When they'd been in school, she'd been too shy to explore Jaq's body, and Jaq had been too distracted by hers to care.

Bronwyn kissed softly down the side of Jaq's neck, eventually moving back up to trace her ear with her tongue and the warmth of her breath. As she sat back up, Jaq held her gaze and started to move Bronwyn's hips with her hands, sliding her back and forth, tight against her body. Bronwyn's wetness slicked between them, and she started to gently rock her hips against Jaq's as she leaned back, then dragged her nails slowly up the inside of Jaq's thighs.

"Jesus."

Jaq's voice was rough, hands tightening around Bronwyn's hips as she guided her into the right rhythm, Bronwyn's center sliding hard across her own. Her abs tensed and she bit her lip as Bronwyn rode her, matching her pace. Bronwyn watched as Jaq's breath started to deepen, her eyes closed, every muscle in her body tight.

"Fuck, baby," she said, the words falling and disappearing between them.

Bronwyn leaned back, her hands braced behind her on Jaq's thighs. Heat built between their bodies and she rocked harder against

Jaq's clit as she held her hips. Jaq's muscles tightened underneath Bronwyn's hands, her eyes dark and locked on where Bronwyn's body met hers.

    She slowed and brought Bronwyn down to kiss her, the familiar scent of her skin bringing sudden tears to her eyes. Jaq held Bronwyn's forehead to hers until Bronwyn kissed her cheeks gently, then sat back up and started sliding her hips against Jaq's again, holding her eyes until she was too close to do anything but feel. Seeing her like that was too much. Jaq's breath quickened, then caught, and she cried out as she came. She pulled Bronwyn's hips harder against her until a sudden orgasm whipped through Bronwyn's body like a crack of lightning and she collapsed against Jaq, wondering if she'd ever catch her breath again.

Chapter Eight

"So this is where you live?"

Bronwyn looked up at the industrial building as she parked. It was five stories tall, with a crumbling plaster exterior that exposed the brick underneath, and tall oak arched doors.

Jaq nodded, gripping the keys in her hand. "It used to be a furniture factory, and the converted lofts still have that gritty look, which is probably why I like it so much."

"That sounds like you," Bronwyn said, looking over at Jaq. She felt suddenly desperate to memorize her lips, the angles of her face, the way her fingertips moved over her body, but she just leaned her head back in the seat.

"Come upstairs with me," Jaq said, turning toward her.

The late afternoon sun fell across Bronwyn's eyes, and she closed them before she spoke, tears soaking through her lashes.

"I can't," she said, her voice a whisper. "If I do, you know I won't leave."

Jaq looked out the window for a long time before she spoke. "I don't want to lose you again."

A tear slipped down Bronwyn's face. She took a shaky breath and turned to look at Jaq. "It's too late. I can't do this to Ian."

"Can I see you again?"

Bronwyn shook her head, wiping the tears from her cheek with the cuff of her sweater. She started to speak, but a sob stole the words from her mouth, leaving only one. "No."

Jaq shut her eyes and ran her hands through her hair, then

turned back to Bronwyn and held her face in her hands, kissing her gently and touching her forehead to Bronwyn's.

"I'm here," she said. A tear dropped from Jaq's face onto Bronwyn's cheek. "I love you. I always have."

She got out of the car, put her bag on her shoulder, and shut the door.

❖

The second Bronwyn stepped into her house and dropped her bags on the floor, she knew Ian was there. She walked down the hall to the kitchen, where she saw him sitting at the table with a vodka bottle and a shot glass.

"Where the fuck have you been, Bronwyn?"

Bronwyn sank into the chair beside him, taking in his crumpled shirt and the tired lines of his face. "I've been stuck in Northumberland. They finally got my car fixed this morning."

"Did you even go to the wedding?"

"Of course I did," Bronwyn said. "You can ask my dad and Moira, they were both there."

"Why didn't you call me?"

"I lost my phone. Moira's was the only number I had memorized. She said she'd let you know."

Ian filled the shot glass and threw it back in one swallow, setting it back on the table with a sharp clink. "Right."

"Have you been here the whole time?"

"Since yesterday. Moira spun me that same line of bullshit about your phone, so I wanted to be here when you got home."

"It's not bullshit, Ian." Bronwyn sighed and leaned back in her seat. Ian hadn't turned on a single light, and the kitchen was dark as if no one was in the house at all. Shadows from the trees outside the windows were strewn across the floor as if someone had tossed them there.

"The day of the wedding my phone quit, and I just left it at the hotel. You know I've had the same one for way too long."

Ian walked over to the kitchen counter and came back to the table with a new iPhone in his hand that looked exactly like her last one. "I got you a new phone."

Bronwyn didn't take it when he handed it to her and Ian set it on her side of the table. "You didn't have to do that," she said.

Bronwyn got up from her chair and picked up the bag she'd dropped by the table. Suddenly, she was exhausted, too tired to think, or move, or argue with someone who thought she was lying. And he was right.

"Ian, I'm exhausted, we can talk about this later. I'm going upstairs for a bath," she said, looking back at him. "Can you lock the door on your way out?"

Ian stood and set her bag on the floor before he pulled her into his arms. His unshaven face scraped her cheek, and he smelled of vodka and dry cleaning. Bronwyn felt herself stiffen.

"You know I love you, right?" He pulled her back slightly and looked into her eyes. "I may not always show it as I should, but I panicked when I didn't know where you were. I don't know what I'd do without you."

"I know." She stepped back and picked up her bag. "But you don't have to worry. I'm back now."

Ian squeezed her shoulder and grabbed his jacket from the back of the kitchen chair as he headed toward the front door.

"I almost forgot," he said. "A parcel came for you earlier today. I put it upstairs on your bed."

He shut the door behind him, and Bronwyn slid down the wall to the floor, silent tears crowding her cheeks, the memory of Jaq's arms around her already fading into a pale gray.

Later that night, she opened the plain brown box she'd found on her bed. Inside was a new pair of the same black leather boots she'd worn in high school. There was a note tucked into one of them, and Bronwyn opened it, her hands shaking.

For the next time we dance.

❖

The next day was sparkling with unexpected October sunshine, the breeze ruffling the leaves at Bronwyn's feet as she walked from her house across town to meet Moira at her local pub. They always met there; the pubs in Notting Hill were a bit too stuffy for Bronwyn. The hipster crowd had taken over in the last few years, and now you couldn't get a pint without someone in a beard asking you whether you fancied a mushroom stuffed with goat cheese or something equally obnoxious. She texted Moira as she walked, turning sideways as a crush of giggling schoolchildren passed her on the sidewalk, their backpacks bumping against her and almost knocking the phone out of her hand.

Almost there, where are you sitting?

Her phone pinged almost instantly with Moira's reply. *Where I've sat for the last ten years. Already got you a chocolate martini.*

Bronwyn raised an eyebrow, typing quickly as she crossed the street to the pub on the other side. *You'd better be kidding.*

Okay, it's for me. But if you're not here in three minutes, I'm drinking your pint.

People sitting outside, soaking in the last of the afternoon sun, packed the World's End Pub. The building was lacquered a bright red, with an old black door that was usually propped open with an old whiskey barrel, even late into the fall. Flowers fell several feet down the front wall from the second story windows, competing with the ivy growing around the corners and up to the mossy slate rooftop. She edged her way inside then out to the back garden, spotting Moira sitting at a picnic table, tapping her nails on her glass. She gave her a quick hug from behind and slid onto the bench on the other side.

"Did you have a nice holiday weekend?" Bronwyn dropped her bag under the table and smiled sweetly at Moira.

Moira rolled her eyes. "Oh my God, Bronwyn, if you don't start talking right this second, I'm going to lose my mind."

Bronwyn laughed and took a sip of her pint. It was a hard golden cider, more sharp than sweet, and Bronwyn's favorite.

"How the hell did you get back in touch with Jaq Bailey?"

"I didn't, well, not on purpose anyway. We ran into each other at a country pub outside Northumberland."

"What were you doing there?"

"Well, here's the short version. I got lost in that storm Friday night, my car got stuck in the mud, and I walked to the nearest pub dragging my suitcase behind me in the rain. I looked a right state by the time I got there."

"Ooh." Moira looked thrilled, sipping her chocolate martini and giving herself a tiny chocolate mustache in the process. "So you were stranded and walked in looking like a sopping stray cat? This is even better than I thought."

"Cheers, Moira," Bronwyn said with a wink. "Although you're not wrong."

"So what, she was just sitting there when you walked in?"

"Apparently," Bronwyn said, smiling at the memory of how Jaq looked when she walked over to her by the fire. "But she waited until they told me there were no vacancies for the night before she said anything. She walked up behind me, and I knew it was her before I saw her."

"God, it's that deep sexy voice of hers." Moira paused and added to her mustache. "Even I'd recognize that."

"Exactly," Bronwyn said. "And she looked…well, you saw her at the wedding."

"She was hard to miss. You looked gorgeous too, by the way. That suit was amazing." Moira paused, getting back on track. "Wait, what happened after you saw her in the pub?"

"Well, she was nice enough to let me use her room to dry off and lend me a sweater." Bronwyn ran a hand through her hair, smiling at the memory. "When I came back down, she'd ordered me dinner, and we just talked for ages."

"If you're going to try to make me believe you had a cozy little supper with Jaq Bailey, then politely got into a cab and went on your way, don't waste your breath."

"Okay," Bronwyn said. "I stayed the night in her room, but nothing happened."

"Oh my God." Moira leaned forward in her seat. "This just keeps getting better."

"Well," she said, "nothing happened that night."

"Spill it, B," Moira said. "You slept with her after the wedding, didn't you? Even Catherine noticed the tension. She literally couldn't keep her eyes off you."

"Well, it almost happened then, but we held off until the next night. But God, it was amazing."

"That's not hard to imagine," Moira said. "Who started it?"

"I did. She was worried I'd regret it and kept asking if I was sure."

"Such a gent," Moira said, pulling her lip gloss out of her pocket and expertly swiping her lips without a mirror. "If that's the term to use, anyway."

"To be honest, I can't stop thinking about it."

"Can't stop thinking about...it?" Moira said, leaning forward over the table until Bronwyn stopped avoiding her eyes, "Or her?"

Bronwyn didn't say anything. She didn't have to. She swiped at the sudden tear on her cheek as Moira reached out and took her hand.

"So you're going to let her go because you think you have to keep Ian happy? I've never seen you as happy as you were with her, B."

"But I'm engaged." Bronwyn picked up her pint and sat back with her arms crossed.

"Yes, you are engaged," Moira said, looking at the diamond on her hand with one eyebrow raised. "To a complete knob."

"Moira! You just don't know him. He's not always that bad."

"Bron," Moira said, "if you let Jaq go, you'll regret it for the rest of your life. We've been best friends for fifteen years. I know you."

"Shit." Bronwyn pushed her pint to the side and dropped her head down on her arms. "What the hell am I going to do?"

❖

"Where have you been hiding, Bailey? I haven't seen you all week."

Trina Hanson, the no-nonsense detective who worked in the

office across the hall, leaned into Jaq's office on her way downstairs to the coffee stand on the main floor.

Jaq looked up from her desk, startled. "I've been down in Brighton since last week, finishing up the Riley case."

She nodded. "Better you than me. Brighton always gives me a migraine. Wait, didn't you go to a wedding up north before that for the bank holiday?"

Jaq fished her phone out of her jacket pocket, scrolling through pictures until she found what she wanted. "I did," she said. "And it turned out to be pretty interesting."

She held the phone up to Trina, who leaned in and grabbed it out of Jaq's hand with a delighted squeal. It was a picture of Bronwyn with her father and Catherine at the table during Victoria's reception.

"You met Catherine Flack? How the hell did that happen?"

It had been almost two weeks since she'd seen Bronwyn, and Jaq still hadn't been able to concentrate on anything else. Talking about Catherine was a distraction, at least. "She's a friend of a friend and was seated at my table for the reception."

"You know she hosts my favorite show every summer, right?"

"I've heard you mention it once or twice." Jaq peered over to look at the picture. "Scroll over to the next one."

Trina swiped to the next photo and looked suddenly like she might faint. "Jaq, oh my God! Send that to me this very instant!"

Jaq laughed and took her phone back to text the picture to Trina. She'd asked Catherine during one of the slower speeches whether she'd mind posing for a picture for her workmate. She was very gracious about it and had borrowed a pen to write something on her napkin, then held it up in the photo, pointing at it with a big smile. *Trina's Biggest Fan.*

Jaq could still hear her chattering about it halfway down the hall, which was pretty entertaining because ordinarily, Trina was all business and hard as nails. Jaq sat back in her chair and stared at the window, the spreadsheets she had open on her monitor forgotten. She was waiting to be briefed on a new case from her boss, Terry Macmillan, but he was late for their meeting.

Jaq had never given law enforcement a thought until she was actively recruited in the States and flown back to London for an interview. As she started learning more about what they needed, she realized why they'd chosen her. Computers only went so far—they needed a human link to identify numeric codes and patterns and give the other detectives an edge as they delved deeper into the cases that required forensic accounting. Jaq had always been able to identify codes that computers missed, so the combination of that and her additional knowledge of specific case details proved to be invaluable. It had pushed her abilities in an unexpected direction, and she'd loved it from the first day.

For the first three months in London, she worked with law enforcement professionals to develop the physical skills she'd need on the job, much like boot camp for American police officers. Unlike the States, almost none of the law enforcement personnel in the UK were authorized to carry guns, except for those at higher levels who received special clearance, and Jaq was one of those. More often than not, if forensic accounting was brought in to help solve a case, there was a good chance it was linked to the drug trade and trafficking. If you followed the money, what you found at the end was typically drugs, which amped up the danger for anyone involved.

A few minutes later, Terry Macmillan arrived at her office, trying to hold on to a stack of folders and peel the backing from a nicotine patch at the same time.

"These things will be the death of me," he said, handing the files to Jaq and slapping the patch onto the underside of his arm. "But my wife says she'll leave me if I don't quit smoking. Frankly, I'm not sure which is worse."

Jaq smiled. Anyone who'd ever stepped into Macmillan's office, his walls thickly lined with photos of his wife and three redheaded boys, knew that wasn't true.

"Now," he said, leaning over Jaq's desk and dropping the nicotine patch wrapper into her trash, "let's go over this case. We've been working on this thing for three months, but there's something we're missing here."

"How so?"

"Technically, it's a money laundering case, but I'm fairly certain it leads straight into the center of the cocaine trade here in London. All the money patterns follow the known drug shipments, but whoever is at the helm knows what they're doing. It's been difficult to track and even harder to figure out who's calling the shots."

"So why haven't they shut down the account?"

"If we do that, they'll ghost us, which means she'll just go underground and we won't have continued access to them."

"It's a woman?"

"It is, although I'm positive there's more than one person involved here, most likely a small group. She may just be the front person," Terry said. "I was almost sure whoever was moving the money was using an account they hijacked, so first thing we did was track down the person whose name and national insurance number is on the account."

"That's like an American social security number, right?"

"Just the same," Terry said, "But that woman died in 1982."

"So they used a dead woman's details to open a fraudulent account?"

"They most likely did it online," Terry said, leafing through the folder as he spoke. "Either that or they have a connection within Barclays Bank or one of its subsidiaries. It's difficult, but it can be done."

"So you can't freeze the account and tip them off, and there's no way to know when they'll visit a particular bank to be able to arrest them there?"

"Exactly. There are more than thirteen hundred branches of Barclays in the UK." Macmillan turned his pen over and over between his fingers as he spoke. "Once we make a move, it doesn't take long before they realize we're onto them, sometimes only hours, and once they do, we won't have a chance in hell of seeing them again. They'll be gone faster than a fart in the wind."

Macmillan suddenly looked at his watch, grabbing his suit jacket and shoving his arms through it as he headed for the door.

"Shit, I was supposed to be at my kid's lacrosse game ten minutes ago."

"Go," Jaq said, pulling the folders over into a stack and waving him off. "I've got it. I'll go through these, and we'll talk in the morning."

❖

Later that night, Jaq sat on her leather sofa, her office folders and stacks of papers spread out on the coffee table in front of her as she ate the last of the takeaway she'd picked up on the way home from the restaurant around the corner. A kind Pakistani family owned the place, and their four-year-old twin boys were always running around in the front of the restaurant when Jaq stopped by after work a few times a week. They'd gotten to know her by now. A few months ago, she couldn't decide what she wanted, so she just left it up to them, and since then she'd never ordered anything specific. She'd just come in and sit by the window until the boys ran over with her food in a bag, and she handed over the money with an extra pound for each of them.

When she was a kid, she'd almost burned the trailer down one night while her mom was at work, and she hadn't cooked since. She'd tried to make Kraft mac and cheese from the box, but she was only seven and somehow missed the part about adding water to the pan with the dry macaroni. She'd turned the burner up to high so it would be ready faster, and the pasta caught fire. By the time she'd run outside and dragged the garden hose through the front door of the trailer, the flames were almost to the cabinets, and it seemed like forever before they reluctantly backed down, hissing under the spray. She'd slid down the wall of the trailer and sat in the pool of water and black, oily ash until her mom came home. She was already drunk and tripped over Jaq on the way to her room, locking the door behind her. Over the years, Jaq shoved it to the back of her mind, but the memory of being invisible never faded.

She made it through all but one of the files, then leaned back and stared at her phone on the table. Streetlights shone through the tall loft windows and scattered across the wood floors in broken amber squares. Jaq got up, poured a bourbon into a short glass, and swirled it around in the fading light. She drank it without a flinch and poured another. She stood by the windows, watching people pass on the sidewalk underneath, and pushed her hair back with her hand. The silence was heavy and dark as she reached through it for her phone and pressed a button.

❖

"I was starting to wonder if I was going to hear from you again."

Amelie Linder walked through the door as soon as Jaq opened it, tossing her purse on the couch and walking to the bar, where Jaq had already poured her favorite brandy. An executive at Veuve Cliquot, the top champagne producer in the world, she was based in Paris but had met Jaq one evening at a restaurant in London's West End, where they were both dining alone at separate tables. Forgotten food and stacks of paper surrounded Jaq, her pencil moving across the page faster than Amelie had ever seen someone write, and strangely, she could see it was numbers, not letters. She'd invited Jaq to join her, and by the end of the evening, she was naked in her bed, hands braced hard against the headboard, while Jaq brought her to an orgasm so intense she thought she might pass out. Since then, they'd seen each other whenever they found themselves in London or Paris at the same time.

She swirled the brandy in the glass, then walked back over to Jaq, pressing the length of her body into hers. Jaq didn't kiss her, just slid her hand around the back of her neck and pulled her gently back.

"Drink that."

Amelie smiled. Jaq turned her on in a way she'd never experienced. She was always in control, yet treated her with intense respect. Amelie had done things with Jaq she'd never done with anyone else, simply because of the way she treated her. She drank the brandy, Jaq's eyes locked onto her mouth, and handed her the glass. Jaq stroked her bottom lip gently with her thumb before she spoke.

"Go to the window, please, and face it."

Endless floor to ceiling windows made up the entire front wall of the loft, and Amelie walked over to them, stopping at the center window. She heard Jaq walk to the couch and sit, just far enough behind her that she was an invisible voice.

"Take your coat off."

Amelie loosened the belt of her trench coat, letting it drop behind her and pool at her feet. She was wearing a black turtleneck cashmere sweater, sleek black heels, and nothing else.

She heard Jaq get up from the couch and closed her eyes as Jaq stepped between her body and the window and slowly sank to her knees.

"Hands against the window, please."

Jaq's voice was quiet and strong, and Amelie spread her hands on the window as Jaq placed one of her thighs over her shoulder. She paused until Amelie begged, then Jaq's tongue enveloped her clit in a sudden hot rush and she moaned, moving against Jaq's mouth, every stroke so intense she felt it might push her over the edge. Jaq wrapped one hand around her hips and held her while she sank her fingers deep inside, pulling Amelie's swollen clit into her mouth without mercy, working it with her tongue until Amelie tensed and moaned, fingers spread and white against the cold glass.

She ran her tongue over every inch of her until Amelie's nails dug into her shoulders. She continued to stroke her, pulling Amelie hard into her mouth and holding her there until she shuddered to a shattering orgasm, hands spread against the icy glass, the only barrier between her and the glittering night sky.

Chapter Nine

Bronwyn pulled on her favorite painting jeans, splashed with every color of smeared paint and falling apart at the knees. It had been almost two weeks since she'd seen Jaq. She still woke up every night, thoughts of her swirling around her in the dark, stealing the hours until dawn. She'd even thrown her coat over her pajamas three nights ago and driven to her building, just to be closer to her. She'd almost called but stopped herself at the last minute. She was being ridiculous, and she knew it. She'd made her choice, and that meant going back to the life she had before instead of throwing everything away for the fantasy of Jaq Bailey. But somehow, everything was different now, in a way she couldn't shake, and she woke up every day feeling like half her heart was missing.

It was late afternoon as she opened the door to her attic and watched the dust dance in the beams of sunlight. She'd converted it to an art studio a few months ago in preparation for the semester off Stratford had given her to paint. They had given her the opportunity in hopes she would return and take over the somewhat stale chemistry department and move it in a new direction, but so far, she'd resisted. She loved science and was particularly interested in making it more exciting to girls and students of color. When she was in school, she'd always felt science as a career was only considered a real possibility for white male students, and whether that had been true or not, she wanted to do what she could to make it more accessible to everyone.

She was setting up her easel when she saw it. She'd forgotten it was even there, but behind one of the wardrobes where she kept her out-of-season clothes, a door led to a hidden storage space. She'd wandered into it one afternoon when she was a little girl, and it was so dark inside she couldn't find the door again. There was no doorknob, just a string to pull it closed, and Bronwyn had just sat there and cried until her grandmother came upstairs to see where she'd gone.

The wardrobe was pulled away from the wall slightly, and from where she was standing against the window, she saw a sliver of light coming around the door. When she moved the wardrobe away from the door, she saw that someone had installed a lock on the door of the storage space; in fact, they'd installed three rather complicated-looking locks in a vertical row. But they'd left the light on, which caught Bronwyn's eye as she set up her easel. She never knew there was a light in the storage room but was now more interested in who had been in there to leave it on. She eased slowly toward it, as the temperature in the attic seemed to drop. There was just enough of a crack between the door and doorframe to get a glimpse of what was inside, and when she saw it, she jumped back and pushed the wardrobe back in front of the door. Then she called Jaq Bailey.

❖

Bronwyn went to the kitchen to wait for Jaq, making herself a cup of tea then leaving it forgotten on the counter as she paced. The doorbell rang eventually, and she padded down the hall in her bare feet, remembering too late she was in her ancient painting jeans and the only thing she'd done to her face that morning was pull on her glasses. She pulled open the door, and Jaq stepped in as she locked it behind her.

"Sorry, I know this doesn't make anything easier," she said, tapping her finger on her lower lip the way she'd always done when she felt nervous or anxious, "but I didn't know who else to call."

"It's okay, Bella," Jaq said. "We'll figure it out, just tell me what happened."

Jaq pulled her into her arms and held her, feeling Bronwyn's heart pound against her chest. After a minute, Bronwyn relaxed enough to tell the story. Jaq listened, then looked upstairs.

"Take me there."

Bronwyn led her upstairs and into the attic, where Jaq pulled the wardrobe away from the door, then crouched in front of the locks and pulled a small leather roll of tools out of her pocket.

"You were right. I will need more than a pocketknife," she said. "Whoever did this doesn't want anyone to get through this door."

Her tools looked like thick steel pins with tiny grooves and levers, and one by one, she popped the locks open. She pulled her sleeve down over her hand and opened the door. Shelves had been built into the walls, utilizing every inch of the limited space, and on them were dozens of stacks of bound hundred-pound notes, two black cases, and what looked like endless plastic-wrapped bricks of white powder. Bronwyn went to pick one of them up, and Jaq grabbed her hand.

"Don't touch that, that's evidence."

Jaq stepped out of the room, gesturing for Bronwyn to come with her, then closing the door behind them. "You've never seen this before?"

"No, I played in it as a kid, but I'd forgotten it was even there. The wardrobe has been in front of it since I moved in, and I've never had a reason to move it. I only noticed it today because of the light inside when I was setting up my easel."

"Have you told anyone else about it?"

"No, just you."

Jaq pulled out her phone and walked over to the window, spoke quietly into it, then clicked it off and went back to the door and opened it again, snapping several pictures of the inside. After she finished, she turned back to Bronwyn.

"We need to go downstairs. We're about to have company."

"Do I have time to change? I look an absolute mess."

Jaq's eyes swept her body then slowly looked up at her. "You look beautiful, but if I have your permission to open the door when they get here, you can take all the time you need."

Bronwyn nodded and went to her room to change. What exactly

did one wear to welcome an influx of police investigating cocaine bricks in your attic? The thought of calling her mother for advice popped suddenly into her head, and she laughed. Her mother always thought she was on the verge of ruining her life. Being at the center of a drug investigation and sleeping with Jaq Bailey might send that right over the edge.

She chose faded jeans and a navy cashmere sweater, threw her hair into a quick bun, and put on a touch of eye makeup before she came back downstairs. When she got to the kitchen, there was only one other person besides Jaq, which was surprising. For some reason, she'd expected hordes of people to be milling around in her house, looking grim and dusting things for fingerprints. Or that's what it seemed like they did on the telly, anyway.

Jaq looked up as she walked in the room. "Bronwyn, this is my boss at Scotland Yard, Chief Terrence Macmillan."

He had wild Irish red hair, and one of his lapels was tucked under his overcoat. He extended his hand to Bronwyn with a warm smile and told her just to call him Terry, all of which was oddly comforting given the circumstances. He reminded Bronwyn a bit of her father—younger, but with the same crinkles around his eyes that made him look kind.

"Jaq tells me you walked into a bit of a situation in your attic today."

Bronwyn laughed and went to put the kettle on. "That's a good way to put it."

"When was the last time you were in that room?"

Bronwyn thought for a second. "This was my grandmother's house, so I was probably about eight years old. The last time I was inside, there wasn't even a doorknob. It was just a storage space."

"And did you touch the door today?"

"No, I didn't want to get that close. I thought there might be someone in there. I just leaned in far enough to get a glimpse."

Terry nodded and wrote her answer down in a small notebook he pulled out of his pocket. "And how did you know to call Detective Bailey?"

Neither Jaq nor Bronwyn answered, just looked at each other as the kettle whistled and Bronwyn hurried to turn it off.

"We went to school together at Stratford," Jaq said to Terry, her voice low. "But we have a bit more history than that."

"Understood," Terry said, glancing over at Bronwyn as she made the tea and set out the milk and sugar on the table.

"Okay, Bronwyn," Terry said, opening a new page in the notebook as they sat down. "Who other than you has access to this house?"

"The list is fairly short," Bronwyn said. "My mum has a key, of course, my best friend Moira, and my fiancée Ian."

"And when was the last time you were in the attic?"

"Yesterday, and I painted well into the evening, so if a light had been on then, I would have seen it."

"Would Moira have had a reason to come into the house at all?"

"She's never done that to my knowledge, and as far as I know, she was in Manchester at a social services conference until noon today. She works with the Strangeways young offenders program."

Terry looked at Jaq, who shook her head, then he turned back to Bronwyn.

"Okay, that takes care of Moira, and I think it's safe to assume your mum probably doesn't have anything to do with this, so let's talk about Ian. What does he do for a living?"

"He's an investment banker at Barclays here in London."

Jaq glanced at Terry, who raised his eyebrow. "On Bridges Street?"

Bronwyn nodded.

"And has he been in the house since yesterday?"

"I spent most of the morning at Mum's house in Camden handling wedding details, and he was here when I got home. I'd told him when I left this morning I was going to stay for lunch at her house, but she was doing my head in so I decided not to and came home early."

"Does he often just let himself in?"

"He's welcome to, but no, not any other time that I remember."

She looked from Jaq to Terry. "Do you think this has something to do with Ian?"

"We don't know anything at this point, but there's an ongoing investigation that this may or may not tie into, which makes this situation a little trickier to handle." Terry shut the notebook and looked at Bronwyn. "And it's certainly possible this could have absolutely nothing to do with him. We just need to find out."

"Anything else?" Terry looked at both Jaq and Bronwyn.

"There are two gun cases upstairs in the closet," Jaq said. "I didn't open them, but I'd bet the farm there aren't knitting needles inside."

"Do you have somewhere you can stay tonight?" Terry asked Bronwyn, who'd started rubbing her temples with her fingers at the mention of guns. "We need to leave everything like it is and put surveillance on the house. It's vital you not say anything to anyone about what's going on, even to your parents."

Bronwyn shook her head. "My mother will know something's up if I show up twice on the same day. I never spend the night there without a good reason. And I'm not sure Moira is even back in town."

Terry tapped his pen on the table. "Unfortunately, a hotel is not an option. That's an obvious sign something's not right."

"She can stay with me, if it's not a conflict of interest." Jaq looked over at Bronwyn. "I'd feel better if I knew she was safe."

"It's not a conflict. The fact that she's the one that reported it pretty much eliminates her as a suspect." Terry stood and tucked the notebook in his pocket. "Bronwyn, why don't you pack a bag and I'll take a look in the attic with Jaq, if that's okay with you."

Bronwyn nodded and put the teacups in the sink.

Once they reached the attic, Jaq stopped Terry before he got to the closet. "Do you remember after I got home from that wedding and told you about the tracking device I found under a friend's car?"

"Let me guess," Terry said, trying not to smile. "Bronwyn was the friend?"

"She was," Jaq said. "She'd spun out in the mud during the rainstorm, and I had someone pull it out for her the next morning.

I was standing to the side and saw it by the axle. I also found a tracking app on her phone when I scanned it with my laptop."

"Damn." Terry pulled the wardrobe aside and eased the door open with a pen. "This isn't looking good for Ian. Do you know him?"

"No, and I hope I never do. He's gotten violent with Bronwyn in the past. She told me a bit about it over the weekend up north."

"So we know he's been tracking her to determine when she's not at the house, he tends toward violence, and he happens to work at the very same investment firm we're looking at for money laundering. He sounds like quite a catch." Terry raised an eyebrow. "How did *he* land a girl like Bronwyn? She's a knockout, if you don't mind me saying."

"Not at all." Jaq grinned at Terry and pulled on the pair of latex gloves he handed her. "I completely agree."

Jaq found a pile of handwritten financial notes, line after line of numbers and calculations, on the top shelf and glanced through them. She snapped a picture and put them back where they were. They scrutinized the guns, photographed the serial numbers, and replaced them in the cases. They also did a rough count of the money, as much as they could do without disturbing the stacks.

Jaq took a last look around the inside of the closet and took another photo before they pulled the door shut and headed downstairs. "So if we just took this now," she said, "there'd be no way to connect it to Ian."

"Exactly," Terry said. "So we wait."

❖

It was almost nine before they'd gotten out of the house and picked up a takeaway for dinner. Jaq carried it and Bronwyn's bag up the stairs and let them into her loft. Bronwyn looked lost as she walked over to the front wall of windows and looked out, still and pale as a ghost.

Jaq turned on the lamps, then went to the bar and poured her a brandy, handing it to her and returning to make a scotch for herself.

"Well," Bronwyn said, piling her hair on top of her head and squeezing the back of her neck. "Today went a bit tits up, didn't it?"

Jaq laughed, clinking her glass to Bronwyn's as she sank down beside her on the leather couch.

"Tell me what you're thinking?" Bronwyn looked over at her, then leaned her head onto her shoulder.

Jaq slowly tipped the amber scotch in her glass and thought before she spoke. "I think there's something you're not telling me." She picked up Bronwyn's hand and stroked the center of her palm with her thumb. "And that's okay, you don't have to tell me anything at all, but I can't keep you safe if I don't know what's going on."

Bronwyn looked out the windows at the London skyline, and it was a minute or two before she answered. "I lied to you."

Jaq didn't say anything, just waited.

Bronwyn sat up, finished the rest of her brandy, and gave the glass back to Jaq, who went to refill it. There were tears in Bronwyn's eyes as she sat back down.

"It's okay, Bella," Jaq said gently. "I know you. You had reasons. Just tell me."

She caught a tear on Bronwyn's cheek with her thumb and handed her the glass. Bronwyn sat back on the couch while Jaq slipped her shoes off and pulled Bronwyn's feet into her lap, warming them in her hands.

"When we were in Blackpool, you asked if Ian had ever done anything else to hurt me after that time I went to stay at my parents'." She looked down into her glass. "I told you no, but that wasn't the truth."

"I knew that then," Jaq said gently.

"I was ashamed," Bronwyn said. "After he hit me again, I knew if I backed out of the wedding, he'd do something worse, and I couldn't bear for you to know I was that weak."

Jaq leaned forward and tipped her chin up with her fingers. "Don't ever let me hear you say that again." She waited until Bronwyn met her eyes. "You're the bravest girl I've ever known, and doing what you had to in order to stay safe isn't weakness. It's strength."

Bronwyn set her glass down and waited. She knew what Jaq was going to say.

"Tell me what he did, Bella."

She took a deep breath and let it out, her eyes closed. "We were arguing, I honestly don't even remember what about, but what I do remember is that he got so angry so fast. I don't even know what happened. I was backing out of the room to go downstairs, and he told me not to take one more step toward the door."

"And you did?"

"Of course," Bronwyn said. "He grabbed me by the throat and slammed me up against the wall. Then," she paused, "I felt suddenly calm. It was like I knew I was going to die."

Bronwyn paused so long Jaq thought she might not go on.

"He let me go the second before I passed out. I heard the front door slam a few seconds later, and he didn't come back until the next day. When he did, it was like it never happened."

"Did you tell anyone?"

"I called Moira. She came over right away, but I wouldn't tell her what happened. She stayed the night, but I made her go home in the morning before Ian came back."

"Did you have bruises?"

Bronwyn nodded slowly as if she was just thinking about it for the first time. "Moira took pictures. She begged me to come home with her but I wouldn't, and I never admitted that Ian had done it."

"When was this?"

"About a month ago. When I saw the cocaine today, it suddenly made sense. His eyes looked different that night, like he was high on something."

Bronwyn's phone rang inside her bag next to the couch, and she jumped. "Shit," she said, digging it out of her bag and holding it up to Jaq. "What do I do?"

"It's okay," Jaq said, her hand steady on Bronwyn's thigh. "Just let it ring. We'll call him back."

Her phone was set to vibrate as well as ring when calls came in, and when Bronwyn dropped it on the couch, it squirmed with every ring like some medieval sea creature.

• 113 •

Finally, it stopped, and Jaq looked at Bronwyn. "Has he had access to this phone since you got a new one?"

"He gave me this phone. He had it ready when I got home from the wedding. Moira told him some bullshit story about me having lost my previous one, so I assumed he was just thoughtful."

Jaq's voice was quiet and steady. "Can you think of any reason why you'd be in this part of the city right now? Something he'd believe?"

"Sure, Moira lives two blocks over. I can tell him I'm staying at her flat tonight doing wedding stuff. She's my maid of honor."

"Perfect. I need you to call him back and tell him that. If the tracker he used is the same as the last one, it's fairly indistinct. You being here will look the same as you being at Moira's."

She picked up the phone, but Jaq stopped her before she dialed.

"Can you text me Moira's number?"

Bronwyn nodded, taking a deep breath before she dialed Ian. Jaq stepped out the door into the hall and called Moira.

"Hello?" That accent was like a fingerprint. Jaq smiled in spite of herself.

"Moira, this is Jaq Bailey."

"Jaq, is Bron all right?" There was instant panic in her voice that made sense now that Jaq knew what she'd seen.

"She's fine, she's safe with me in my flat, but I need you to do something for me."

"Absolutely," she said. "Anything."

"If Ian calls you tonight, for any reason, tell him that Bronwyn is staying the night with you. Can you do that?"

"Done."

"Then let me know right away on this number." Jaq paused, wondering how much she needed to say. "Whatever you do, don't call Bronwyn until you hear from me again."

"Well, obviously," she said with a sigh. "She's at my house. Why would I do that?"

Jaq smiled. "I'll tell you as much as I can later, okay? You can call this number anytime."

Just as they were getting off the phone, there was a pause.

"Jaq," Moira said, "there's more to Ian than meets the eye. I can't pry details out of her. She won't admit it, but he's dangerous."

"I'm on it," Jaq said. "I know what happened last time, and he's never coming near her again."

"Thank fucking Christ," she said. "It's about time."

Jaq came back through the door of the flat just as Bronwyn was hanging up, her hand visibly shaking as she put the phone back down on the table. Jaq shook her head, held her finger to her lips, and picked it up, making sure it was disconnected before she spoke.

"Okay," she said, "What happened?"

"I acted like everything was fine," she said. "I told him Moira had a fight with James and I was staying over."

"Does he think James is still in the house?"

"Yes, I said that specifically."

"Okay, I think we're good for now. I let Moira know to cover for you if he calls."

"He won't call her. He knows she thinks he's a dickhead." She smiled. "Her words."

"God, I like that girl more every day."

"I think the feeling is mutual. She tried to talk to me about you when I came back from the wedding, but I knew leaving Ian wasn't an option." She looked out the window. The night sky was dense and starless, like polished onyx. "It wasn't safe. He would have come after you." Bronwyn let out a long, slow breath and rested her forehead on Jaq's chest.

Jaq held her for a moment, her hand wrapped gently around the back of her head, then scooped Bronwyn off her feet and into her arms. "Time to sleep, baby."

Bronwyn felt suddenly exhausted, the kind of tired that makes your stomach ache, the kind that hits you in the gut and tells you there's not enough safety or sleep in the entire world to make that feeling ever go away. She let Jaq undress her and pull the duvet up around them, the only light the full moon through the window casting a silvery path across their bodies.

Chapter Ten

"Has he been back to the flat at all?"

Bronwyn padded into the kitchen the next morning to find Jaq on the phone, showered and dressed in black jeans and a black and white striped turtleneck sweater. Her leather boots were unlaced at the top, and she'd perched on the back of the sofa.

"Just a drive-by? Did he make any of our vehicles?"

Jaq smiled at her sleepily wandering around the kitchen and walked over to pour her a cup of coffee from a steaming French press on the counter, adding milk and brown sugar before she handed it to her.

"Thank you," Bronwyn whispered as Jaq pulled her in and kissed her forehead.

Jaq listened for a moment, the phone still to her ear. "And do you need to hear that from her?" Jaq handed the phone to Bronwyn. "It's Terry. He needs to ask you something."

Of course. Scotland Yard needed to speak to her about her drug-dealing fiancé before her first cup of coffee. In Jaq Bailey's loft. Why the hell not?

She put Jaq's phone to her ear. "Hello?"

"Good morning, Bronwyn. I need your permission for something, if that's okay."

"Of course. How can I help?"

"We've got surveillance outside your house, but we'd like to go in and set up some cameras in the stairwell and attic areas with your permission. I'm guessing he'll show up eventually, and we'd like to have a record of what he does while he's inside. We can pick him up at any point on suspicion, but we can't hold him if we don't have proof."

"Of course."

"The bad news is I'm not sure when it will be safe for you to go back to the house. Is there anything you need?"

"There's a new pair of black boots in a box beside my bed. Would you mind having someone collect them for me?"

"I'll do it personally."

Out of the corner of her eye, Bronwyn saw Jaq smile from the kitchen.

Bronwyn paused before she handed the phone back. "There's one more thing you might want to know?"

"Of course, even something small may make all the difference."

"If you're putting cameras in the house, you may want to make sure you get a good view of the bay window in the kitchen. Ian's phone doesn't work well anywhere but there, so that's where he stands if he's sending a text."

"Cheers, that's brilliant. Will do."

After she hung up, she walked over to where Jaq was sitting on the kitchen counter and leaned into her, holding her eyes. She kissed her, the memory of dancing in Blackpool warm and soft between them. Bronwyn pulled back slowly and touched her forehead to Jaq's. "Thank you for giving me back my boots."

❖

After she'd showered and dressed, she walked back into the great room of the loft. Jaq was on the sofa, typing on her laptop, and didn't seem surprised when Bronwyn took it away and sat across her lap.

"There is zero chance I'm going to be able to concentrate with you in the house," Jaq said, her hands already under Bronwyn's sweater, kissing her neck, the soft drape of Bronwyn's hair falling against her face. "But I like it."

"You can tell your boss it's all my fault."

• 117 •

"That might work," Jaq said, cupping Bronwyn's ass with her hands. "I don't think he'd blame me."

"Do you have to go to work today?"

"No, it's Sunday, and Terry said the AV guys are all over the house today. I'm meeting him at the office early tomorrow morning."

"Well," Bronwyn said, "if you don't have anything to do later, do you think you could help me with something?"

"I'm all yours," Jaq said, bringing Bronwyn's hand to her mouth and kissing her palm so softly Bronwyn had to close her eyes to feel it. "Providing we can eat something first, I'm starving."

"Perfect," Bronwyn said. "I have to make one phone call, then we can go."

❖

By the time they'd finished eating, it was early afternoon, and a cold pewter mist hung in the air that was steadily turning to rain. Jaq took her jacket off and held it for Bronwyn to slip into, then took her hand as Bronwyn led her down the high street.

"Where are we going, by the way?"

"That's none of your business, nosy."

Bronwyn smiled and twisted her hair into a quick bun as they walked. Her hair was wavy on the best of days, but at the first hint of moisture in the air, it defiantly twisted into curls that were currently refusing to be captured and coaxed into a bun. She slowed as they approached Selfridges, and they ducked inside just as it began to rain in earnest. Jaq ran a hand through her hair and followed her to the escalator.

It was hard not to think about the possibility of actually getting to be with Bronwyn. Jaq assumed she wasn't going back to Ian, but they hadn't talked about it yet. Being with her would mean telling her mother about their relationship and coming out as queer, and even if Bronwyn didn't realize it yet, Jaq knew from experience that it would change every aspect of her life. Or maybe she did realize it. Either way, it didn't matter. Jaq knew she was already in too deep to rescue herself.

Bronwyn led her into an upstairs dressing area with plush couches, beautiful cherry furniture, and mirrors facing every direction. An impeccably dressed man with light blond hair and a quick smile hugged Bronwyn as soon as they walked in.

"Jaq, this is my friend Andrew. He helped me choose the suit I wore for the wedding."

He quickly looked Jaq up and down and then glanced back at Bronwyn with one eyebrow arched. "Wow. I did not see this coming."

Bronwyn laughed, and he quickly extended his hand to Jaq.

"Please excuse my rudeness, Jaq. It's lovely to meet you. Bronwyn is one of my favorite people in the world."

"Well, we have that in common, then," Jaq said, smiling and shaking his hand.

Bronwyn smiled and shrugged off Jaq's jacket, which Andrew took and hung up behind the counter.

"This is very smart, Bronwyn, I'm impressed," he said, straightening the collar. "Beautiful fabric."

"It's Jaq's. Which is kind of the reason we're here." She paused. "I think…"

Jaq and Andrew both looked at Bronwyn and tipped their heads in the same direction, waiting for her to go on. She hesitated, suddenly not sure if Andrew would laugh or think this was a ridiculous idea, and she'd also realized too late that she didn't have any idea how to describe what she needed. In the absence of any other option, she decided just to say it.

"I think I'm sick of my mother's taste in clothes."

Andrew took that in for a moment, then brought his hand to his chest and looked to the ceiling. "Thank baby Jesus," he said. "I've literally been waiting *years* for you to say that."

Over the next couple of hours, Andrew collected clothes he thought Bronwyn might like, then sat on the couch with Jaq to watch her try them on. The two of them had surprisingly similar taste and gently steered Bronwyn toward pieces that she would have never thought to try on if she was alone. Almost everything had to be altered to fit her body, but gradually she'd collected a pile of more masculine pieces like wool trousers, jackets, and dress shirts that she loved, mixed with a few softer elements she liked, like a black cashmere cardigan. When she stepped out of the dressing room in it, Jaq and Andrew both instantly insisted she go down two sizes, then refused to budge on the issue, despite her hesitation.

"Bronwyn Charles," Andrew said, getting up from the couch and standing behind her in the mirror. "You've been hiding that gorgeous body for too many years. Stop it."

"Well said," Jaq called over from the couch.

Maybe he's right, Bronwyn thought, seeing herself the way he did for the first time as she looked in the mirror. Until she'd worn the suit Andrew chose for the wedding, it had been years since she'd even thought about her clothes. She'd forgotten how it felt to wear something she loved.

❖

By the time they'd left Selfridges, the gray afternoon was turning violet at the edges. Buses and people crowded the streets, vying for space, and Jaq led her quickly into a waiting taxi, climbing in behind her and shutting the door.

The driver glanced at Jaq through the rearview mirror. "Where to, sir?"

"Thirty-three Greycoat Street, please."

He nodded and took off into a jumbled maze of careening rush hour traffic.

Jaq put her hand on Bronwyn's thigh and spoke into her ear, her voice low. "I thought it might be smart to lessen the chances of Ian seeing us together. The other option was just not to touch you, but it seems I can't manage that."

Bronwyn covered Jaq's hand with her own and moved it higher on her leg. Jaq took a breath and held her eyes, fingertips stroking Bronwyn's inner thigh.

"Be careful, Bella. Sometimes you get what you ask for."

She slid her hand around the back of Bronwyn's head and pulled her closer. She kissed her, then tipped her chin up and held it there with her thumb as she kissed slowly down the side of her neck, finally pulling away with a soft bite on Bronwyn's lower lip.

When Bronwyn caught her breath, she remembered to borrow Jaq's phone, and by the time they arrived at Jaq's loft, she'd ordered everything she needed to make dinner from Marks & Spencer's grocery delivery, and scheduled it to arrive at the door within the hour. Jaq looked at the screen when she handed it back, then looked again.

"You're going to cook?"

Bronwyn nodded and followed her out of the cab. "I thought I might. Is that okay?"

"I've just never really had girls in my flat who…did that." She winked at Bronwyn as she punched the code into the front door and held it open for her to go in. "I'm afraid to get used to it."

Bronwyn laughed and took her hand, standing on tiptoe to kiss her in the lift. "I like cooking for you. I always wondered if I'd ever get to do it."

The door opened, and they rounded the corner into Jaq's corridor. Jaq pulled her back suddenly and stepped in front of her.

"Stay here, Bella."

"Why?"

"Just don't move. I'll be right back."

As she walked toward the door of her loft, Bronwyn realized what Jaq had seen. A sealed cardboard box was in front of her door, and Jaq slowed as she approached it. Bronwyn started to walk toward her.

Jaq didn't turn around or take her eyes off the box. "Stop, Bella. Let me check this out before you come closer."

Bronwyn stopped as Jaq looked more closely at it, then pulled her phone out of her pocket. She dialed and held it to her ear, eyes still on the box.

"Terry, did you have someone deliver Bronwyn's boots to my door?" She listened for just a moment, then motioned Bronwyn down the hall. "Great, no worries, I just wanted to make sure it was you." She clicked the phone off and picked up the boots, holding the door open for Bronwyn.

"Next time I tell you not to move, Bella," she winked at Bronwyn and pulled her close, "don't move."

"I'll consider it, Detective Bailey," Bronwyn said. "But don't hold your breath."

As soon as she took her coat off and hung it by the door, Bronwyn heard her phone ringing. Jaq went to the coffee table and picked it up. "It's him."

Bronwyn took it and set it down, clicking the answer button and turning it on speakerphone. Ian started talking before she'd had the chance to say hello.

"Where the hell have you been?"

"Shopping, why?"

"I've been trying to get in touch with you all day."

"I'm sorry. I just didn't take my phone with me."

The silence on the line then made it clear he didn't believe her. "You know I hate that. What's wrong with you?"

Bronwyn sighed and rubbed her forehead. "Sorry."

There was a long silence before Ian spoke again. "When are you getting home tonight?" The irritation in his voice was barely controlled.

"I think I'm staying another night with Moira."

"No, you're not. She's an adult. She can solve her problems with her husband."

"Ian, I don't *have* to be here, I want to." Bronwyn shook her head. "She's my best friend."

"Fine, but then you're coming home."

Bronwyn looked at Jaq but didn't say anything.

"I'll see you tomorrow," Ian said, then hung up the phone.

Bronwyn sat back on the couch and dropped her face into her hands. "Shit. I've been trying not to think about the fact I have to go home to him eventually."

"Bella, you don't have to do anything. I can't believe he speaks to you that way."

Jaq clicked off the phone and looked over at Bronwyn. There was nothing to say. It was her choice, and she wasn't going to be another person telling her what to do.

"Don't worry. It's been a long time since he's been violent, and he's been a lot more irritated than this since. I just don't want to see him."

"Come here, baby." Jaq pulled her into her arms and kissed the top of her head. "You don't have to see him. We can get him out of there and try to make the case with what we have."

"No," Bronwyn said. "I want to do it." She looked up at Jaq. "I'm tougher than I look."

Jaq smiled in spite of herself and kissed her. "I've never doubted that for a second."

This time Jaq's phone rang, and Bronwyn jumped. Jaq picked it up and answered, then set it down on the coffee table and clicked it onto speakerphone mid-sentence.

"That asshat called me three times in the last five minutes, so I finally answered. He's in fine form tonight."

"Moira, so that you know, I put you on speakerphone and Bronwyn is sitting here with me."

"Great, she needs to know what a prick he is." She paused to take a quick breath. "He said if Bronwyn didn't come home by tomorrow night, he was coming over here to get her. Can you believe that? How old does he think you are, twelve?"

"What did you tell him?" Jaq asked, trying not to smile.

"What do you think I told him? I called him a bellend and told him to fucking try it."

Jaq looked quizzically at Bronwyn while Moira paused for breath.

"It's Scouse for 'dickhead,'" she whispered. "She likes to stay with the classics."

Bronwyn leaned back toward the phone. "If you see him, will you call us right away?"

"You won't have to," Jaq interjected. "We've had an undercover car parked two houses down from yours since yesterday. He'll call it in before Ian even gets to the door."

"I figured as much when I saw someone devouring a bacon butty and staring at my front door at six this morning. He can stay. He's cute."

Jaq laughed. "Not much gets past you, does it?"

"Well, not Ian Norton, that's for damn sure."

After they got off the phone, Jaq went to open a bottle of wine while Bronwyn changed her clothes. She made it as far as the bathroom and sat down on the edge of the clawfoot tub, her legs suddenly weak. Ian was angry. He was more on the edge than she'd admitted to Jaq, and she could hear in his voice that he knew she was lying. What she wasn't saying out loud was that she needed him to go down for whatever crimes he was involved in, because if she left him for Jaq Bailey and he wasn't in jail, they might as well add murder to that list.

"Damn." Jaq turned around and stared at her as she walked back into the kitchen. "How do you make my ancient sweater look like that?"

Bronwyn smiled and took the glass of wine Jaq held out. She'd pulled on the wool sweater she'd claimed in Blackpool and paired it with red silk shorts and bare feet. "Like what?"

Jaq pulled her close and slipped her hand under the sweater and across the velvety warmth of her breasts, lifting it just as the downstairs buzzer rang. Bronwyn laughed, and Jaq reluctantly went to buzz the grocery delivery guy up and took the bags. She peered down at them as she set them on the counter. "What are you making?"

"Just some tikka masala and naan."

"Just tikka masala? That sounds like every late night kitchen fantasy I've ever had." Jaq dropped her eyes down Bronwyn's body and smiled. "Well, maybe not every fantasy, but it's up there."

Bronwyn swatted at her with a tea towel and got to work on the dough for the naan. It was quick to put together, and she set it aside to rise under a towel. She peeled a white onion and chopped it into perfect squares, mincing them so finely they were almost a paste by the time she slid them off the knife into a warm pan with a glug of olive oil.

Jaq looked mesmerized. She watched Bronwyn season the chicken breast, then fry it to a golden brown in a second pan while she caramelized the onions with some brown sugar and vinegar in the first.

"Where did you learn to cook?"

"I haven't, really," Bronwyn said. "I've just watched enough Jamie Oliver to get it right every once in a while."

"I don't believe that for a second." Jaq pulled her eyes away from the food and looked over at her. "There's got to be more to the story."

Bronwyn left the chicken to simmer in some butter and spices while she floured a cutting board and started kneading the onions into the naan dough.

"Maybe," Bronwyn said, looking up at Jaq with a smile.

She stretched the naan and rolled the edges, popping them into the oven to bake while she started the sauce.

Jaq started to say something, then hesitated and seemed to think the better of it. Then she said it anyway. "I can't believe I'm asking you this because I'm almost positive I don't want to know." She took a long sip of her wine. "But how's the sex with Ian?"

"Jaq Bailey, I can't believe you just said that!" Bronwyn looked up and tossed a tomato in her direction.

Jaq caught it with one hand and waited. "Feel free to decline to answer. I fully recognize it's none of my damn business."

Bronwyn looked over at Jaq, then dropped her eyes to the counter. "It's fine."

Jaq reached over and tucked a stray lock of hair behind her ear. "Bella, I'm sorry. I shouldn't have asked you."

Bronwyn paused, then looked up. "Actually, do you want to know a secret?"

"I'm pretty positive I should say no here," Jaq said. "But of course I want to know any secret you want to tell me."

"That night in Blackpool was the first time I've had an orgasm with someone other than myself since high school." She smiled. "Since you, specifically."

Jaq stared at her. "You're kidding, right?"

"Nope." Bronwyn crushed some fragrant leaves into her hand

and threw them into the hot pan with some other dry spices. "I slept with a couple of guys after college, but I wasn't serious about either one, so I'm not surprised it didn't happen then."

"What about Ian?"

"Not once," she said. "But in fairness, it's not Ian's fault."

"Oh really," Jaq said, refilling Bronwyn's wine glass and trying not to smile. She leaned back against the counter and crossed her arms. "You're going to have to explain that one to me."

"I don't know," she said, "I guess he just never asked and I never told."

Jaq took that in for a moment. "He never asked if you came during sex?"

Bronwyn shook her head.

"Were you faking it?"

"No, not even once. He just never noticed, I guess."

Jaq shook her head. "More like he never cared."

Bronwyn nodded toward the garlic on the other side of Jaq, and Jaq reached over and handed it to her.

"Sorry, I'm not trying to shit-talk your fiancé, but if you weren't faking it, there was no reason for him to think you ever came. And if he wasn't getting you there, he should have been on that from the first time."

Bronwyn smiled but shook her head. "He's not my fiancé," she said quietly.

Jaq looked at her hand and realized for the first time her ring was gone.

"And he'll never touch me again."

Jaq didn't say anything. She just pulled Bronwyn over into her arms and kissed her until they were both breathless and the herbs in the pan caught fire.

❖

Jaq finished the dishes and wiped down the counters, switching on the lamp and turning off the main kitchen lights before she sank down by Bronwyn on the couch.

"That was the best food I've ever eaten in my life."

Bronwyn stretched out on the couch and put her head in Jaq's lap, looking out the windows at the city lights below.

"Lying is a sin." She looked up at her and smiled. "But thank you."

Jaq smoothed her hair back from her face. "You can think I'm lying all damn day, but that's the truth."

Bronwyn was quiet for a moment, running her fingers up and down Jaq's arm. "Can I ask you something?"

Jaq looked down at her. "After that meal, you can ask me anything you want."

"Do you," Bronwyn hesitated, visibly choosing her words one by one, "think I'm gay?"

Jaq leaned her head back on the couch. "That's a loaded question." She looked down at Bronwyn and held her eyes. "And only you can answer it."

Bronwyn gave her a look. "You said I could ask anything I want, and that suggests an answer is on offer as well. Like it or not, that's how it works, Bailey."

Jaq laughed. She'd known Bronwyn long enough to choose an early surrender when faced with certain defeat.

"Fine." Jaq looked down into Bronwyn's eyes. They looked lit from behind even in the semidarkness of the room. She decided to tell the truth. "I've always known."

Bronwyn was quiet for a moment. "Me too. Maybe that's why I chose Ian, so I didn't have to think about it."

"You wouldn't be the first."

Jaq didn't throw words at the silence. It belonged to Bronwyn. She ran her finger across her lip and waited until she spoke.

"Will you take me to bed?" Bronwyn sounded almost hesitant, but then she caught Jaq's finger and brushed the tip of it with her tongue.

"Go get ready for bed, Bella," Jaq whispered. "I'll make sure everything is locked up."

Bronwyn took off her makeup and brushed her teeth. She reached for the pajamas she'd brought into the bathroom, then

• 127 •

thought for a moment and let them slip from her fingers. Jaq came to bed a few minutes later, the scent of her skin warm and familiar.

"Jesus," Jaq said, pulling Bronwyn's naked body into hers. "You have no idea what this does to me."

Bronwyn kissed her, her thigh between Jaq's, then ran her fingers slowly over the muscular lines of her stomach. Jaq kept her close, the heat between them intense and palpable. She slipped her thumb underneath the waistband of Jaq's underwear.

"Take these off for me?"

Jaq slipped them off and dropped them beside the bed. She lay back and ran her fingers over Bronwyn's back, watching her. Bronwyn leaned in and worked Jaq's nipple with her tongue, then a scrape of her teeth, stroking it until she felt Jaq's breath deepen and her hand at the back of her head. She ran her tongue slowly down Jaq's body until her mouth met the curve of her hip, then paused, her breath warm and still on Jaq's skin. Jaq ran a hand through her hair and let out a slow breath, resisting the urge to pull Bronwyn into her arms.

Bronwyn moved over Jaq's body and settled between her legs, pulling one knee up beside her and kissing slowly down the inside of Jaq's thigh until she groaned, biting gently until she felt Jaq's hand in her hair.

"Bella..." Her voice was like gravel.

Bronwyn didn't look up, just took her time, her mouth moving over every inch of Jaq's inner thigh, and then the other, raking her nails lightly across the outside of her legs. After what seemed like forever, she laid her hand warm and low across Jaq's abs and looked up at her. Jaq put her arm under her head and traced the edge of Bronwyn's face with her thumb.

"Are you sure you want this, Bella?"

Bronwyn's eyes were soft. "Since the day I met you."

Jaq lay back and scraped her hand through her hair. Bronwyn touched Jaq with her breath, then ran her tongue lightly over her, dipping inside to taste her, then drawing one of her lips into her mouth just hard enough to get her attention.

Jaq growled, her thighs tense under Bronwyn's fingers. She

explored Jaq with her tongue for what seemed like forever, slicking into her center, dragging the tip slowly across the wet heat of her, touching everywhere but her clit. She got close, over and over, her tongue so near Jaq's swollen clit that Jaq felt her breath.

"Fuck, baby." Jaq's voice broke as she pressed the heel of her hand to her forehead. Every muscle in her body was tight. "Are you trying to kill me?"

Bronwyn laid her palm low on Jaq's stomach, holding her eyes as she finally slid her tongue slowly over Jaq's clit, listening to her groan as she drew it slowly in and out of her mouth the way she remembered Jaq doing to her.

"Oh my God." Jaq's fingers tangled in her hair.

Bronwyn held Jaq's clit in her mouth while she swirled her tongue around it, achingly slowly, memorizing the feel of her. Jaq's body told Bronwyn what she wanted. Hips bucked toward her mouth when she needed more pressure, her hand at the back of her head telling her to stay when Bronwyn fell into a rhythm, breath begging her not to stop, her abs tense and still as Bronwyn got her as close as possible without tipping her over the edge.

Then she felt Jaq's clit harden under her tongue, taut with tension, and realized her breath had gone quiet. Jaq silently pressed her hips into Bronwyn, and she drew her clit further into her mouth, stroking it until she heard Jaq cry out, her breath wild, the sheet wrapped hard into her hands as she came. Bronwyn stayed with her, Jaq's clit slick and hard under her tongue, until Jaq wrapped her hand lightly around the back of her head, her breath slowing and hoarse.

Bronwyn moved into her arms and Jaq enveloped her, covering every part of her with her body. "I can't believe you just made me come like that," she whispered into the warmth of her hair.

"I can," Bronwyn said, settling onto Jaq's chest, listening to her heart as Jaq's arms closed around her. "I'm in love with you."

Chapter Eleven

The next morning Jaq woke just after dawn and reached for Bronwyn. She was gone, her pillow cold as she ran her hand over it. Jaq had never known her to wake up first, even in school. She looked toward the bathroom but it was dark. Her heart sank all at once and she lay back onto the pillows, kicking herself for not realizing last night would be too much.

After a few minutes, it occurred to her that Bronwyn might have left a note; she pulled on a pair of jeans and headed down the hall to the kitchen. As she rounded the corner, she saw her, wearing one of her shirts, standing at the farthest window. She was on the phone.

"Ian, this is not your choice. It's mine."

She pulled the phone away from her ear and leaned it against her forehead. Jaq could hear him shouting from across the room.

"I realize I should have done this in person." She paused. "But I'm doing it now. I don't want to be in this relationship anymore."

She listened for a long time. When she spoke, Jaq could hear the tears in her voice. "You can't make me change my mind, Ian. I should have done this the first time you put your hands on me."

Jaq listened as she asked him to go to her house later in the day and take anything he had there, then leave the key on the entry table when he left. When she finished, she clicked the phone off and leaned into the glass. It wasn't until Jaq walked over and pulled her into her arms that she started to cry.

❖

Jaq got to work early, walked into Terry's office just as he arrived, and told him about Bronwyn's breakup with Ian.

"Bloody hell." Terry shook his head. "I mean, I get why she wants rid of him, but she just woke up this morning and decided today was the day?"

Jaq didn't answer, just looked at him and raised her eyebrow.

"Ah, I get it." Terry smiled, looking down at the stack of folders on his desk. "I can't say I blame you, but this complicates things a bit from here on out. I'll need you to take a back seat if there is any kind of safety issue with Bronwyn. You're too close now to stay objective."

Jaq nodded. "There shouldn't be. She asked him to take anything he still had at her house by the end of the day and leave the key."

"Smart girl. That tightens up the time frame significantly. I'll get some more officers down there first thing. I had the tech guys go over every inch of her car over the weekend, so it's clear," Terry said. "Did you happen to bring in her phone?"

"I did. I already dropped it with the techs. I ordered her a new one, and it should come to the flat by this afternoon."

"How is she doing?" Terry asked, leaning back in his chair and tapping his pen on the desk. "This is a lot to take in for her, I'm sure."

"She's a tough girl. I think she's been ready to see the back of him for a while."

"That's not hard to imagine." Terry smiled. "I'm happy for you. I like her a lot."

"Thanks," Jaq said. "I'll feel better when we've got him and he can't get to her."

Terry stood and picked up his jacket. "You ready to go?"

"Always." Jaq dropped her takeaway coffee cup in the trashcan at the side of his desk. "Where are we going?"

"I think it's time we paid a little visit to Mr. Norton at work, don't you?" Terry strapped on his holster and made sure Jaq had done the same before they left and shut the door behind them.

By the time they got to the bank where Ian worked, people were streaming in the door, shoulder to shoulder. The lobby was massive, built with endless white granite, and everything they said seemed to ricochet off the walls, even at a whisper. They stopped to ask the woman at the front desk what floor held Ian's department.

"Investments will be the sixteenth floor, to your right as you get out of the lift."

Terry pressed the button in the lift and looked at his watch. "I was hoping to be a little more low-key than this, but I guess we should ask someone where he is. This place is like Manhattan shoved in a skyscraper."

Terry dug into his shirt pocket and slapped a nicotine patch on his arm as the doors opened and they walked down the hall. Jaq looked over and smiled.

"I still hate these bloody things. There's nothing in them but misery."

They stopped at the main reception desk, and Jaq asked for Ian Norton's office.

The receptionist, a delicate-looking blonde, looked slightly confused. She turned to her computer and typed in his name, then looked up at them.

"Ian Norton doesn't work here anymore. This says he was terminated just over a year ago."

Terry turned to Jaq. "Well, I can't say I saw that coming."

"Can you refer us to whoever was his direct superior?" Jaq asked.

"Of course, sir. That's Maeve Thomas, in the corner office on the west side."

They started walking toward the office, and Terry looked over at Jaq, trying not to laugh. "You get that a lot?"

Jaq rolled her eyes. "All the damn time."

The hall opened up into an enormous room full of cubicles, ringed by offices on every side. The noise hit them like a wall, computer keys clicked from every inch of available space, and the people passing them from every direction made it seem like they'd been dropped into a human beehive.

"Jeez, I thought the Yard was crazy."

Terry looked over when Jaq didn't answer to find she'd stopped about three meters back, standing with her eyes closed, people swirling around her in every direction as if she wasn't even there.

"You'd better be having a stroke or something," Terry said when she finally reached him. "I looked like an idiot talking to myself just then."

Jaq put up her hand and turned her face to the left. He watched as she walked in that direction, holding her fingers tight to her right ear. Terry just shook his head and followed. Apparently, all geniuses were a bit odd, and Jaq was no different. He had to admit it was worth it; he'd never worked with a more promising detective. He'd balked at first, when she was being interviewed—bringing in a random American at such a high level with no law enforcement experience was ridiculous by anyone's standards. But Jaq had won him over the first time she scanned a fifteen-page case file in less than a minute and singled out an inconsistency that instantly solved a case the department had been sitting on for a year. Initially, she'd been hired to head up forensic accounting, but as time went on, Terry increasingly pulled her in to look over stalled cases from every department. Her mind worked faster than a computer and she instinctively thought like a detective, which he knew from experience couldn't be taught. He didn't have favorites, but if he did, it would be the ridiculous American.

"Excuse me," Jaq said, stopping at a cubicle occupied by a plain girl in a cardigan, typing on her computer. She looked up and raised an eyebrow. "Can you tell me where I can find Ian Norton?"

Her eyes flicked from Jaq to Terry, then settled back on Jaq. "He no longer works here. Why?"

"You were his secretary when he was here? Or assistant in some way?"

"I was his assistant." She gripped the edge of her desk with one hand, and Terry noticed her fingertips were white. "Why are you asking me this?"

"Are you still in touch with him?"

"I don't have to tell you that." She sat back in her chair and crossed her arms, her mouth a thin, tense line. "You need to leave."

As they walked back into the hive toward the hall, Jaq whispered, "She's going to pick up her phone in about five seconds."

Terry stopped and stepped back until he could see into her cubicle. "Office or cell phone?"

"Cell."

"Damn," Terry said, shaking his head and falling back into step with Jaq. "I'll never understand how you do that."

❖

By the time they'd gotten back into the car, Terry had touched base with the team surrounding Bronwyn's house to tell them Ian was tipped off and might be on his way. He pulled out into traffic and turned back toward Scotland Yard.

He turned to look at Jaq and narrowly missed a wayward double decker bus on his right. "So how did you know she was involved with Ian?"

Jaq got her phone out and opened her pictures, swiping until she got the one she wanted, then held it up for just a second before she put it back in her pocket.

"Don't worry about the picture. I'd actually like to survive the trip back to the station. I'll just tell you about it."

Terry swerved to avoid a black cab and nodded. "Probably wise. I was a better driver when I smoked."

"Do you remember those handwritten notes we found in the attic? A woman wrote them."

"How do you know a woman wrote them if it was just numbers? Those all look the same."

"I don't know. It's hard to explain," Jaq said, tucking her phone back into her jacket. "But every ninth number on those notes had a hesitation, a slightly bigger space between it and the number that followed it. Usually when a person has that kind of unconscious pattern, it repeats itself in other ways, like a fingerprint. So I just listened for that same pattern as we walked in."

Jaq leaned against the door and held on to the dashboard as Terry took the corner into Scotland Yard and skidded to a stop. "We were lucky she was typing. I would have had to figure out some other way to identify her in that zoo otherwise."

"Well, however you found her, she's the right girl." Terry unbuckled his seat belt and let it snap back against the wall as he reached for the door handle. "I recognized her from the bank's security videos. She's the one that's been making the deposits."

❖

Moira finally knocked and Bronwyn opened the door, pulling her inside and into a hug. "God, it's good to see you!"

Moira hugged her back hard and kissed her cheek, then looked around her at the loft. "Christ, this place is gorgeous!" She walked into the living area, tossed her purse onto the sofa, and looked down onto the street from the windows. "It's easy to imagine Jaq living here."

"I know," Bronwyn said. "Everything about it looks just like her."

Moira spun around and headed for the kitchen. "I'm going to pop the kettle on, and you're going to sit there and tell me everything." She filled the kettle and flipped the switch, then looked in the fridge for the milk.

"It's in the door."

Moira rolled her eyes at Bronwyn over her shoulder. "That's not the information I'm looking for."

"Okay, what story do you want first?" Bronwyn let out a long breath. "That I split up with Ian this morning? Or how I decided to stop dressing like a kindergarten teacher?" She paused for effect. "Or how it was to go down on Jaq last night for the first time?"

Moira skidded sideways onto a barstool and slapped her hand down on the counter. "I can't believe you're even asking me that!"

"Okay," Bronwyn said, pretending to consider her options. "Let's start with Jaq."

"You went down on her? What was that like? No, wait, maybe you shouldn't tell me if I'm going to be jealous."

Bronwyn laughed. "You might be."

"I'll take that chance," Moira said, leaning onto the counter on her elbows. "Spill it."

"I was so nervous, but once I got going, it was like I'd been doing it all my life." Bronwyn poured milk into her tea and looked back up. "It was literally the hottest experience I've ever had, and that's saying something. That girl has always been amazing in bed."

"Great," Moira said. "Now I'm officially jealous." She paused. "And just trust me, do not, under any circumstances, breathe a word of that to Catherine."

They chatted for hours, until the sun started to go down and Moira realized she needed to get home and start dinner. Bronwyn walked her to the door and hugged her, but Moira hesitated just as she was leaving.

"What is it?" Bronwyn said. "I can tell you've got something to say."

"Just be careful. I've seen an ugly side to Ian in the last few days. Don't see him if you can avoid it."

Bronwyn nodded and watched her friend walk down the hall. "Moira?"

Moira spun around right before she rounded the corner to the lift.

"Stop flirting with the cop in the surveillance car."

"What?" she said. "How did you know about that?"

"I didn't. I just know you."

Moira blew her a kiss and disappeared.

❖

Five days later, Ian still hadn't put in an appearance. He hadn't shown up at the house, hadn't called, and no one Bronwyn knew had heard from him. He'd just disappeared.

Scotland Yard tested everything in the attic storage space for prints, including the firearms, cocaine, even the notes Jaq had found on the top shelf. There was not a single print on anything. They tested the entire attic for fingerprints, from doorknobs to walls, and every print they found belonged to Bronwyn, and there weren't many of those. Clearly, someone had been in the house and wiped everything down after Jaq and Terry came to get Bronwyn but before the cameras were installed. Their fingerprints never showed up in the attic and they should have been in several places. Neither had put gloves on until they actually entered the storage space, so they should have been on the locks and armoire at the very least.

Since Ian's fingerprints were nowhere to be found, unless they caught him with the cash or cocaine, even on camera, they had nothing. Terry pulled surveillance outside Bronwyn's home in hopes he'd assume he was in the clear. They left the cameras running continuously inside but Bronwyn couldn't go back to the house until the issue was resolved.

Terry called Jaq into his office at the end of the fifth day, and they spent an hour or so going over everything again, hoping to find something they'd missed.

Jaq looked up from the files, finishing the last of the coffee in her cup. "Bronwyn broke off the engagement. Maybe he just doesn't want to go back to the house. Is it possible that he's just written this off as a loss?"

"No way," Terry said. "The street value of the cocaine alone is close to a million pounds, and that's without the four hundred thousand or so in cash and guns. There's no way he's just going to walk away from that."

"Fair point," Jaq said, rubbing her temples. "But if he knows we're onto him, he knows there's no way in hell he's going to get back into the house and back out with everything in that closet without us being all over him in two seconds."

Terry leaned back in his chair. "I'm not convinced he knows anything. He probably wipes everything down every time he leaves the closet, but had to come back and do it the next night because Bronwyn came home early that day and surprised him."

"What about the investment accounts he's been moving money through?"

"I checked those, and there's still activity, but nothing out of the ordinary, roughly on par with his past patterns. I left a copy of them on your desk right before I called you in."

Terry leaned over and pulled a cigarette out of his left desk drawer, holding it up to his nose and inhaling the scent as if he was embracing a long lost lover.

"Oh hell no," Jaq said, holding out her hand. "Give that to me."

She tried not to laugh as he scowled and handed it over like a scolded schoolchild.

"What's got you so nervous you're sniffing cigarettes?"

Terry shook his head and turned his pen through his fingers several times before he answered.

"I think Ian is up to something," he said, his eyes settling on Jaq's. "And I think it has a lot more to do with Bronwyn than what's in that house."

Chapter Twelve

That night, Jaq got home before Bronwyn and fixed herself a drink, sitting on the couch in the dark and staring out over the London skyline. She wasn't surprised to hear what Terry had to say about Ian. His silence had felt increasingly odd to her since the first day. He'd been possessive of Bronwyn for years; he saw her as his, and it didn't make sense that he'd just give her up without a fight. Every day she hadn't heard from him made Jaq more nervous, and hearing Terry say the same thing today just solidified it. She got up and walked to the window, looking down to find the undercover car she knew would be there. When Bronwyn told her that morning they'd pulled the car they'd had at Moira's house, she knew Terry would just have it sent to her loft for Bronwyn.

The key rattled suddenly in the door, and Bronwyn walked in, switching on the lights before she saw Jaq in the great room.

"Jaq?" she said, dropping her bag on the chair and walking over to her. "What are you doing just standing here in the dark? What happened?"

Jaq pulled her into her arms and rested her chin on Bronwyn's head. If Ian wanted a fight, he was going to get one.

Bronwyn tightened her arms around Jaq's waist, snuggling into her chest. "Are you okay?"

"Now I am," Jaq said, setting her drink down on the side table. "Grab your coat. I'm taking you to my favorite restaurant for dinner."

Jaq watched Bronwyn walk up the stairs wearing a pair of the perfectly tailored wool trousers she and Andrew had picked out for her, a close-fitting denim shirt, and black Chuck Taylor sneakers. Somehow, on her, it all worked, and she looked cute as hell.

She came back down the stairs, and Jaq took her hand, leading her out the door and locking it behind them.

"So where are we going?"

"Well, fair warning, it's my favorite restaurant in London, but it's not posh." She waited for the light to change at the intersection of Banks Avenue and Harley Street and crossed, Bronwyn's hand in hers. "In fact, it's not even in the neighborhood of posh."

"Well, my favorite place to eat in the world is the chippy on the corner just down from my house, so it has some stiff competition."

"I'll have to try it. I have some pretty strong opinions when it comes to fish and chips, which is your fault, by the way, because you took me to Blackpool and raised the bar." Jaq smiled down at her and squeezed her hand. "What do you like about it?"

A cold wind whipped around the corner as they turned onto the high street, and Jaq pulled her closer, guiding them through the Friday evening crush of people on their way home after work.

Bronwyn wrapped her scarf tighter around her neck and tucked the ends into her coat. "They put mint in their mushy peas. It's heaven."

Jaq slowed as they approached the restaurant and held the door open for her. As they stepped into the warm air inside, scented in sheer layers of cardamom and green coriander, two little boys came running out from behind the counter. When they saw Bronwyn, they came to a shocked halt, both looking up at Jaq.

"I think we're going to eat here this time, guys," Jaq said. "Can you tell your mom there's two of us?"

They nodded and ran into the back, the dented aluminum kitchen door swinging shut behind them. Jaq took Bronwyn's coat, hung it up by the door with hers, and led her to a corner booth. There were two other couples in the tiny red dining room, but it was still quiet and intimate.

"That was the cutest thing I've ever seen," Bronwyn said,

looking back over her shoulder to the door they'd disappeared behind. "Are they twins?"

"They are. They're the owner's sons, Azran and Zahaar. They're about four years old, I think."

"They certainly know you." Bronwyn smiled, as someone came to fill their water glasses. "I'm guessing you come here a lot?"

"You could say that," Jaq said. "I don't cook, so they pretty much cook for me."

"What's your favorite thing to eat here?"

"I'm not sure, which is also why we don't have menus." Jaq unbuttoned the top button of her shirt and sat back in the booth. "I ordered off the menu for the first couple of months, and then they just started making me dinner on the days they knew I came in and handed it to me. It was always the same price, so I just hand over the money to the little guys and they give me my food."

"That's adorable."

"Yeah, they're pretty cute."

The waitress brought two chilled glasses of white wine and a small plate of fragrant, savory cakes with green chutney.

"Oh my God, that smells amazing." Bronwyn twisted her hair into a bun and watched Jaq spooning the chutney onto the plate beside the perfectly browned cake. "Have you ever thought about having kids someday?"

Jaq looked up at her, surprised, and handed her the plate. It was a moment before she answered. "I'd love to. I just don't know if I'd be a great parent."

Bronwyn watched her cut into the cake and top it with the bright green chutney. She hesitated before she spoke again. "Because of your mum?"

Jaq nodded. "That, and the fact that I never had a dad. I'd want better than that for my kid." She looked out the window beside them and put her fork down on her plate. It was starting to rain. Just enough to soften the light from the streetlamp into an amber glow that filtered through the raindrops on the window like stained glass. "And I don't know if I have what it takes."

Bronwyn touched her hand to Jaq's. "You may not know, but I do."

Jaq's eyes softened, and she leaned across the table to kiss her. "Thank you, Bella."

Bronwyn took her first bite of their appetizer and immediately closed her eyes. "This is gorgeous," she said. "What is this?"

Jaq laughed at her look of sheer bliss. "No idea, but I love it too."

"My friend Jules and her husband would love this place. We'll have to bring them here."

Jaq smiled. She was starting to feel like they were a couple, but Jaq put the thought out of her head. Better not to jinx it.

Every course after that was beautiful, complex, and unrecognizable. The spices were always perfectly balanced, the flavors and textures bold, but somehow still delicate and seamless. They finally had to tell the waitress they couldn't eat any more, but Azran and Zahaar brought the desserts to them anyway, setting both dishes in front of Jaq and running off.

Bronwyn smiled as Jaq handed one of the bowls to her. "They love you."

Jaq looked at them playing behind the counter. "Yeah, sometimes when I've had a rough day I stop in just to see them. The food is a bonus."

After they'd paid and thanked the owner, Jaq and Bronwyn stepped out into the October wind and hurried back to the flat, the rain letting up just long enough for them to round the corner to Jaq's loft before it started coming down again, slicking the streets with dark sheets of water. Jaq nodded to the surveillance unit as they walked in the front door to the building, and when she unlocked the door to her loft, she asked Bronwyn to wait at the door until she'd checked it out. Jaq walked through every room, then turned on the lamps and brought Bronwyn in from the hall.

"What was that about?" she said, hanging her coat on the hook by the door and looking at Jaq. "There's something you're not telling me."

Just then, they heard her phone ring, vibrating in a circle on the coffee table. Jaq picked it up and gave it to Bronwyn.

"Oh God." She was whispering even though she hadn't yet answered the phone. "It's my mother."

Bronwyn was the strongest woman Jaq knew, but she knew one word from her mother was usually all it took to make Bronwyn fold. Bronwyn clicked the phone on and put it to her ear. Her mom was already talking.

"Mum, I can't just drop everything and meet you for brunch tomorrow. I have plans." She listened for another moment then put the phone back down on the coffee table. "She hung up on me." Bronwyn rubbed her forehead with the pads of her fingers, which did nothing to smooth the worry lines that had instantly etched themselves into her brow the second she'd picked up the phone. "And now somehow I have a brunch date with my mum tomorrow at noon."

Jaq smiled and held out a small glass of brandy. "Come sit."

Jaq sat on the couch and pulled Bronwyn into her arms. The streetlamp cast gold light through the window, and the candles Jaq had in the fireplace caught her eye.

"You have those in there because..." Bronwyn smiled and pulled the pencil out of her hair and let it fall around her face in loose waves, waiting for Jaq to finish the sentence.

"Because I've never been able to build a fire in that stupid thing," Jaq said, smiling. "I'm convinced it hates me."

Bronwyn hesitated. "I know this is a lot to ask, and you certainly don't have to do it." Bronwyn turned and spoke into Jaq's neck, her fingertips slipping under her shirt and over her abs. "I mean, even I wouldn't go if I didn't have to, but it just sounds like she's going to be in exceptionally bad form, and—"

Jaq put her finger on Bronwyn's lips. "Of course I'll go with you."

Bronwyn climbed over into Jaq's lap and hugged her hard. "Brilliant, thank Christ. I just can't face her alone this time. I've been dreading this moment since I was sixteen."

Jaq slid her hands around Bronwyn's ass and pulled her close. "You thought about coming out to your mom way back then?"

"Yep, and if she hadn't intercepted our mail, I would have eventually. I think she knew that."

"So," Jaq said, her eyes teasing, "where is this brunch and will your mother be armed?"

Bronwyn sighed. "It's at the Duck and Waffle on Bishopsgate; and no she won't, but you might want to consider it."

Jaq took Bronwyn's hand and put it low on her hip.

"Jesus, you *are* armed." She bent down to get a closer look. "How did I miss that?"

Jaq laughed. "I'm from Texas. I wear it well."

Bronwyn untucked the rest of Jaq's shirt and ran her hands up the inside and across her nipples. Jaq's breath caught, and she tightened her hands around Bronwyn's hips. "It's sexy," Bronwyn whispered, her words warm against Jaq's neck. "I like it."

Jaq's phone rang next, just as she'd opened every snap on Bronwyn's shirt with one flick of her wrist.

Jaq looked at it and had to laugh. She held it up to Bronwyn.

"My father now? Seriously?" Bronwyn rolled her eyes and reluctantly got up from the couch. "I'm going to run a bath. Good luck with that."

Jaq waited until she'd rounded the corner to click the green answer button. "Good evening, Mr. Charles, this is Jaq."

"Hello, Jaq," he said, pausing before he went on. "Is my daughter around, by chance?"

Jaq looked back toward the hall. "No, she's gone to run a bath, but I could take the phone to her, if you'd like."

"No, I called to speak to you, actually. I just thought we'd be able to talk more easily if she wasn't around."

"Of course."

"First of all, I admire the professionalism you showed in not making me aware of what's happening with Bronwyn and Ian. I know your hands were tied."

"I appreciate that," Jaq said, hoping the relief she felt didn't show in her voice. She'd been worried Bronwyn's father would be upset she hadn't contacted him, but ethically, there was just no way around it. "If I'd had a choice, I'd have told you right away, but I'm glad you've been made aware of the situation now."

"Bertrand Roundtree is the chief superintendent at Scotland Yard. We went to university together and have been friends for forty years, so he gave me a call today after speaking to Terry."

"I'm glad he did."

Mr. Charles paused. "I never liked Ian, and that's putting it mildly. I'm calling you to let you know he's been in touch with Bronwyn's mother. I don't know what they've spoken about, and as far as I know, she's unaware of any police involvement, but I did want you to know they've been speaking for the last few days."

"Thank you. That's good information to know."

"I'll leave it at that," Angus Charles said, clearing his throat, "But Terry mentioned that Bronwyn is staying with you, which eases my mind. Thank you for looking after her."

"Of course, sir." Jaq hesitated, choosing her words carefully. "I feel the same about Bronwyn now as I did when we first spoke at the pub."

"I was hoping that was the case. Please let me know if I can help in any way."

Jaq smiled. "Of course, sir."

"One more thing?" He paused before he went on, and when he spoke, Jaq could hear the smile on his face. "I think it's about time you started calling me Angus, don't you?"

❖

The next morning, a wide beam of sunlight streamed through the window and fell across Bronwyn's face, warming her cheek enough to wake her. She wrapped herself in the sheet and wandered into the kitchen, wordlessly accepting the mug Jaq offered her. Jaq was already on the phone with someone from work, her hand flying across the page, writing into a yellow notebook.

She hung up soon after and walked over to Bronwyn, lifting her onto the counter and kissing her, pulling Bronwyn's hips against hers. "You look amazing in a sheet, Bella."

Bronwyn wrapped her legs around Jaq's waist and let the top of the sheet fall to her waist. "Let's go back to bed," she whispered, leaning into her neck and running her tongue along the edge of her ear.

Jaq reluctantly glanced at the clock on the wall. "Unfortunately, it's already ten thirty. When do we have to meet your mom?"

Bronwyn dropped her head onto Jaq's chest. "I forgot about brunch. Can't we just skip it?"

Jaq picked her up and set her back on the floor. "Shower first, baby. Then I'll bring you home after brunch and we can do anything you want."

"Will you at least get in with me?" Bronwyn's lower lip made an appearance and Jaq surrendered. Five minutes later, they were standing under the water, Jaq sliding her hands across Bronwyn's breasts, kissing down her neck, and turning her slowly to face the wall, the water falling like warm rain between their bodies.

"Lean forward and put your hands on the wall for me, Bella."

Jaq's words were soft and powerful against her ear, and Bronwyn placed her hands against the slate wall. Jaq pulled Bronwyn's hips against hers and rested one hand gently between her shoulder blades. The other she moved down between them, two of her fingers sliding into Bronwyn and finding the sensitive spot she knew would be directly under her fingertips.

Bronwyn moaned and pushed back against Jaq's hand. Jaq kept her where she was, whispering in her ear, stroking until she felt her swell and throb beneath her fingers, then used a bit more pressure until she moaned, her voice deeper than Jaq had ever heard it, whispering for her not to stop. Jaq kept her face next to Bronwyn's until her breath told her she was close, then reached around with her other hand and slicked her fingers firmly across her clit in the same rhythm. Bronwyn held her breath, her forehead pressed against the slate, the muscles of her back tense, pressing back against Jaq's fingers as she started to come hard against both of her hands, her orgasm longer and deeper because of where Jaq was inside her. Her knees finally started to tremble, and Jaq caught her on her way to the floor. She lifted Bronwyn back into her arms, holding her until her breath slowed, softly kissing her forehead.

"Remember that, baby."

Bronwyn looked up at her, eyes still soft with the last of her climax. "Remember what?"

"Remember how you felt just now when your mom is staring you down."

Bronwyn smiled, wrapping her arms around Jaq's neck as she lifted her again and backed her up against the wall.

❖

The Duck and Waffle restaurant was a brunch staple for the visibly rich in central London, and one of Mrs. Charles's favorite places to be seen. The dining room only accommodated eighteen people, and the restaurant was located on the fortieth floor of the building, giving the lucky few inside the sensation of being suspended in the sky.

"I'm sorry we're late, Mum," Bronwyn said as they walked up behind her at the table, her mother's face falling into stone as she realized her daughter had arrived with Jaq Bailey.

Bronwyn gave her a quick kiss on the cheek, and Jaq extended her hand. "Nice to see you again, Mrs. Charles. You look well."

She ignored Jaq completely and sat, locking her eyes onto her daughter. "You didn't tell me you were bringing a guest."

Bronwyn took a deep breath. "Jaq is here because I asked her to come. Please try to be polite."

The waiter came and somehow managed to pour the coffee through the tension so thick it hung like fog between them. He offered Bronwyn a glass of prosecco, but she just shook her head. Mrs. Charles ordered a double vodka on the rocks, handing him her empty glass to take away.

"I don't like what I've been hearing, Bronwyn." Her mother smoothed her hands over her hair and locked eyes with her daughter.

• 147 •

"Whatever childish game you think you're playing needs to stop. Your wedding to Ian is in seven weeks, and if you keep this up, you're going to lose your only chance at a normal life." She didn't look at Jaq, but she didn't have to.

Bronwyn visibly steeled herself as Mrs. Charles' double vodka appeared at the table. Jaq added cream and sugar to her own coffee and switched it with Bronwyn's. Bronwyn smiled and squeezed Jaq's hand under the table, which did not escape the attention of her mother. She shook her head and glared across at Bronwyn, picking up where she'd left off.

"And to tell that poor man over the phone that you were breaking off the engagement was just unforgivable."

Bronwyn's eyes narrowed. "How did you know I broke up with him over the phone?"

Mrs. Charles looked around them briefly and lowered her voice to almost a whisper.

"Honestly, Bronwyn, after everything he's done for you too. You were a lot to take on, what with the rumors still flying around about you." She paused to give Jaq a pointed stare. "Frankly, I was surprised a man of Ian's caliber was even interested in you. Everyone was."

Jaq saw Bronwyn's shoulders slump beside her, and it was all she could do to keep her mouth shut. She covered Bronwyn's cold hand with her own and squeezed it, keeping it there to warm her fingers.

Bronwyn's mother clinked the ice against the sides of her glass, clearly warming to her own words. "I finally felt like the embarrassment you put me through when you were expelled from Stratford was coming to a close."

"Mother, I was not expelled from Stratford. You lied to me and forced me to withdraw."

The menus arrived as well as another drink for Mrs. Charles, who turned an icy glare in Jaq's direction as soon as the waiter stepped away.

"Is that what you've been telling her? To cover up the fact that you ruined my daughter's life?"

Jaq didn't reply but she didn't look away, either.

Bronwyn took a deep breath and did her best to remain calm. "Mother, I'm not sixteen anymore. I'm an adult. What you did is obvious. It has nothing to do with Jaq."

Jaq watched Bronwyn's mother as she drained her second double vodka in twenty minutes. She was willing to bet that the empty glass on the table when they'd arrived had contained the same thing, and the sudden sense of déjà vu made her nauseous.

"And after all that," she said, her volume rising as she started to slur her words at the edges, "you turn up to a civilized brunch with this *he/she* and expect me to welcome you with open arms? I said this to Ian yesterday, and I meant it, I'm very disappointed in how you've turned out, Bronwyn."

Bronwyn leaned toward her mother and looked her dead in the eye, her voice as hard as steel. "Don't ever speak that way to my girlfriend again."

Her mother stifled a laugh. "Is that what you're calling it?"

"No, Mother, that's what she is." Bronwyn kept her voice down, and Jaq knew that in spite of her mother's cruelty, Bronwyn was still doing her best not to embarrass her. "You forced us apart twelve years ago, and I've spent every day since in love with someone you made me believe never felt the same way. I'm not going to let you do that again." Bronwyn's voice broke and she swiped at a tear on her cheek. "If you want a relationship with me, you'll have to accept that I'm gay and treat the person I love with the respect she deserves."

Out of the corner of her eye, Bronwyn spotted two senior men a few tables over. They'd apparently heard what was happening; everyone had. They both held her with soft eyes, intensely kind, one of them giving her an almost imperceptible nod of support. Bronwyn suddenly felt not quite so alone and raised her chin just a touch as she gathered her coat and stood beside the table with Jaq, giving her mother a chance to reply.

Mrs. Charles stood, unsteady on her feet and suddenly very aware the entire restaurant was silently watching them, including their waiter, who'd stopped in the center of the dining room, unsure whether to stay or go. Bronwyn's mother glared at her and brought her hand back to slap her so quickly that Bronwyn didn't realize what was happening.

Jaq caught her wrist instantly and stared her down, her face just inches from hers. "Sit down, Mrs. Charles."

Surprisingly, she sat, just as her next drink was delivered. As she picked it up, Jaq reached into the bag at her feet and took her keys.

"I'm going to call you a cab that will be outside the main door in fifteen minutes," Jaq said, her voice firm and even. "Then, if at some point you sober up in the future, you'll need to apologize to your daughter." She picked up her jacket from the chair. "But don't ever even think about hitting Bronwyn again."

Jaq took Bronwyn's hand and they walked out the door and back onto the busy London sidewalk.

Chapter Thirteen

As soon as she'd called the cab and they were out of sight of the restaurant, Jaq pulled Bronwyn into an alley and wrapped her arms around her. Bronwyn was silent, in shock until Jaq kissed her, and she started to cry.

"I can't believe she was going to slap me."

Jaq pulled her back into her arms. She knew that feeling. "I would never let that happen, baby."

"I know," she said, wiping her eyes. "It's just that she intended to. In front of all those people."

"She'd had quite a bit to drink, Bella. I don't think that was necessarily how she would have reacted if she was sober."

Bronwyn took a deep breath and stepped back suddenly, covering her mouth with her hands. "I can't believe I embarrassed myself like that. It's like I totally forgot we were in public."

"What do you have to be embarrassed about?" Jaq said. "That was the bravest thing I've ever seen someone do."

Bronwyn wiped a tear off her cheek and attempted to rescue a bit of her eye makeup. "Really?"

"Are you kidding?" Jaq tried not to smile at the memory. "You stepped up and owned that situation, Bella. No one's ever stood up for me like that."

Bronwyn sank back into her arms.

Jaq smiled down at her. "Did you mean it?"

Bronwyn raised an eyebrow.

"That you're my girlfriend again?"

Bronwyn stood on tiptoe and kissed her. "I think that's a done deal, Bailey."

❖

As they climbed into a cab to go home a few minutes later, Jaq remembered she needed to stop by the office and grab a file she'd forgotten on her way out the door Friday evening.

"Do you mind if we stop by the Yard so I can grab the financials on Ian's case?"

"That's great, actually," she said. "I've been dying to see where you work."

Jaq gave the cab driver the new address and he dropped them off at the door a few minutes later. Jaq punched in the security code for the main doors, then scanned her fingerprint. There were a few people working, but most of the detectives were gone. As they walked to her office, Bronwyn stopped in the hall and pointed at an open door.

"Isn't that Terry?"

It was indeed Terry, who was at his desk, tapping his forehead against the surface, audibly muttering to himself.

Jaq stared. "I don't know whether I should take a picture or call the mental health hotline."

"What's the matter with him?"

"I don't know," she said, trying not to laugh, "but we should find out." Jaq knocked lightly on the doorframe of his office. "You okay, boss?"

Terry raised his head and ran his hands through his already unruly red hair, effectively standing most of it on end. "I just looked at the calendar."

"And?"

"It's the twenty-seventh, my wedding anniversary. The very same date I forgot last year."

"Oh no." This from Bronwyn, standing by Jaq at the door. "That's not good."

Terry just shook his head. "She's going to kill me. I told her ages ago I'd come up with something special for tonight, which of course is impossible now. None of the nice restaurants will have open tables on a Saturday, and that's what she loves the most." Terry paused, searching for the word. "She's one of those people who watch food shows all the time and run around trying new restaurants."

Bronwyn nodded. "A foodie."

Terry snapped his fingers. "That's it."

Bronwyn glanced at her phone. "Will you two excuse me for just a moment?"

Terry nodded and Bronwyn walked a few paces away, the phone already to her ear.

Jaq asked, "Okay, restaurants may be out, but what about presents? Is there anything you know she wants that you can get this afternoon before she expects you home?"

"Bugger," Terry said, shaking his head. "This is when it would have been handy to actually listen to her every once in a while."

Bronwyn almost made it back to the office, then got another call and stepped away, mouthing "sorry" to Jaq.

"What about a holiday booking?" Jaq said, turning back to Terry. "You still have a few hours. You might be able to make it look like you planned it all in advance."

"She'll see right through me. She always knows when I'm lying." He leaned back in his chair, head in his hands. "I'm screwed. At least I won't have to remember it next year after she leaves me tomorrow."

Bronwyn finally made it back to the office a few minutes later and handed Terry a small notecard with a handwritten address on it. At the bottom, she'd written *8pm* and underlined it.

15 WESTLAND PLACE
LONDON N1 7LP
T. 020 3375 1515

"What's this?" Terry turned it over in his hand.

"It's the details for your dinner reservation for tonight at Jamie

Oliver's restaurant, Fifteen Westland Place. It's usually booked three or four months in advance, but his wife, Jules, told me once they sometimes keep a table open for emergencies."

Jaq looked over at Terry and had to laugh. His mouth was literally hanging open.

"How do you know his wife?" Jaq asked, since Terry seemed to have lost his ability to speak.

"Dad produced one of his shows a few years back. I love to cook so I tagged along while they were filming. Jules was there too, and we've been friends ever since. She and Moira are close too."

"Are you kidding me with this?" Terry looked like he might cry.

"I wouldn't do that." Bronwyn smiled. "We're in luck, actually, because Jamie's there tonight, which is rare these days, so he'll be making your meal personally. He'll come out and introduce himself after you're seated and talk to your wife about what she'd like to eat."

Terry finally got himself together and walked over to Bronwyn, pulling her into a huge hug.

"Thank you for this," he said as he let her go, still shaking his head. "This is incredible."

"And just so you know, Jules has already called and told Jamie not to breathe a word about how this happened, so you can tell her anything you'd like. I wrote his mobile number at the bottom, just in case you have any questions."

"Jamie Oliver's mobile number?"

"Yes," Bronwyn said, smiling. "So keep that close to your vest."

"Wow," Terry said, shaking his head and looking at Jaq. "Just wow."

Jaq grabbed the file she needed from her office as they said goodbye and headed for the lift, leaving a much saner Chief Macmillan leaning back in his chair, smiling at the note in his hand.

❖

That evening, the sun was just setting when Bronwyn realized she hadn't eaten all day. They'd never gotten a chance to actually eat at brunch, and after they left Jaq's office, they had to drop by Selfridges to pick up the rest of Bronwyn's tailoring and give Andrew a chance to flirt with Jaq. Not that Jaq looked like she had any idea what was going on. Andrew pulled a suit on a whim while they were there and convinced Jaq to try it on, just to see it on her.

Bronwyn tried not to laugh as she and Andrew sank down on the couch and waited for her to come out of the dressing room, shoulder to shoulder.

"You do realize she's not a boy, right?"

"I know," Andrew said, his eyes locked on the dressing room door. "I can't help myself. I don't know what's wrong with me."

"I totally understand," Bronwyn said, leaning her head on his shoulder. "I can't take my eyes off her either."

"How did you two meet, anyway?"

"It's a long story, but she was my first girlfriend. We were roommates at Stratford Academy. My mum pulled me out of school when she found out about us and made sure we stayed apart until Jaq graduated. We met again at the wedding."

"Well, thank God," Andrew said, rolling his eyes. "I thought I was going to have to break the news to you that you're gay five minutes before your wedding or some shit."

They were both still laughing when Jaq came out of the dressing room, looking like a tousled version of a male model, complete with the requisite concerned stare off into the distance. It was actually in the direction of the clock, but it worked all the same. The suit hung from her lean frame perfectly, and she'd put her leather belt on the trousers and worn them low on her hips. She walked over to the couch and raked her hand through her hair, stopping in front of them. Andrew stared and dropped his eyes to the hem of her jacket.

"What's that on your hip?"

Bronwyn looked over at Andrew, not even trying not to smile. "It's a gun."

"Jesus." Andrew leaned his head back on the couch and looked at the ceiling. "You've got to get her out of here. I'm losing my fucking mind."

❖

They arranged for the remainder of the tailoring to be delivered to Jaq's loft later that week and walked out of Selfridges onto the high street, Jaq leading her into a series of back alleys on the way back to her flat.

"We could take a cab, but I feel like walking," Jaq said, glancing at her. "If you don't mind?"

"Not at all. It's going to be dark in a few minutes anyway. Fancy heading to that chippy down the road from my house? I'm starving."

"God, me too," Jaq said. "That sounds great."

"You looked amazing in that suit, by the way." Bronwyn slid her hand across Jaq's ass in the empty alley, then laced her fingers back into Jaq's, looking perfectly innocent as they turned back onto the main road down from her house.

"So, was that suit fitting for your benefit or Andrew's?" Jaq looked over at her and winked.

"You caught that, did you? I thought you might be working it just a tiny bit for his benefit, which was sweet of you." She reached up and kissed Jaq's cheek. "Something tells me that happens to you a lot."

"Maybe once or twice. Mostly by gay men trying to figure out if I'm a man or woman."

"Do they even care when they figure it out?"

"Not usually." Jaq laughed, leaning down to kiss her. "Now, where is this toothpaste-flavored chip shop? Suddenly I think I may die unless I eat something."

"I can't believe you just said that about my favorite chippy, but you're in luck, because we're here."

Bronwyn pulled her into a crowded chip shop, half-lit neon signs and yellowed racing schedules hanging on the walls. A chalkboard over the counter held the menu, at least what hadn't been rubbed off, and Bronwyn ordered for both of them. Jaq shook an alarming amount of vinegar on her chips before they left and grabbed two wooden chip forks from the bin.

By the time they walked out with their food, night had fallen in earnest. They walked toward the park, crossing the street just down from Bronwyn's house, and settled into a bench under an oak tree in the semidarkness.

"Just being here makes me jittery," Bronwyn said. "I didn't expect I'd feel that way." She squeezed a lemon slice onto her fish and looked up at Jaq. "I just don't know what he's thinking. I feel a little nervous that he's been so quiet."

"How so?" Jaq knew exactly what she meant, but any information was good information, and Bronwyn was still the closest person to him, unfortunately.

"Not that I wanted him to, mind, but I expected him to get a bit nastier about the breakup. Other than speaking to my mum, and God knows what they talked about, I haven't heard anything from him. It just makes me nervous."

"I know. I've actually been thinking the same thing."

"Has he been back to the house at all?"

"Not that we know of. We monitor the video feed daily, and there's been zero activity. I almost thought he might be writing the contents of the closet off and moving on, but Terry thinks not."

Bronwyn handed her fish and chips to Jaq, her appetite suddenly gone. "Terry's right. There's no way he'd just give in like that. Which makes me nervous."

Jaq looked across the park, then got up from the bench and peered over the street into the darkness. Bronwyn joined her, pulling her jacket around her and zipping up the front.

"Shit," she said suddenly, walking past Jaq and toward the edge of the park.

"Bronwyn, stop." Jaq caught up to her and stopped her from stepping into the light, holding her back under the shadow of the trees.

"But look," Bronwyn said, pointing at her house. "Do you see it?"

"I do, baby, but we have to be careful. We can't just go walking over there."

Jaq got her phone out of her coat pocket, and Bronwyn looked at the contact she pulled up.

"Don't you dare call Terry," she said, looking at her watch. "It's his anniversary."

"Shit, I forgot about that."

"It might be nothing."

"The attic light should not be on, but I can get a car out there and have the techs review the footage from today with a fine-tooth comb. They'll let me know if there's anything out of the ordinary. If not, we'll check it out Monday."

"Does that mean we get to go home?" Bronwyn took Jaq's hand.

"It does," Jaq said. "Your car should be there by now as well. I had someone drop it off today."

"Good, because for some reason, I'm exhausted. I think the drama with Mum took it out of me."

Jaq flagged down a cab on the way out of the park and pulled Bronwyn close in the back seat, remembering how it felt to hear the girl she loved call her flat home.

❖

Bronwyn sank down into the couch when they got back to Jaq's flat, and didn't wake when Jaq picked her up and carried her to bed a few hours later. Early the next morning, Jaq ended up having to go into work anyway to get a look at the security footage, and Bronwyn drove to her dad's house to let him know what had happened the previous day with her mother, before she had a chance to tell him an amplified version. If she remembered what happened at all.

Catherine answered the door and pulled Bronwyn into a hug as soon as she'd stepped into the foyer. "I heard what happened with your mum, Bronwyn. I'm so sorry."

Clearly, she'd left it too late and her mother had already painted her version of the story to her father, but at least she could talk to him about it and explain what happened.

"She's not here, is she?"

"God no, she came yesterday to see your dad, but I just made myself scarce until she was gone. He's in his office if you want to go back and see him."

"Thanks, Catherine. It's lovely to see you," Bronwyn said, smiling. "You look beautiful as always."

"Same to you," Catherine said, squeezing her hand and dropping her voice to a whisper. "You look happier than I've seen you in a long time."

Bronwyn got to her dad's office and peeked around the door. "Hi, Dad, do you have a few minutes for a chat?"

Angus Charles looked up from his computer, then got up to hug his daughter, kissing her forehead as he let her go. They sat on the navy velvet loveseat in the window nook, and Bronwyn kicked off her shoes and tucked her feet up underneath her.

"So I guess Mum told you what happened yesterday?"

"Well, she did give me an overview after she'd sobered up somewhat."

"It was awful, Dad." Bronwyn's eyes burned with sudden tears that quickly overflowed without warning. Her dad offered her the handkerchief in his jacket pocket. "She was vile to Jaq and called her a name I won't even repeat, and then went to slap me in front of the entire restaurant."

"Jesus." Angus squeezed her shoulder and shook his head. "She left that part out, of course. I'm sorry, Bronwyn. I won't let her get away with that."

"She would've slapped me, but Jaq grabbed her wrist before she even realized what was happening, then sat her back in her chair. She was brilliant. She even took Mum's keys on the way out and called her a cab."

"I should have known Jaq would handle the situation. Thank her for me, will you?"

Bronwyn looked down, twisting the handkerchief in her hand. "The wedding is off, Dad."

Catherine came in just then and set down a tea tray with two mugs and some chocolate biscuits, then turned without a word and ran back to the kitchen when the smoke alarm sounded.

"Is she trying to cook again?"

"Yes," Angus said. "This time it's a roast." He looked toward the door. "Or was a roast."

Silence fell between them and Bronwyn started to continue what she was saying.

"Let me stop you there, Petal," he said, using his nickname for her from when she was a little girl. "You had a rough enough time coming out to your mum yesterday, so I'll make this easy for you, if that's okay."

Bronwyn took a deep breath, unsure why the tears wouldn't stop rolling down her face. "Yes, please."

"I already know you're gay. I've known since your mother took you out of school that year, without my permission by the way, and I've been telling her for years she should have given you the space to be yourself a long time ago." Angus put his hand over hers and squeezed. "So if that's what you thought you had to tell me, you can relax."

Bronwyn let out a deep breath and smiled. "And…I'm back together with Jaq Bailey."

"Good, I've always liked Jaq," Angus said. "She has integrity, and I don't say that about too many people." He smiled, catching the last tear on her cheek and wiping it away. "I can't think of anyone I'd rather see you with."

"I heard that you two kept in touch."

"Nonsense," Angus said, biting into two chocolate biscuits at the same time, one on top of the other. "Why would I do that?" He smiled at Bronwyn as he handed her a cup of tea.

"So, where is Mum now, then?" Bronwyn asked, not actually sure if she wanted to know.

"Your mother," he said, "is at a spa in the Swiss Alps for an extended period of time."

"Seriously?" That news was not at all what she'd expected. "She actually went to rehab?"

"Yes," he said. "A very, very expensive one."

"What did you say to get her to do that?"

"Frankly, I was at my limit with her even before I heard what happened yesterday, and it was just getting worse. She's been drinking too much for years. It's the reason we got divorced."

"I thought you left her for Catherine!"

"Not at all, though your mother told everyone the opposite. When I told her I'd leave if she didn't stop drinking, I hadn't even met Catherine. I didn't start producing *Romance Island* until six months after the divorce."

"And she didn't stop drinking at all?"

"No, she didn't even try," Angus said, the hurt still there in his voice. "She just wasn't willing to give it up, and she said as much."

"So what made her do it this time?"

"After I heard what happened, I told her she'd end up losing her only daughter if she didn't dry out. She was already crying when she got here yesterday from brunch—the cab dropped her off at my front door. Believe it or not, I think she felt bad about what happened. It was kind of a breaking point for her. An hour later, I was driving her to the airport."

"Wow," Bronwyn said, "I can't believe it."

"She's at a spa, mind; if anyone finds out she went to rehab, I'll never hear the end of it." He popped the last chocolate biscuit in his mouth and smiled. "A very boring spa."

❖

On the way home, Bronwyn ordered a grocery delivery while she was stuck in traffic and scheduled it for later that evening. Before she'd even realized it, Jaq's place had started to feel like home. She'd loved cooking dinner for her and sleeping tangled together in bed like they used to when it all first started. But she needed to get her head around the fact that she was going to have to go back to her own house sooner or later. She couldn't just stay with Jaq forever, however tempting it might be.

By the time she got back to the flat, Jaq was there, sitting on the kitchen counter and opening a bottle of white wine. She was still wearing her office clothes, slim gray trousers and button-up shirt, topped with her black leather jacket.

"Great timing, gorgeous," Jaq said, pulling another glass down from the cupboard. "I just walked in a few minutes ago."

"Is this what you do?" Bronwyn teased, dropping her bag and settling herself between Jaq's knees, sliding her hands around her hips. "Just sit on your counter and wait for women to walk in and kiss you?"

Jaq leaned down and pulled Bronwyn's face to hers. "Actually, yes," she said, her fingers so gentle they felt like breath on her skin. "I've been waiting for the last twelve years for the only woman in the world to walk through my door." Then she kissed her, slow and close, looking into Bronwyn's eyes before she let her go.

Bronwyn leaned into her chest, laying her head on her heart, trying to memorize the rhythm. When she and Jaq were in school, she used to lie in her arms at night, listening to the beat of her heart. As long as she could hear it, she knew she was safe.

Jaq shrugged off her jacket and wrapped it around Bronwyn's shoulders. "Let's go," she said. "I have something to show you."

"I took my shoes off at the door. Should I go get them?"

"No need, we aren't leaving the building."

Jaq led her into the lift and up to the top floor, where they took another short staircase to a narrow door.

"What is this?" Jaq opened the door, holding it open for Bronwyn to walk through. When Bronwyn stepped out onto the roof, she realized suddenly it was a rooftop garden. The last autumn roses glowed in the twilight, fruit trees dangled low branches over the perimeter, and fig vine covered every inch of the concrete walls that surrounded the garden. A huge fountain sat in the center, made of royal blue and bright white Spanish tile, the turquoise water splashing into the pool underneath.

"Jaq, this is gorgeous," Bronwyn said. "Is it a community garden?"

"Yes and no," Jaq said. "Every flat owner has a corner to

cultivate, but they also hire professionals to keep it looking like this."

"Where is your corner?"

Jaq took her hand and led her to the far west wall, where rich, pillowy moss covered a three-foot by two-foot space, and a single vine had been trained around a little handmade fence at the back. Bronwyn leaned in to sniff the vine.

"Is this honeysuckle?"

"It is. I used to love the smell of it as a kid, and I try to keep a little wherever I am, although it can be hard to find. There was an old wire fence behind my trailer when I was a kid, and honeysuckle grew up it every summer, just took over. When it got August hot, I could smell it from my bedroom window. It reminds me of Texas summers."

"That's adorable," Bronwyn said, standing on tiptoe in her bare feet to kiss Jaq. "I can picture you as a kid in the summer with your nose buried in a honeysuckle thicket."

"That's about right." Jaq smiled.

"What else do I smell? Is that lavender?"

Jaq led her around the corner from where they'd come in to the east wall, where dozens of terra-cotta pots were mounted between pallet slats on the walls. Thyme and oregano fell over the sides, and lavender was dotted among the herbs, surrounded by sweet basil, lemongrass, cilantro, and spearmint.

"It's getting a bit late in the season for these, but apparently when it gets too cold they move the pots to the greenhouse in the back." Jaq rounded the next corner to the wall opposite the entrance. A small greenhouse, just big enough for two or three people to stand in, sat there in the last of the fading light.

"I love this," Bronwyn said, looking around. "I never would have guessed it's here, but when you open the rooftop door, suddenly it's like walking out into an English country garden."

Jaq glanced back around the side of the wall, then led Bronwyn between it and the greenhouse, pressing her hard against the stone wall. It was one of those times Jaq was almost rough, when she pushed Bronwyn against the wall with a sudden urgency, as if she couldn't breathe unless every inch of her body touched hers. The first time, Bronwyn had tensed until she realized Jaq had wrapped her hands around the back of her head, taking the impact with her arm as they hit the wall.

Jaq buried her face in Bronwyn's neck, her mouth warm and insistent. "There's only so long I can go without kissing you, Bella."

Bronwyn melted into her arms, instantly wet when she felt Jaq's thigh between hers. Jaq slid her hand around Bronwyn's neck, thumb holding her chin up to let her bite gently down her neck and across her shoulder, then bring Bronwyn's mouth back to hers.

Bronwyn pressed into her, untucking Jaq's shirt and sliding her hands under it and around her waist. That's when she felt it. She leaned back, her hand falling between their bodies, looking up at Jaq.

"I'm strapped on, Bella," Jaq said, her eyes heavy with desire. "But I don't have to be. Just tell me what you want."

Bronwyn never dropped her eyes, just loosened her belt, unfastening the button of her jeans and sliding the zipper down. Jaq unzipped her own trousers and took Bronwyn's hand, wrapped it around the length of the shaft, then held her hand over Bronwyn's, her breath deep and hard. Bronwyn leaned her head against Jaq's chest, sliding her fingers slowly down the shaft and back up, memorizing the feel of it, still warm from Jaq's body. Jaq watched her, looking for any sign it was too much, but Bronwyn just looked up at her, then slid her jeans down her hips and off. Jaq dropped to her knees, sliding her panties down and folding them into the pocket of her jacket. She sank her mouth into the heat of her, working Bronwyn's clit, holding her hips hard, her thumbs pressed just inside her hipbones. She knew something about that spot took her breath away; it had since Jaq found it the first time in her bed at Stratford, right before Bronwyn jerked her hips hard and came into her mouth, her thighs trembling and tight around Jaq's face.

Jaq stood and picked Bronwyn up easily, wrapping her legs around her waist. She held her against the wall, Bronwyn's fingers light and hesitant at the back of her neck.

"You have to ask me for it if you want it, baby."

Bronwyn's tongue slid over hers, whispering *please* into her mouth as Jaq guided the tip into her, then dropped her body down just enough to slide the rest of the way inside her. Bronwyn moaned, arching her back and tightening her legs around Jaq's waist. Jaq's hands slid to her ass, pulling her hard onto the shaft, then letting her go only to pull her back again, over and over, until Bronwyn's nails dug into her shoulders.

Jaq tipped her hips forward, pulling Bronwyn's body closer into the smooth front of the harness, holding her there and grinding it into her clit as she thrust deeper inside her. She held her tight against her hips, stayed deep, kept her clit slicked against the leather harness, until Bronwyn arched her back and cried out, her hands behind her flat against the wall, spread and tight, Jaq's still gripping her ass, trying like fuck not to come just watching her.

❖

Eventually they found Bronwyn's clothes and made it back to the flat, where the groceries had been delivered to the door.

"I'm going to guess since I can see lettuce on the top that the box has something to do with you?"

"Good guess, Detective Bailey," she teased. "Hungry yet?"

"Oh my God," Jaq said. "I was hoping you were going to ask that. I'm starving."

Jaq picked up the box and unlocked the door, holding it open for Bronwyn.

"I might fancy a shower before I start dinner," she said. "Do you have time to put those away for me?"

"I'm on it," Jaq said, pulling a pint of cream out of the box and looking at it. "What are you making?"

"Just spaghetti Bolognese with béchamel; it's really quick to put together," she said as she pulled the pencil out of the twist of hair at the back of her head and headed for the bathroom.

Jaq rounded the corner from the kitchen and pulled her close before she went further, resting her forehead on Bronwyn's. It was a moment before she spoke.

"No one has ever cooked for me like you do."

Bronwyn kissed her cheek and held her face to hers.

The water was hot almost instantly when Bronwyn turned it on and she stepped in, letting it run over her face and shoulders. Every day, it was harder to think about going home to her empty house. She loved everything about being here with her. Jaq's hungry little face always made her laugh, she loved how all she had to do was walk into the kitchen in the morning and a mug of steaming coffee appeared in her hand, and Christ, the sex. The explosive sex that took her breath away every time she thought about it, erasing the memory of anyone she'd ever known before Jaq.

She pulled on her silk shorts and one of Jaq's hoodies after her shower and pressed the water from her hair with a towel. She needed to start the mirepoix for the sauce and leave it to simmer in some stock before she went back to dry her hair.

As she rounded the corner from the hall, Jaq was standing by the box the groceries had been in.

"Come here, baby."

Bronwyn's stomach dropped. She knew by now when Jaq was worried, and this was it.

"What's wrong?"

Jaq nodded at the box and Bronwyn looked inside; there was a small black envelope lying at the bottom with her name on the front, typed on a small piece of white paper.

"Jesus."

"I was hoping you'd know what that is?" Jaq studied her face.

"No idea." But she did know, the second she saw it. It was Ian's stationery.

Jaq pulled on a pair of latex gloves from the counter. "Do I have your permission to open it? I won't read anything in it, I just need to make sure there's nothing hazardous inside."

Bronwyn nodded and Jaq slid her finger under the seal that popped open easily. There was no note inside, but Bronwyn could tell from Jaq's face that whatever it was wasn't good. Jaq held up her engagement ring.

"Fuck," Bronwyn said, sinking back against the counter. "How does he know where I am?"

Jaq just shook her head. "The only people that know where I live wouldn't give that information to anyone, like Moira and your father." She paused. "Does your mother know where you are?"

"I don't think so. She'd have no reason to think I'm not still at the house, and even if she did, there's no way Dad would tell her anything." She paused, suddenly remembering what her dad had told her that morning. "She's on an extended stay at a spa in the Alps for a couple months, anyway."

Jaq looked up. "She's what?"

"That's British for rehab."

She smiled. "Okay, do you remember where you left it in the house?"

"I left it on the hall table in an envelope. If he came back into the house, I wanted him to see it, and that was the only place I was sure he'd see it as he came in. I went back to the house when you were at work and left it there."

Jaq dropped the ring back into the envelope and sighed, setting it on the counter.

❖

"Sorry to call you so early," Jaq said, opening the door for Terry the next morning. "I was hoping to catch you on the way to the office." She looked down then and tried not to laugh. "You didn't have to bring me flowers."

"They're for Bronwyn, smartass," he said. "Our anniversary date was amazing. The wife is still thanking me."

"Stop right there. I don't want any details," Jaq said, holding up one hand and taking the bright yellow roses wrapped in brown paper with the other. "It's bad enough that people actually have heterosexual sex, I don't want to hear about it."

Terry laughed, giving Jaq's shoulder a playful shove as he came in. "I'll try to keep that in mind."

He looked around suddenly, remembering why he was there. "What did you need to show me, by the way?"

Jaq pulled on a glove and held up the envelope. "This arrived last night in the bottom of a grocery delivery box." She shook the ring out into her hand. "It's Bronwyn's engagement ring." Terry looked at it and then at Jaq. "Let me guess—it was in the house."

"Bingo."

He leaned back against the counter. "I got your message about the light on in the attic as well. I went over every bit of that footage myself afterward. There's no one on it. And the light is off now."

"What the hell?"

"I have no idea," Terry said, "But I do know that bastard is playing with us. What bothers me is that it's clearly aimed at Bronwyn, and I feel like it's going to get worse."

"What do we do at this point?"

"There's not a lot we can do until he gets sloppy somehow," Terry said, "Except bust our asses to stay ahead of him or catch him with the contents of the closet. Preferably both."

Jaq tapped her thumb on the counter, her face set. "I have a bad feeling."

"You and me both. We need to step up our game here."

Jaq looked toward the hall when she heard a door open, then poured coffee into a cup on the counter with sugar and milk already in it. She'd just stirred it when Bronwyn rounded the corner, barefoot and rubbing her eyes. She was wearing the shirt Jaq had worn to the office the previous day. It was wrinkled and buttoned wrong not quite halfway up, falling off one shoulder. She took the steaming mug from Jaq's hand and kissed her cheek, then turned and walked back down the hall to the bedroom.

"Sorry about that." Jaq smiled. "She didn't even see you."

"Bloody hell," Terry said, shaking his head and looking at the floor, not even trying not to smile. "I'm not even going to comment on that."

"You're telling me," Jaq said, putting the coffee pot back on the counter. "It's been difficult to get work done with her here, to say the least."

"Spare me, mate." Terry laughed, rolling his eyes. "I'm finding it difficult to work up any pity over here." He pulled on a glove from his pocket and picked up the envelope. "Let's get to the office and see what forensics can lift from this."

❖

It was a long day from that point. There was nothing on the tapes, no forensics on the envelope, and no way to connect Ian to anything. They knew where he was, but unless they could pin something on him, it was useless to pick him up. They might as well just haul him in just to tell him that he'd won. The ring was a statement, about not only the broken engagement, but also that Ian knew she was at Jaq's flat, which clearly he could reach anytime with no problem. Ian was putting himself in a position of power. It was just a matter of time before he used it.

Chapter Fourteen

"Hello, love, I think it's about time we talked, don't you?" Ian's voice was even and calm, as if he was speaking to a child. "Let's have one last meal at the house together. I'll make your favorite curry, and we'll put this whole ugly situation behind us." He paused, then went on. "I'll expect you at seven p.m. Friday evening."

Then, nothing. His phone clicked off, and the message on Bronwyn's voicemail ended. She'd picked it up to call Moira when she saw that he'd called. She hadn't even heard it ring.

❖

"Hi, Terry, I asked security to call your secretary for clearance. Do you have a moment to talk?" Bronwyn said as she stuck her head into Terry's office early that evening, just as he was furiously trying to shake the sticky side of a nicotine patch off the tips of his fingers.

"Absolutely," Terry said.

Bronwyn slid into one of the chairs across from his desk and took the patch off his fingers, pulling the other half of the backing off easily. Terry stuck out his arm, and she smoothed it on, tossing the paper into the trash. "Thank you for the flowers, by the way. They were gorgeous."

"Do we need to get Jaq down here?"

The look on her face told him it wasn't good news. She nodded as he picked up his phone and asked his secretary to find Jaq.

"You're an angel for setting up that dinner at Jamie's

restaurant." Terry leaned back in his chair, smiling. "Not only did you save my ass, but he took the time to eat dessert with us at our table and chatted with my wife about foodie stuff until the restaurant closed. He sent her home with all the recipes he used written out by hand. She's still smiling."

"I'd love to meet her someday," Bronwyn said. "Jaq told me she's a sweetheart."

"She is," Terry said, looking at the family picture on his desk. "I completely don't deserve her."

Jaq rounded the corner, smiling when she saw Bronwyn. The smile faded when she saw her phone in the center of Terry's desk.

"Great," Jaq said, sinking down into the chair beside Bronwyn and unbuttoning her shirt at the collar. "Let me guess, Ian's feeling chatty?"

Bronwyn pushed the button and played the recording. Jaq and Terry were silent as it finished, each of them looking at the other. Then Bronwyn jumped as Terry's office phone rang. He was still looking at Jaq when he went to pick it up.

"What tells me this isn't good news?"

He listened for what seemed like forever, then rubbed his forehead with the heel of his hand. "You're fucking kidding me with this, right?"

He clicked the phone over to the speaker and put down the receiver, walking over to shut the door of his office.

"No, sir, I'm not." The male voice on the other end of the line hesitated. "We've had eyes on and in that house since this started. The only person in there was the owner, so I can't tell you how it happened, but I just had an officer confirm it. The closet in the Charles residence is empty."

Bronwyn drew in a sharp breath, and Terry watched the blood drain from her face as he hung up the phone.

"How could that happen?" Jaq looked like someone had punched her in the gut. "So we have nothing on him now?"

Terry shook his head and Jaq saw he was angry. His face flamed to red in a matter of seconds when he was upset, even if he was controlled and calm on the outside.

"Terry," Jaq said, "do you have those pictures we took inside the closet?"

He nodded, shuffling the papers around on his desk until he found the small manila folder he'd put them in. Jaq pulled them out and spread them on the table, looking at each carefully.

"That attic is wired with more cameras than the White House," she said, tapping one of the pictures with her fingers. "Yet nothing showed up on any of the tapes, and we know Ian's been in there because he got Bronwyn's ring."

Terry and Bronwyn sat silent, looking at Jaq. Jaq pushed one picture to the center of the desk and they leaned in toward it.

Bronwyn drew in a sharp breath. "The skylight."

Terry looked up at her. "What? What skylight?"

"There used to be two skylights in the attic roof, one on either side before that space was used for storage. Dad always worried about them leaking, so he had them both removed and shingled over years ago and just patched the inside ceiling with drywall."

All three of them looked down at the barely visible small square, barely wide enough for a person's shoulders, just behind where they'd been standing looking at the shelves. It was only visible in one photo, the last photo they took before they locked everything back up. It was a wide shot of the entire closet interior from just inside the door. Terry and Jaq hadn't seen it because it was behind them, on the portion of the ceiling opposite the shelves.

"So he just dropped himself through the ceiling from the roof and never had to set foot in the attic at all?"

"Yep," Jaq said, raking her hand through her hair. "He bypassed every one of the cameras."

All three of them sat in silence, staring at the photo.

"Wait," Bronwyn said finally, tapping her nails on the arm of her chair. "We may not have anything on him at this point, but we can get it."

She looked at her phone lying on Terry's desk. Jaq and Terry both shook their heads at the same time.

"Hell no," Terry said. "I'm not sending you in there with that bastard. He'll have a gun with him for sure, and we won't be able to get in there fast enough if he decides to use it."

Jaq was still shaking her head. "Absolutely not."

Bronwyn looked at Terry. "Are we sure he even knows you're onto him about the cocaine?"

"No, but—"

"Then it's possible he has no idea that's even a factor and he just wants to talk to me about my relationship with Jaq. But if I can get him to talk about the coke, you've got your evidence."

"I don't care, Bella," Jaq said. "I don't want you anywhere near him."

Bronwyn sat back in her chair and looked at both of them. "If this is about me, which I think it is, both of you know he's not going to stop."

Terry and Jaq looked at each other but neither answered.

Bronwyn sat back in her chair and let out a long, slow breath. "He's not going to stop until I come back, and if I don't do that, he'll kill me before he lets me be with someone else."

Terry glanced at the office door to be sure it was still closed. "If we're even going to consider this, and I'm not saying I am, I need a little more information about your relationship, if you feel comfortable telling me."

Bronwyn nodded just as Terry's secretary opened the door slightly to ask if he needed anything before she headed home.

"I'm fine, Marta, just shut the door on your way out, if you don't mind."

She nodded and closed the door softly. Most of the detectives were gone for the day, so the office area was quiet. Scotland Yard was always busy, even in the middle of the night, but the detectives tended to keep daytime hours and most of their offices were located in the same area along with Jaq and Terry's.

"Would you like me to bring a female detective in while we talk?" His voice was gentle. "Or would you rather talk without Jaq or me here? I can bring someone neutral in."

"No, I'm okay," Bronwyn said. "I trust you."

"She's tougher than she looks," Jaq said, squeezing her hand.

"I certainly wouldn't want to mess with her," Terry said, raising his eyebrows and leaning back in his chair. "And I'm the one with the gun."

That was enough to make Bronwyn laugh and ease the tension a bit.

"I'm asking these questions to get a feel for what Ian may or may not do in the future. It's not perfect, but past behavior is a decent indicator of whether future behavior might escalate." Terry looked over at Jaq. "And unfortunately, it's all we have to base this decision on. I couldn't care less about the cocaine at this point—I'm concerned about you. But I think you might be right about him coming after you. We know we have something on him, so if we can get an admission on tape and get him put away for the next thirty years or so, that's going to keep you a lot safer."

Bronwyn nodded. "I understand. That's what I'm going for, too."

Terry leaned forward in his seat and opened a notebook. "Okay," he said. "Was he ever abusive during your relationship?"

"He's hit me, enough to leave bruises a few times. He choked me once until I almost blacked out," Bronwyn said, dropping her eyes. "I don't know why, but at the time I tried to just write it off as him having a temper. But it was escalating enough at the end that I knew if I left him for Jaq, he'd come after both of us."

"But then we found his stash in the attic and you didn't have a choice."

Bronwyn nodded and Terry took a deep breath. Terry was always professional, but Jaq could see this was difficult for him.

"Has he choked you more than once?"

Bronwyn nodded. "Yes, but it wasn't until the last time that I thought he would actually kill me."

"What about any possessive behavior?" he said. "Was he controlling at all?"

"Just this last year. He was fairly normal before that. Then everything just seemed to change after he got fired, although I didn't realize that had even happened at the time."

Terry sat back in his chair. "Jaq, I know you're close to the situation here, but I'd like to know what you think." He looked over at Bronwyn. "Is there any chance she can just walk away from this?"

Jaq shook her head. "I think she may be right." She sighed, rubbing her forehead with her fingers. "But I'm not willing to put her in danger."

"But I'm already in danger." Bronwyn looked at both of them and leaned forward in her seat. "If I was someone you didn't know, would you consider sending me into this dinner on Friday to get what you need to prosecute?"

"On the drug charges?" Terry looked over at Jaq. "It's a possibility."

"Then send me in. I'm not concerned with the drugs either, but if he's not in prison, he won't stop until he kills me."

Jaq shook her head and looked at the ceiling. Terry was quiet for a long time before he spoke. "This has to go through more people than just me," he said, "But I'll present it to them tomorrow and see what they say."

Jaq and Bronwyn gathered their things and walked out of the office. There was nothing left to say.

❖

The next day was Thursday. Jaq got to the office early after holding Bronwyn all night, drifting in and out of sleep and panic.

"Got a minute to talk?" When she looked up from her desk, Terry was leaning on her office door, a takeaway coffee in each hand.

"Sure, come on in."

Terry took a seat and handed Jaq her coffee. She took a sip, then made a face, narrowly avoiding spraying it across her desk.

"What the hell is this?"

"What?" Terry said, looking over and raising an eyebrow.

"Whatever's in this cup is not coffee, I can tell you that."

Terry took a sip from the cup he was holding and handed it to Jaq, switching it for hers. "So I like a few pumps of strawberry syrup in my java," he said, shrugging. "I'm secure in my masculinity."

"You'd better be," Jaq said, laughing and downing half a bottle of water. "Because that, my friend, is lip gloss in a cup." She raised an eyebrow in Terry's direction. "Not that there's anything wrong with that if that's what you're into."

Terry smiled and shook his head. Neither one wanted to bring up the elephant in the room.

"You know I hate the thought of putting Bronwyn in that situation, right?" Terry said.

Jaq nodded. "I do know that."

"I'm only considering this because I think she's right. If she weren't positive she was in danger, she wouldn't want to do it, and we wouldn't let her."

"I know," Jaq said. "None of this is your fault. I know you care about her."

"I think the world of that girl," Terry said. "But I also value our friendship. So if you don't want this to happen, I'll pull the plug. I know I should be impartial here, but I'm not going to run over you with this."

"Did you get clearance for her to go in on Friday?"

"This morning."

Jaq nodded. "This is her decision, not mine. I'm not going to be another person in her life telling her what to do."

"You know we'll do everything we can to keep her safe. And I promise you, if I didn't know she could handle it, I wouldn't send her in there." He held Jaq's eyes. "She can do this."

"I hope you're right," Jaq said, "Because she's everything to me."

❖

When Jaq got home that night, Bronwyn was in the kitchen making dinner, dancing to the Backstreet Boys.

"Really, baby?" she said, leaning on the doorframe. "The Backstreet Boys?"

"You're home," she said, coming over to kiss her, her body

melting as Jaq pulled her in, holding her, memorizing the warm weight of Bronwyn's hair in her hands. Jaq finally picked her up and put her on the counter, resting her hands on her thighs.

"They're going to let you go in, Bella," she said, fighting the burn of sudden tears. "Terry got the approval this morning." Jaq leaned into her, resting her head on Bronwyn's chest.

Bronwyn kissed her, breathing her in. Neither one spoke for a few long moments. "I just found you," Bronwyn whispered. "I can't lose you all over again because someone else doesn't want us to be together."

"Baby…" Jaq closed her eyes and let out a long breath. "Just promise me you'll be careful."

She nodded. "I will. I promise."

"And we'll be right outside in a surveillance vehicle. We already have cameras inside, and you'll be wearing a wire. If we think you're in danger, we'll be in there before he can take his next breath."

Jaq held Bronwyn's waist, wishing she could say something to change her mind, then reminding herself that it wasn't her choice.

"Tomorrow afternoon they'll go over everything you need to know, what they need to hear him say, etc., then fit you with a wire."

Bronwyn nodded, then handed Jaq the wine opener lying next to her. "In the meantime, will you see if you can talk some sense into that wine over there?" She nodded in the direction of the bottle, surrounded by jagged bits of cork lying on the counter. "It hates me."

❖

Jaq watched as Bronwyn finished making dinner, sliced filet of beef topped with chopped cilantro, fresh mint, and heirloom tomato. They ate in the living room, watching the sunset in layers of orange and violet over the London skyscrapers.

When they were done, Bronwyn lay back on the couch and Jaq pulled her feet into her lap.

"The farther I get from the past with Ian, the angrier I get with myself," Bronwyn said. "This wouldn't have even been happening if I'd left him the first time he hit me."

"None of this is your fault, baby."

"But it is." A tear slid down Bronwyn's cheek as she stared out the windows. "I don't know why I didn't leave. I so badly wanted everything to be okay that I was actually the one apologizing to him. I just wanted everything to go back to normal."

"I get that," Jaq said, warming her feet with her hands.

Whenever Bronwyn was upset or scared, her hands and feet seemed to turn to ice. Jaq had always done her best to warm them, hoping it would fix what was wrong.

"Has there ever been another time in your life you've felt like that?"

"Like what?"

"A bit desperate, like you just wanted everything to be okay again?"

Bronwyn thought, her brow crinkling before she answered. "I guess. Not really when I was young, but from about twelve and older, whenever my mum would get upset, there was a lot of drama. Even if I knew I was right, or she'd done something glaringly awful, I'd apologize over and over, just to make things okay again." She paused. "So I could breathe."

"That sounds familiar," Jaq said.

She looked down at Bronwyn's feet in her lap, wrapping her hands around them.

"My mom would come home from work wasted when I was a kid," Jaq continued. "And if she'd had a bad night, she usually got mean. I learned pretty quick that it'd only get worse if anything else upset her. I stressed myself out every day trying to make sure there was nothing that could make her angry."

Jaq looked up at Bronwyn, her eyes dark with the memory.

"I didn't even know I was doing it until I got to Stratford and suddenly realized I didn't have anything but school to stress out about. It was a huge relief."

Bronwyn nodded and laced her fingers into Jaq's. Jaq was so strong she sometimes forgot she'd once been a kid who had to rely on her mum.

"I always knew that if something went wrong, Mum would start drinking, so I did whatever I could to keep that from happening," Bronwyn said. "One time I even replaced all the clear liquor with water, which only got me a slap, so that backfired."

She looked down and pulled at a thread at the bottom of her shirt. "But when she did start drinking, I just kept pretending whatever she was angry about was all my fault until she calmed down."

She scooted down until she was lying on the couch, looking up at the ceiling, a single tear falling from the side of her face. She didn't speak for a minute or two after that. "Which is exactly what I ended up doing with Ian."

Jaq didn't say anything, just waited.

"Every time he got violent, he told me all the reasons why what he did was my fault, and I believed him. And if he didn't try to blame it on me, I did it for him. I just wanted everything to be better again, and it was the only way that ever happened."

She swiped at a tear with the back of her hand. Jaq wanted so badly to pull her into her arms, but it wasn't the time. Memories need space to unfold.

"And then I guess I just started to actually believe it myself after a while."

Jaq unbuttoned her shirt, pulling Bronwyn's icy feet onto the heat of her stomach and wrapping them back up with the shirt, holding them there with her hands.

"And now?"

"Since I met you again, there's been something in the pit of my stomach, like I was just waiting for you to hurt me, but you never have. I don't think I ever realized how tired I was of trying to protect myself until I didn't have to do it."

"I know," Jaq said. "You get so used to bracing for the worst that it's hard to see when you don't have to do it anymore."

• 179 •

Jaq pulled Bronwyn up onto her lap and laid her hand, warm and soft, in the center of Bronwyn's chest. "I'm not going to let anyone hurt you again."

Bronwyn leaned down and Jaq kissed her, pulling her in tighter as Bronwyn's hands slipped under Jaq's open shirt and across her breasts.

"Take me to bed?" Bronwyn kissed along the outside of her ear, then down to her mouth, until Jaq's breath deepened and she took Bronwyn's face in her hands.

"We don't have to do this, baby, not tonight," Jaq said, kissing her forehead and looking into her eyes.

"I need to be with you," Bronwyn said, then hesitated. "I just need us to be us tonight."

That was all Jaq needed to hear. She stood leading Bronwyn down the hall, then laid her back on the bed while she lit the candles on the mantel and across the windowsills.

"Where did all the candles come from?" Bronwyn said, her eyes sparkling. "They're beautiful."

Jaq smiled as she picked up the last candle and lit it. "It's all part of my secret plan to make you want to never leave my bed."

Jaq took Bronwyn's clothes off and quickly shed her own, then got into bed and pulled Bronwyn into her, hands sliding across her back as she dipped her head and caught Bronwyn's nipple in her mouth. She swirled her tongue around it and pulled it deeper, her fingers working on the other side, intensifying her touch as they responded. Bronwyn rolled onto her back and Jaq raised Bronwyn's arms above her head, holding them there, her mouth still slick and warm against her nipples. Her fingers found Bronwyn's clit and she deepened and slowed her touch, feeling her clit harden underneath her fingers in response.

"You're already driving me crazy, Jaq," Bronwyn said, laughing and covering her face with her hands. "I think you love to torture me."

"I'm going to keep you on the edge tonight, baby," she said, raising Bronwyn's hands back above her head and holding them there, kissing her then softly biting her lower lip. "And there's nothing you can do about it."

She moved down her body, touching everywhere, fingers moving like water over her clit. She didn't hold back, and the next time Jaq had her close, Bronwyn moaned, pressing her hips into Jaq's mouth and tangling her hands hard into her hair, keeping her where she needed her as she started to fall over the edge. Jaq slipped quickly out of her grasp just in time and moved up her body, trying not to smile. She stopped when her face was an inch from Bronwyn's and tried to look serious.

"One more time, Bella," Jaq said. "Do that again, and I'm going to tie you to that bed."

Jaq moved back down to her clit with her tongue, and it only took a few seconds until Bronwyn's hands were back in her hair. Jaq smiled as she crawled back up her body and off the bed, reaching into the back of her closet and pulling out two black ropes.

She held them up and raised an eyebrow. "Just in case you think I'm kidding."

Bronwyn held Jaq's gaze and hesitated. "I think I want you to do it."

Jaq thought for a second, then climbed back in bed with her, bringing the ropes but putting them on the nightstand. The last thing she wanted to do was make Bronwyn feel powerless. She said that, gently, stroking her hair and listening closely when Bronwyn finally answered.

"I don't," Bronwyn said. "With you, it's the opposite. When you take over, I can just…feel. It's the one time I know I'm safe."

Jaq held her face in her hands and kissed her, feeling suddenly emotional at Bronwyn's show of trust.

She reached across for the ropes. "Have you done this before, baby?"

Bronwyn shook her head.

"The only thing you have to remember," Jaq said, "is that if you tell me to, I'll stop what I'm doing, no matter what, and untie you."

She looked down into Bronwyn's eyes and dropped her voice to a low scrape that sounded like sex. They were in school the first time Bronwyn had heard it, and she could count on one hand the number of times she'd heard it since.

"But if you don't do that, no matter what you say, I'm going to take you right to the edge and push you." She paused. "Like you've never been pushed."

Jaq's eyes were dark and intense, glittering in the candlelight, and Bronwyn watched as Jaq tied her wrist to a metal loop hidden just below the surface of the headboard, then did the same with the other side. She closed her eyes, suddenly wet and aching in a way she'd never experienced, and felt Jaq move back down her body and her tongue slide back over her clit.

Jaq was not in the mood to be merciful. She worked Bronwyn in a steady rhythm with her tongue until she started to come, then backed off completely and watched her pull at the ropes, her mouth a millimeter from Bronwyn's straining clit. She added two fingers as soon as Bronwyn's breathing started to calm, moving them inside her until Bronwyn bit her lip. Sweat shimmered between her breasts and the flickering candlelight caught the drops as they fell down the side of her body to the bed. A deep flush covered her chest and arms, tensed against the ropes.

Jaq climbed back up her body and kissed her, waiting until she opened her eyes to speak. "Bronwyn," she said, "how much do you want?"

She opened her eyes slowly, drunk with lust and pleasure. "What do you mean?" she whispered.

Jaq paused, thinking. When they'd started, she hadn't intended to go in this direction, but Bronwyn's body was telling her she was ready. "Let me put it this way," Jaq said softly. "When I was inside you just now, did you want more?"

Bronwyn nodded. "I wanted everything."

Jaq traced her lower lip with her thumb. "Do you trust me?"

Bronwyn nodded, both of them aware they were moving past the point of intimacy into surrender.

Jaq pulled Bronwyn's clit into her mouth, circling it with her tongue, giving it to her exactly the way she wanted it until she saw her arms flex against the ropes. Jaq slid two fingers into her and stroked inside, her G spot already tense and swollen under her fingers. She touched it softly, then with more intensity, listening to every breath, and adding a third when a soft moan told her it was time. She turned her fingers slowly inside Bronwyn, pushing deeper until the base of her fingers met resistance.

"God, baby," Bronwyn whispered. "That feels…"

Her voice trailed off as Jaq slid her fourth finger inside. Bronwyn's breath caught and her body tightened around her hand. Jaq stopped, holding her fingers inside her, letting her get used to the sensation. She brought her mouth to Bronwyn's clit again, using deep, rich strokes with the flat of her tongue, giving her everything she wanted, dipping lower and licking where her fingers met Bronwyn's body, tasting and soothing her, feeling her slowly relax around her fingers.

Jaq met Bronwyn's eyes as she went back and slid her swollen clit under her tongue. Bronwyn arched against the ropes as her excitement built, groaning when Jaq moved at the last second, working the skin of her inner thighs, pulling it into her mouth to remind Bronwyn what she could be doing elsewhere.

"I can't take this, you've got to let me come," Bronwyn said, her breath quick and desperate.

"You don't want me to stop, baby," Jaq said, smiling, her other hand moving across Bronwyn's stomach to rest between her breasts. "Trust me."

Jaq turned her fingers again, slowly, and went back to her clit with her tongue, stroking the underside before she pulled it gently back into her mouth. Bronwyn was panting now, straining at the ropes, and wetter than Jaq had ever seen her.

"Can you take more, baby?"

Jaq covered her clit with her tongue, waiting until she heard the *yes* between Bronwyn's moans to continue. Jaq pressed her hand slowly deeper. Bronwyn was breathless, words a whisper, her body stone still. Jaq moved down to drag her tongue again around the edge of her hand as she slowly curled the fingers inside her toward her palm and tucked her thumb into the center. She didn't move, just looked up at Bronwyn and whispered. Bronwyn answered before the words were out of Jaq's mouth.

"God, yes. Now."

Jaq slid the rest of the way inside her, filling her slow enough to let her feel every inch of her fist. Bronwyn arched and tensed, the words balancing on her lips, as light as air.

Then she opened for Jaq. And when she did, she fell into an orgasm so dark, rich, and endless that tears slid from her eyes when the end she thought didn't exist finally came. Jaq stayed inside her, then raised her eyes to Bronwyn's, dense love shimmering in the air between them. Finally, she laid her palm on Bronwyn's stomach. "Take a deep breath, baby."

Bronwyn closed her eyes and took a deep breath, then as she let it out Jaq slowly relaxed her hand, moving back up Bronwyn's body to untie the ropes around her wrists. When she had them off, she lay back and pulled Bronwyn into her arms, holding her against her heart.

"Jaq," Bronwyn whispered, her mouth warm at Jaq's ear. "How did you do that?"

Jaq pulled her closer. "I didn't, Bella. You trusted me, and we did it together."

Chapter Fifteen

The next morning, Jaq went into work early, and Bronwyn met her there late that afternoon. She'd already showered and dressed for her date with Ian. It was surreal to think about seeing him again—being with him seemed like it had happened in another lifetime, although once she thought about it, that was more accurate than not.

She arrived at Terry's office right on time, and he made a call to a department he referred to as "the tech guys." They came up to the office and explained how the surveillance system would work. Jaq joined just as they started.

"It's Bronwyn, right?" One of the two techs looked up at her and smiled as she handed him her phone.

"It is."

"Okay, Bronwyn," he said, plugging her phone into his laptop and pulling up what he needed on the screen. "We're sending you in with a virtual wire, not a wire that's physically attached to you. I'm installing an app that will run in the background on your phone but can't be seen. It will send audio and video to the Phantom in real time."

"The Phantom?"

Bronwyn looked over at Terry, who was distracted by a cigarette that had somehow jumped into his hand from his drawer. Bronwyn raised an eyebrow, and he rolled his eyes and put it back. "The Phantom is a hardware box that talks to the iPhone and decodes it."

He looked up at Jaq, Bronwyn, and Terry, clearly proud of the technology, only to find not one of them had understood what he'd said.

"So," Jaq said, "she just has to have her phone on her? And even if Ian looks at it, he won't know the app is running?"

"Exactly. And the recording is not actually on the phone at all. It's off-site in the Phantom, so it can't be destroyed even if he does figure it out."

The tech reached toward Bronwyn and took her glasses off her face. "I'm also going to attach a tiny microphone to the earpiece of her glasses, just as a backup. This one is visible, although you'd have to look super close to see it, so just try to make sure your hair hides it."

He gave the glasses back to Bronwyn and pointed out the microphone. It looked like a black Tic Tac stuck onto the side of her frame toward her ear.

"This one transmits remotely as well?" Jaq asked.

"It does, but the sound quality is poor compared to the Phantom setup, so it's only there as a backup."

Terry thanked the tech department as they left, and looked at his watch. "It's almost six now, so let's go over what we need to get on tape before you drive over there. We already have our surveillance vehicles in place, so all we have to do is get in once you're there."

"I'm driving there alone, right?"

"You are," Terry said. "Everything needs to look as normal as possible, and that's what you would ordinarily do. Just park wherever you parked when you lived there."

For the next forty minutes, Jaq and Terry went over what they needed to get on tape, which turned out to be exactly what she'd expected. They needed him to take ownership of the drugs and money, and to admit his part in the distribution. Once they had that, she could leave, albeit very carefully.

"Just tell him you forgot something in the car and keep walking," Terry said. "We'll move in once you're clear."

Bronwyn took a deep breath and looked over at Jaq and Terry.

"You two look like you're being pushed off a cliff." She laughed, sliding her glasses back on. "I'll be fine. Stop worrying."

But in reality, as she got into her car a few minutes later and started the drive to her house, she was gripping the steering wheel so hard her knuckles were white. When she finally arrived and found parking on the street, the fact that she'd walk into her house and find Ian inside was suddenly very real. Too real. She paused at the door, then turned around and sat on the stoop, fighting a sudden wave of nausea. Her stomach turned over, and just for a moment, she thought she was going to be sick.

❖

"What the hell is she doing?"

Terry looked at his watch then back at the stoop, where Bronwyn sat with her head in her hands. They'd just gotten to the surveillance van and done tests to make sure the audio and visuals were running, but everything looked good. They had a good view of the kitchen area and the hall, and they'd expected Bronwyn just to walk into the house.

Jaq kept her eyes on Bronwyn. "I have no idea."

They watched as Bronwyn appeared to pull herself together and stood to face the door. She ran her hands through her hair and pushed her glasses up on her nose several times, something Jaq knew she did when she was upset and trying to settle herself. Then she turned the knob and walked into the house, shutting the door behind her.

As soon as she came in, Bronwyn smelled curry and heard Ian in the kitchen. He heard her shut the front door and came out to greet her as she hung her coat up in the hall.

"It's good to see you, love." He held her close for a moment, then held up a wooden spoon covered in curry. Bronwyn noticed he glanced at her hand to see if she was wearing her ring. "I don't want to get this all over you, so let's take this into the kitchen."

It felt like any other fall evening when Bronwyn came home

from work to find Ian already there, cooking or watching telly, but in another way, the house felt empty, a farce, almost haunted. As if the house itself was watching them from the darkened corners, silent and concerned, willing her to walk back out the door.

"Noodles or rice?"

Bronwyn shook her head clear of her thoughts. "What?"

"Do you want noodles or rice with your curry?" Ian had one box in each hand and held them up for her to see as she sat down and placed her phone on the table beside her.

"Either," Bronwyn said, then tipped her head. "No, wait, noodles."

Ian smiled and put the rice back in the cupboard. "You never could make up your mind when it came to starches."

He put the pasta pot on to boil and handed Bronwyn a glass of wine, sitting down at the table across from her with a glass for himself. He brushed her fingers with his as he handed it to her. They were warm, and Bronwyn's were icy, which he'd known before he did it.

She ran her hand through her hair and tried to relax back into her chair. She saw him looking at her clothes, his eyes slightly narrowed in thought or derision, it was impossible to tell. He took in the camel wool pants, black wool cardigan and the leather boots Jaq had given her, then the faded denim jacket she'd worn under the coat in the hall. She knew she looked different. She was different, now more of a reflection than a presentation. Ian put it together slowly, trying to keep it from settling into hard lines on his face as she watched, unflinching.

Bronwyn sipped her wine and set it back down on the table, the clink of the glass on the table an offering to the silence, instantly rejected.

"This is wonderful," she said, clearing her throat. "What is it?"

"It's that bottle from Sequoia Vineyards we put aside last year from our trip to Napa Valley," Ian said. "I thought now was as good a time as any to open it."

Ian looked over at Bronwyn, taking her in. "You look great," he said. He hesitated, as if he had decided not to say something, but then said it anyway. "Thank you for coming. It's nice to be back in the house together."

Bronwyn nodded. "It is. I felt bad that I ended things on the phone. I should have done it in person."

Ian swirled the wine in his glass, his eyes on the table. "Bronwyn, I want you to know that I understand why you ended it. I didn't take it as I should have at the time, but I deserved it. I was wrong to ever lose my temper like I did with you." He traced a grain line in the wood tabletop with his thumb. "I can't tell you how sorry I am. I know this is my fault."

Bronwyn sat, silent, as she watched Ian try to hide the tears in his eyes. She hadn't known what to expect, but this was not it. He'd never apologized for hitting her, not once.

"I know you didn't mean to hurt me, Ian. And I did a lot to provoke you." Bronwyn dropped her eyes as she said it. The words, and the fact that Ian believed them, made her physically sick.

Ian stood, rubbing his eyes just once with the heel of his hand. "Well, that's not what this meal is about, anyway," he said, trying to smile. "I just really wanted to have a chance to say goodbye properly. And that will be difficult to do without noodles, so let me get those into the water."

Bronwyn smiled and picked up her wine glass.

"She's not falling for this bullshit, is she?" Terry looked over at Jaq.

She kept her eyes on the monitor and didn't answer.

Ian put the curry together as Bronwyn set the table. He drank most of the wine. Bronwyn was hesitant to drink much, in case something went wrong. Ian did seem to be in exceptionally good form, but then again, she'd made that mistake more than once. She finally put her cutlery on her plate and sat back in her chair.

"So how did you know I was staying in the lofts on Greycoat Street?"

Ian folded his napkin and set it next to his plate. "My assistant lives in the building. She remembered you from the office Christmas party." He took a deep breath, and his face softened. "I hope it was okay to send your ring to you. I didn't know when I'd see you next and I just wanted you to have it."

"No, that was fine," she said. "Thank you."

Ian put his hand over Bronwyn's across the table. "I just miss you, Bronwyn, I miss you every day."

Bronwyn left her hand under his and looked over the table at Ian.

"It was more than just the temper," she said. "I just felt like you were hiding something from me all the time. I never felt like you were honest with me."

"Hiding what?" Ian said, surprised. "I swear, I never cheated on you. Not once."

"I never felt like we were really honest with each other. I just couldn't do it anymore."

"I understand," Ian said. "You're right. I couldn't face the possibility of losing you."

"Then tell me." Bronwyn looked over at him. "You can trust me, Ian, and if you're finally honest, then we may have a chance."

Ian got up from the table and took their plates to the sink, then turned around and ran his hands through his hair. "Would you really consider coming back to me?"

Bronwyn got up from the table and walked over to Ian. "Ian, if we can be honest about everything, we can try again."

"What the hell is she doing?" Jaq paced the two or three steps it was possible to take in the crowded interior of the van. "I don't want her anywhere near him."

"I'm not sure," Terry said, his eyes locked on the monitor. "But we've got to trust her. We have no other choice at this point."

Ian dropped his face into his hands, rubbing his forehead. "I lost my job a year ago."

Bronwyn was silent, willing him to go on.

"I didn't want to tell you. I was afraid you'd leave me."

"Why did they let you go?"

"I was moving some money through client accounts in some ways that weren't exactly legal."

"What?" Bronwyn said. "Like money laundering?"

"I just got mixed up in some stuff and had to do some favors," Ian said. "I had it under control."

"But they caught you?"

"Not really," Ian said. "They couldn't prove anything, but the suspicion alone was enough to get me fired."

"Is there anything else?" Bronwyn looked in his eyes. "Now is the time to tell me if there is."

Ian reached out, pulled Bronwyn to his chest, and put his arms around her. He smoothed her hair with his hand and tipped her chin up to look at him.

"I'll tell you anything you want to know." He looked into her eyes, stroking her lips with his finger. "It really doesn't matter since you won't be leaving the house alive."

Jaq lunged for the door of the van, pulling her gun.

"Jaq, stop!" Terry said, pulling her back. "We've got units surrounding that house. One word from us and they'll be in there. She's almost got it."

"You've got to be fucking kidding me." Jaq leaned against the wall of the van, raking her hand through her hair. "He just threatened her life."

"I know, but we haven't seen a weapon yet, and if we go in there now, she will have done all this for nothing." Terry looked up at Jaq. "I trust her."

Jaq and Terry stared at the monitor, radio in hand, waiting.

Bronwyn looked up at Ian, suddenly afraid she was going to be sick. "What are you talking about?"

"Did you think I'd leave that much cocaine in the house without having the house monitored? I've had cameras on that storage closet for the last year. I saw you look through the crack in the door and make your little call to your girlfriend when I reviewed the footage the next day."

Bronwyn was silent.

"What, she's not your girlfriend?" Ian smiled. "My apologies, she must just be some dyke you're fucking behind my back. Easy mistake."

• 191 •

"I don't know what you're talking about." Every drop of blood had drained from Bronwyn's face.

"The only reason you're still here right now is that your little friends lost interest and I was able to collect my belongings from the storage closet. So I thought I'd let you live long enough to have an opportunity to explain yourself, for entertainment's sake if nothing else."

Bronwyn held his eyes and said nothing. Ian smiled at her, his manner calm and solicitous as if he was speaking to a wayward child. He reached into the kitchen drawer beside him and pulled out a handgun.

"Perhaps this will jog your memory."

He'd just clicked off the safety when the front door slammed open against the wall and three agents ran as far as the kitchen doorframe, guns drawn. Jaq and Terry rounded the corner a few seconds later, guns trained on Ian, who, when he heard the front door open, had immediately pulled Bronwyn in front of him, gun to her head. He kept his eyes on Jaq as he reached across her chest and ripped every button off Bronwyn's shirt in one motion, leaving it hanging open, still holding the gun to her temple.

"You came here wearing a fucking wire?"

His voice was still calm as he looked down at her chest, then over at her phone still lying on the table. He looked down at her and knocked the barrel of the gun lightly against her skull.

"Ah, your phone. Clever. I have to admit, you got me on that one."

He hadn't even finished the last word before he flicked the gun toward the phone and shot it, then returned it to Bronwyn's head.

"Ian, we can get this done without anybody getting hurt," Terry said, putting his gun back in his holster slowly, eyes locked on Ian. "Don't make this worse for yourself. Let her go."

Ian laughed, tightening his arm around Bronwyn's throat, pulling her harder against his body. She struggled against his grip, her face a deep red, pulling down on his arm with her hands.

"Now why would I do that?" Ian said. "So she and her little girlfriend here can live happily ever after?"

Jaq locked eyes with Ian as he squeezed Bronwyn tighter, gun still at her temple. Neither one was looking at Bronwyn when she swung the heel of her hand up and back with all her strength, hitting him directly under his nose and snapping his head back. He reeled, his nose instantly spurting blood, and the gun went off as he fell into the table, the impact knocking it from his hand. He took Bronwyn with him, but she managed to slip out of his arm and kick the gun toward Terry. Jaq dove for Bronwyn, scooping her up in her arms and dropping to her knees a safe distance away, while the other officers put Ian in handcuffs.

"Baby," she said, her voice tight with panic, "tell me you're okay."

"I finally got to use one of the self-defense moves you taught me," Bronwyn said. Jaq heard one of the other officers calling for an ambulance, and it was only a matter of seconds before Terry was at her side.

"We need to find out where all that blood is coming from. It's too much to be just from Ian's nose," he said, opening Bronwyn's shirt to both sides. Jaq saw it first. A bullet had gone into the far upper left side of her chest.

"Oh my God, she's shot." The words came out as almost a whisper, and Terry took over as Bronwyn's eyes closed and she went unconscious, her body limp in Jaq's arms.

"Lay her down, Jaq," he said. "You've got to let her go so we can get pressure on that wound." He looked over his shoulder at the officers behind him, raising his voice. "And someone get that fucking ambulance here *now*."

Someone brought a tea towel, and Jaq held it to the wound, telling Bronwyn in as calm a voice as she could to stay with her, that the ambulance would be there soon. Backup officers filled the kitchen as Ian was taken out, still dripping blood. Jaq could hear the medical sirens in the distance.

She looked up at Terry. "She's got to make it."

Terry nodded. "She will, mate, she's a tough one." He held Jaq's eyes. "Keep talking to her."

Dark red blood covered Bronwyn's body, and the towel was

becoming increasingly soaked under Jaq's hand. Bronwyn's eyes suddenly fluttered open.

"The bastard shot me."

"We know, baby," Jaq said, "And those sirens you hear are coming to get us to the hospital."

Terry looked up at the wall behind Bronwyn. "Vanderwall," he shouted back at one of the officers, "get over to that hole in the wall there and tell me if it's a bullet hole."

Officer Vanderwall looked and nodded. "It's lodged in there, you can just see it."

"That's good news, Jaq," Terry said, stepping back as the medical team came through the door. "It's not still inside."

The medical team tried to get Jaq to step away, but she wouldn't until Terry pulled her back.

"You've got to let them do their jobs, Jaq." Terry kept his hands on Jaq's shoulders, both of them soaked with Bronwyn's blood. "She's going to make it, just give them room to work."

❖

Two hours later, Jaq and Terry were pacing the hospital waiting room floor, their clothes covered with Bronwyn's blood. Jaq had called Bronwyn's father on the way to the hospital. He was on location in Istanbul and immediately said he'd return to the UK as soon as he possibly could. Both Terry and Jaq asked the nurse at the front desk if there were any updates so many times that she finally went to the back to get the doctor to come out and speak to them out of self-preservation.

"Who's here with Bronwyn Charles?" the doctor asked as he rounded the corner from the hall, looking around the half-filled waiting room.

"We are." Jaq and Terry both said it at the same time.

"She's recovering now. She lost quite a bit of blood, but we're replacing it now and treating the wound."

"Is she going to be okay?" Jaq said.

"Barring any further complications, yes. The bullet went directly through the soft tissue of her shoulder, missing the major arteries and bone." He shook his head. "I don't know how she got so lucky—a centimeter to the right and it would have been in danger of nicking her heart."

"You're absolutely sure?" Color started flooding into Jaq's face again, and she suddenly felt weak at the knees.

The doctor smiled. "I'm sure, and you're welcome to go back there. She's conscious now. We've got to get some X-rays to make sure, but she may even be able to go home as soon as tomorrow, providing she stays on the antibiotics we give her."

The doctor turned to leave, then stopped and looked back at them. "Which one of you is Terry?"

"I am," Terry said, glancing at Jaq. "Why?"

"She said to tell you she's going to be fine, so there's no excuse to smoke those cigarettes she knows you've got with you."

Terry laughed and pulled the cigarettes out of his jacket pocket, dumping them into the waiting room trash on the way back down the hall to Bronwyn.

❖

The next morning, Bronwyn woke and turned to find Jaq in the chair beside her, reaching for her hand.

"You were supposed to go home after I went to sleep last night," she said, squeezing Jaq's hand and wincing as pain shot through her shoulder.

"I just said that so you'd get some rest, silly. I was never going to leave your side." Jaq looked at her watch. "I think it's time for your pain meds. They should be around with a shot to put in your IV in just a few minutes."

"You look awful," Bronwyn said, smiling and pulling Jaq closer.

"That's what a bullet through your girlfriend's shoulder and sleeping in a hospital chair will do for you." Jaq smiled and smoothed

Bronwyn's hair back from her face. "At least Moira brought me some fresh clothes after you were asleep last night. And left this for you."

Jaq reached over to the drawer and held up a *Chat* magazine and a huge bar of Cadbury chocolate.

Bronwyn sighed and laid back against the pillows. "God, I love her."

"She said in England everyone brings grapes to the hospital, but she thought you'd be dying for some chocolate."

"She's right."

Jaq looked at her watch again. "She and Catherine are actually at your house right now."

"Why?"

"Catherine hired a team of cleaners as soon as they'd released it as a crime scene, and Moira mentioned they were going over there to supervise this morning, which I think means they're pouring a pitcher of mimosas about now and gossiping about *Romance Island*."

"Catherine did that?" Bronwyn smiled, touched at how much trouble she'd gone to. *It can't have been easy*, she thought, as she remembered the slick of blood across the floor as they lifted her onto the stretcher. "She didn't have to go to do that."

"They love you. And you scared the life out of all of us yesterday."

There was a quiet knock, and Terry peeked around the door. "Feeling up to a visitor?"

"Of course." Bronwyn smiled and waved him in. "But I shouldn't even be here. I'm just waiting for them to clear me to go home."

Terry sank down in the chair by Jaq and shook his head at Bronwyn. "Let me just start by saying that you, my dear, are a badass."

Bronwyn laughed, and Jaq asked what was happening with Ian.

"The Phantom worked like a charm, and we have all the evidence we need to put him away for the next twenty years, if not longer. Now he's facing attempted murder charges as well, so they denied bail this morning. You won't have to worry about him for a long time."

Bronwyn leaned back against the pillows and closed her eyes. "I don't think I knew how scared I was until it was over."

"Well, all I know is you shattered his nose behind your back, took a bullet, then made sure the gun got to me before you hit the floor." Terry smiled. "Pretty much put the rest of us to shame."

Just then, the nurse came in with Bronwyn's pain medication, and Terry and Jaq stepped outside.

Terry looked back through the window at Bronwyn.

"Are they going to let her go home today?"

Jaq nodded. "They should let her out in a couple of hours, and I'm taking her back to my house."

"Good," Terry said. "I was hoping that was the case. Why don't you take a few days off next week? It'd make me feel better if someone was taking care of her, and I have to wrap up the paperwork on this one before we can move on anyway. I'll let you know when I'm done."

"Will you email me whatever I need to fill out? I can do it at home and get it back to you."

"Done." Terry smiled and turned to leave, but Jaq stopped him.

"I don't know what to say," she said. "Just…thank you."

Terry folded her into a hug and squeezed her hard before he let her go. "I'll pop round and check on you two in a couple of days," he said.

"Let me know when you're headed that way, and I'll have your lip gloss coffee ready," Jaq said, dodging a playful punch from Terry as he walked back down the hall.

❖

They released Bronwyn from the hospital a few hours later, and Jaq looked over at her as she pulled out of the parking lot. She was pale and quiet, and when Jaq covered her hand with her own, it was cold.

"I probably should have asked, but I was just planning on taking you back to the flat so I can keep an eye on you."

Bronwyn leaned her head back on the headrest and smiled. "That's exactly where I want to be."

The autumn sun warmed the side of her face, and she closed her eyes. She'd gotten so close. Until yesterday, she'd started to let herself believe she might have a future with Jaq Bailey. But deep down there was a part of her that had always known it wouldn't happen, and it turned out she was right.

Now she had a secret that was going to shatter that shiny new life into a thousand glittering shards.

Chapter Sixteen

Jaq came back in from picking up a takeaway for dinner and found Bronwyn curled up on the couch and staring into the night sky. She didn't look up as the door shut, so Jaq dropped the bags on the counter and went to sit with her, pulling her feet into her lap. They were like ice.

"Baby," she said, slipping them under her shirt and against her body to warm them, "what's on your mind? I can tell something's wrong."

A tear slid down Bronwyn's cheek, and she leaned her head back against the sofa. Jaq reached over and caught it with her thumb, then traced the edge of her face until Bronwyn looked at her.

"What is it, Bella?" she said. "Just tell me. Whatever it is, we'll make it right."

Bronwyn looked back out into the darkness beyond the windows. "Not this," she said, her voice barely above a whisper, as if she didn't have the energy to say the words. "Nothing will make this right."

Jaq waited, her hands stroking Bronwyn's legs. Her stomach tightened. She knew Bronwyn like she knew her own heart, and she'd never seen her like this.

"Baby, you've got to trust me," Jaq said. "I've loved you for half my life. I'm not going to stop now."

Tears slipped down both Bronwyn's cheeks. Her eyes never left the window.

"Are you hungry?"

She shook her head. Jaq looked at her for a moment and remembered what Bronwyn used to love when they were at school, the one thing that always seemed to make everything better.

"Can I run you a bath?"

She looked over at Jaq, her eyes softening. "Yes," she said, "I'd love that."

Jaq kissed her forehead and went to start the water. She'd asked Moira a while back what she thought Bronwyn would like, and bought her some bath oil at a posh high street store on her way home from work. She poured it under the running water and watched the white bubbles gather into a velvet blanket on the surface of the water, the scent of freesia rising with the steam to perfume the room.

She felt something on the edge of panic. Whatever Bronwyn was holding on to, it was big. She'd felt something between them the second she walked into her room at the hospital that first time. It hung in the air above them since, heavy and silent, suffocating.

"What is that amazing smell?"

Bronwyn walked into the bathroom, trying to twist her hair into a bun with one hand. It fell back down her shoulders twice, and she started to take off her sling to use her other hand.

"You're kidding me, right?" Jaq jumped up from her seat on the side of the tub to stop her. "That arm is off-limits." She tipped Bronwyn's chin up to kiss her. "Turn around."

Bronwyn turned and faced the mirror as Jaq swept her hair into a ponytail, then twisted it gently into a bun, securing it with the elastic.

"Where in the world did you learn to do that?"

Jaq smiled, unbuttoning her shirt and slipping it gently off her shoulders. "When I was still in Texas, there was a little girl that lived in the trailer next to ours. She came over one morning as I was leaving for the bus stop and asked me to put her hair in a ponytail. She was only about six. Her mom worked the overnight shift at the furniture factory and was always asleep by the time she had to get ready for school."

Jaq went to turn off the water in the tub and returned to remove

Bronwyn's sling, inching down her arm so she could slide her shirt the rest of the way off.

"I did my best, but it looked terrible. That day I gave my lunch money to one of the older girls at school so she'd teach me how to do a decent ponytail."

"It's harder than it looks, isn't it?"

"Damn straight," Jaq said, laughing. "It was two days before I actually had it down."

"Did she come over again?"

Jaq dropped to her knees and eased Bronwyn's jeans and panties down, pausing to let her step out of them.

"No, but I was so proud of myself for learning, I started stopping by every morning and doing her hair on the front step of her trailer before we walked to the bus stop. I even got her some cute hair things eventually and learned to French braid."

Jaq held Bronwyn's hand as she stepped into the tub and sank slowly down into the bubbles, resting her bandaged arm on the side.

"Before I left for Stratford, I spent hours teaching her to do it herself. She got the hang of it by the time I left."

Bronwyn leaned her head back against the tub and closed her eyes. Jaq sat on the counter, watching her. Somehow, it made her feel better that at least her feet had to be warm now.

"I can leave, Bella," Jaq said, looking at the door. "I think it's a pretty well-known fact that girls don't like to be stared at in the bathtub."

That finally got a smile out of Bronwyn, and she opened one eye.

"Will you get in with me?"

Jaq hesitated. "I don't want to jostle your arm and hurt you."

Bronwyn looked over at her and smiled. "And by that, you mean you don't want to smell like an English flower garden for the rest of the day?"

"That's exactly what I mean." Jaq raised an eyebrow at her.

"Get in, Bailey."

Jaq pulled off her shirt and undershirt and stepped out of her

• 201 •

jeans, leaving them in a pile on the bathroom counter. Bronwyn's eyes followed her as she slid her underwear down and walked over to the tub. She stepped in gently and eased in behind Bronwyn, pulling her slowly back between her legs to rest against her chest.

Bronwyn laid her head back against Jaq and let out a long, shaky breath.

"Are you going to tell me what's going on, Bella?"

Jaq whispered the words into her ear as she ran her fingertips over her wet skin. It was a long moment before Bronwyn spoke, and when she did, her words were as fragile as the steam rising off the water.

"I can't tell you this."

Jaq leaned her head back and stared at the ceiling. She felt the divide, felt it growing, pressing them apart, and it wasn't coming from her. It was coming from Bronwyn. The room was so quiet Jaq heard the bubbles popping on the surface of the water, and a single drop of water dripping from the faucet every four seconds. Finally, she felt Bronwyn's breath turn to tears and turned her gently to look into her eyes.

"Bella, do you remember how you felt when you waited for my letters and nothing came, day after day?"

Bronwyn nodded.

"That's how I feel now," Jaq said, trying to keep her voice from shaking. "I adore you. I'll love you for the rest of my life, but if you've changed your mind about us, you have to tell me."

Jaq traced her bottom lip with her thumb and kissed her forehead, then felt Bronwyn slip from her fingers as she turned back around and leaned back against Jaq's chest.

"Jaq, it's not that I've changed my mind." Her voice caught and she stopped. "It's that I don't want to hear that you have. I want to keep this, us, for every second I can before it ends."

Jaq gripped the side of the tub with one hand until her fingers were white, and smoothed the damp tendrils of hair away from Bronwyn's neck with the other.

"Bella, I know you don't believe me, but we're stronger than this. Just tell me."

She felt Bronwyn draw in a long breath, then let it out, trembling. When she spoke, she stared down and dropped the words into the water.

"I'm pregnant."

Her words melted into the heat of the water, then rose with the steam, surrounding them like a curtain. Jaq was stone still, silent. Bronwyn covered her face with her hands and started to cry, wishing she'd waited just one more day before it was over.

Then she felt both Jaq's hands slide around to cover her belly and her voice at her ear.

"We're pregnant?"

Bronwyn turned around to see Jaq's face already wet with tears. Then Jaq was kissing her, the salt from her tears on Bronwyn's lips, one of Jaq's hands tipping Bronwyn's face up to hers, the other still warm and protective around her belly.

"Why didn't you tell me?"

Bronwyn just shook her head.

"Bella," Jaq said, "I've wanted us to be a family since the first moment I looked into your eyes."

Bronwyn leaned into Jaq's chest, quiet sobs of relief shaking her enough to make her wince in pain. With Ian in prison for the next twenty years or more, him being a father to her child wasn't really an option, but it hadn't crossed her mind even once that Jaq might want to be.

Jaq kissed her, holding Bronwyn against her, whispering for her to settle.

"Wait," she said suddenly. "How did you find out? What about the gunshot, what did the doctor say? Is the baby okay?"

Jaq's hand that still hadn't left her belly calmed her, and Bronwyn smiled up at her for the first time.

"I found out when they took me back for the X-rays. They asked me if I could be pregnant and I remembered I hadn't had my period in a while. Everything has been so stressful, I figured that was why and never worried about it."

"And they did a test?"

"They did, and five minutes later the doctor came in and told

• 203 •

me I was going to have a baby." She paused, smiling, looking into Jaq's eyes. "That we're going to have a baby."

Jaq leaned back against the tub and shut her eyes. "Christ, I can't believe I let you go into that house with Ian when you were pregnant."

"I'm glad we didn't know. I wouldn't have taken the risk if I had, and he'd still be out there."

Jaq pulled her gently back into her arms. "What did the doctor say?"

Bronwyn winced. "I'll tell you everything, but I may need to get out and get my pain meds first. I'm almost two hours overdue."

"Wait, can you take those?" Jaq looked slightly panicked. "You're pregnant."

Bronwyn tried not to smile. "My doctor gave me specific non-narcotic medicine that's safe for my stage of pregnancy. It doesn't work nearly as well, but it's safe for the baby."

Jaq got out first, then gently helped Bronwyn step out of the tub.

"You don't need to fuss over me. I'm not that delicate." Bronwyn glanced at her shoulder for emphasis and looked up at Jaq, trying not to laugh at the worry on her face.

"Hell yes, I'm going to fuss over you," Jaq said, her brows pushed together. "You'll be lucky if I let you out of my sight at all for the next…" She hesitated, realizing she didn't yet know how far along she was.

"Six months," Bronwyn said, standing on tiptoe to kiss her. "I'm a little over three months along."

Jaq dried Bronwyn off and got her into pajamas and back into her sling, checking the wound for any bleed-through. Once they were dressed, Jaq warmed up their food and brought it to Bronwyn on the couch.

"Okay," Jaq said, too nervous to eat, "tell me everything the doctor said."

Bronwyn smiled, watching Jaq load up her plate with more lasagna and salad than any one person could eat. "She said the baby looks strong and healthy," she said, squeezing Jaq's thigh, "and that everything looks normal." She tore off a piece of garlic bread and dipped it in the sauce as she looked up at Jaq. "She did say she'd like to see me gain some weight in the next few weeks, but that was the only concern she had."

"Really?"

Bronwyn smiled, smoothing the worry lines on Jaq's forehead with her thumb. "Yes, really."

Jaq leaned back against the couch. "I didn't know it was possible to be this happy and this nervous at the same time."

Bronwyn looked over and her and hesitated. "Would you like to know the gender?"

Jaq leaned forward and kissed her, holding her face in her hands. "I'd love to know the sex, but I'll let him or her tell us the gender in a few years when they're ready."

Bronwyn put her plate aside and melted into Jaq, feeling her heart strain with the love that filled it. "I love you, Jaq Bailey," she whispered, sliding her hands under Jaq's shirt and across her bare back. "You're going to be the most amazing parent our child could ever wish for."

Jaq's phone rang just then, and she leaned over to pick it up. "It's your dad," she said. "He doesn't know your phone is gone, so I'll pick mine up and hand it over to you. Is that okay?"

Bronwyn nodded and Jaq answered the phone.

"Angus, I'm glad to hear from you. Are you at the airport?"

"I'm at Heathrow. I just got in from Istanbul." Jaq heard the airport loudspeakers in the background. "How's our girl?"

"She's great. I brought her home today and she's sitting right here beside me. I'll hand the phone to her now."

"Jaq?" He paused, the airport noise swirling around him. "I spoke to Terry. Thank you for being there for Bronwyn. I don't know what I would have done..." His voice trailed off.

"You never have to worry about that, sir." Jaq smiled, touched. "Here she is." She handed the phone to Bronwyn and finally picked up her fork as she listened to Bronwyn try to speak to her dad.

"I'm fine, Dad, stop fussing. It's barely a scratch." She paused and took a deep breath. "But Jaq and I have some news."

• 205 •

❖

A few days later, Bronwyn was going stir crazy but was still too sore to go out, so Jaq invited Moira and Catherine over to the flat. She made sure there was lots of drinks and Mexican food from the restaurant around the corner, along with a few non-alcoholic choices for Bronwyn. They arrived right on time, bursting past Jaq at the door and stopping just short of hugging Bronwyn.

"It's much better, guys," Bronwyn said, moving her shoulder for emphasis. "You can hug me."

The girls hugged her from one side and kissed her, all of them chattering at once, and settled on the barstools around the chips and salsa Jaq had put out on the counter.

"There are margaritas in the fridge, ladies," Jaq said. "But I'm afraid I have somewhere I have to be." She came over and held Bronwyn's face in her hands for just a second. "I'll have my phone. Call me for anything."

Bronwyn kissed her and whispered in her ear before she turned back to the girls. As Jaq pulled her coat on at the door, she looked over at the love of her life, laughing with her friends. Her eyes were sparkling, her cheeks flushed pink with excitement, and there was the tiniest baby bump beginning to show if you knew to look.

Everything was different now. For the first time in her life, she had a family.

❖

An hour later, Jaq sat at the bar, waiting, scotch untouched in front of her. Another glass sat beside it, wordlessly waiting with her. Everything looked exactly as it had when she'd been there in high school, down to the pig made of hammered copper behind the bar. She straightened her tie and looked at her watch for the third time in sixty seconds. It'd been almost thirteen years since she'd been there, and she was more nervous now than she had been then.

"Jaq." Angus came through the door and shook the rain off his overcoat, hanging it on the hook by the fireplace. "I'm sorry I'm late. It seems all of London's traffic was conspiring against me."

Jaq stood and shook his hand, and they sat, Angus picking up the scotch and taking a short sip. He let it roll around his mouth before he swallowed.

"Laphroaig Islay single malt." The energy in the air shifted. He looked over at Jaq. "This must be a special occasion."

Jaq took a deep breath, the words just out of her grasp. Angus waited, then clapped a hand on Jaq's shoulder.

"Jaq, it's just us," he said. "We've been straight with each other since the first time we were here. Whatever you have to say, just say it."

Jaq cleared her throat. "I'm not sure when I'm going to ask her," she said, meeting his eyes, "but before I do, I'd like to ask your permission to marry your daughter."

The bartender passed just then and Angus asked him for the bottle of Laphroaig, sliding his card across the bar. He nodded and stepped past the door to the cellar just behind the bar, closing it behind him.

"Jaq, you've had my approval for thirteen years," Angus said, raising his glass. "I'd be proud to call you family."

Jaq let out the breath she didn't realize she was holding and clinked her glass to Angus's as the bartender rounded the corner of the bar, carrying a dusty bottle of scotch with the yellowed label. Angus held it up to the light and topped off their glasses, then reached into his jacket pocket and took out a thick leaf of papers, folded in thirds, and pushed it toward Jaq.

Jaq looked up. "What's this?"

"Bronwyn told me you two were expecting, as you know, so I called in a favor at the Yard and paid Ian a little visit yesterday."

Jaq nodded, not sure where Angus was going with this.

Angus smoothed his hand over the papers. "I had a feeling you and I would be having this drink at some point, so I had my solicitor draw up some documents for me."

Jaq opened the papers and smoothed them flat, reading the pages faster than she turned them. "He signed them." Jaq's voice caught. "I can't believe it."

"I asked him how much it would take, and he gave me a lowball number." He took a sip of his scotch and looked at it appreciatively, holding it up to the light. "He's an idiot. I would have paid ten times that amount to get him to sign away any rights he had to that baby. I was out of there in ten minutes flat, done and dusted."

"So I can legally adopt our child?"

Jaq and Angus clinked glasses again.

Done and dusted.

❖

Moira leaned over Bronwyn and grabbed the pitcher of margarita. She topped up her glass and Catherine's, then paused, pitcher aloft.

"Wait, where's your glass?"

"I'm good," Bronwyn said, suddenly very interested in the cheese dip. "I've got water." Silence fell as Moira and Catherine looked at each other then back at Bronwyn.

"Spill it, B." Moira put the pitcher down with a *thunk* and leaned forward in anticipation.

Bronwyn just smiled and nodded.

"You're pregnant! I knew it!" Catherine squealed, followed by the same declaration by Moira. "How far along?"

"A little more than three months. I didn't know until they did a test at the hospital after the thing with Ian."

Catherine scooped up some cheese dip and sat back on her stool. "All I'm saying is that Jaq must have some serious skills."

Bronwyn laughed so hard she had to wipe her eyes. "That's the official story," she said finally, her hand on her belly. "We're definitely going with that."

❖

A few days later, Jaq came through the door after work to find Bronwyn painting by the window, her easel angled to catch the last of the fading evening light.

"Where did you get that?" Jaq said, kissing her and looking under her shirt to check her bandage. "Although I don't know why I'm asking." Jaq winked at her as she eased her shirt back over her shoulder. "I know you just trotted out to the art supply store and hauled this up the stairs like you weren't just shot a few days ago."

Bronwyn leaned into Jaq, untucked her shirt, and slipped her hands across the strong lines of her back. "I had the guy at the front desk bring them up for me, but only because I knew you'd ask."

"Smart girl," Jaq said, leaning into her neck and running her tongue along the edge of her ear. She circled Bronwyn's hips with her hands and gently pressed them into hers. Bronwyn closed her eyes as Jaq's thumb found her chin, holding it up as she kissed her neck, stopping at the base with a soft bite that she followed with her tongue.

"It's unfair to look so beautiful if I can't just pick you up and take you to bed," Jaq whispered, her hands slipping under Bronwyn's sweater and around the warm curves of her breasts.

"God, I'd love that," Bronwyn said, closing her eyes and leaning into Jaq. "But we need to leave here in just a few minutes if we're going to be on time for dinner." She paused and looked up at the clock. "We have a couple of people expecting us."

❖

As soon as Jaq opened the restaurant door, Azran and Zahaar came running up from behind the counter, this time greeting both of them as Bronwyn knelt down and pressed something into both their hands.

"What was that?" Jaq had to laugh as the boys took off at breakneck speed through the kitchen doors. She took Bronwyn's coat and hung it by the door with her own just as the owner came out and showed them to a table. His wife waved at them from the kitchen, her white apron streaked with cardamom powder.

• 209 •

"None of your business, Detective Bailey," Bronwyn teased, settling back into her seat and smiling.

Jaq ordered a glass of white wine for herself and a bottle of sparkling water for Bronwyn as she loosened her tie, rolling up her sleeves and taking Bronwyn in from across the table. She was wearing the black cashmere cardigan and faded jeans, her hair falling around her face as she tucked it behind her ear and pushed her glasses up further on her nose. Her eyes were soft as she looked back at Jaq, and reached across the table for her hand.

"So I got a call from my mum today," she said. "She's in surprisingly good form."

"What did she say?"

"She actually apologized for the brunch disaster. And she's staying an extra month at the spa, so I think that's a good sign."

"Did you tell her you're pregnant?"

"God no." Bronwyn laughed. "I was afraid it would drive her to drink."

A fragrant dish of chicken karahi arrived then, along with two plates, and Jaq dished it up, tucking an extra piece of naan onto Bronwyn's plate.

Jaq started eating, but Bronwyn just pushed her food around on her plate, biting her lower lip.

"What?"

"How did you know I was going to say something?"

Jaq just looked at her and raised an eyebrow. Bronwyn let out a breath and took a sip of her sparkling water.

"I know everything is happening fast," she said, twisting the edge of her napkin in her fingers. "And I know you love your loft. I love it too…" Her voice trailed off and she looked up at Jaq.

Jaq tried not to smile. She'd always been unbelievably cute when she was nervous. Jaq had a good idea of what she'd wanted to say even before she started, so she decided to help her a bit.

"I like the loft," Jaq said, running her thumb lightly across Bronwyn's palm, "but I love you."

Bronwyn smiled, the tension easing just a bit. "I was just thinking. We may need a bigger place with the baby coming, like a family home."

"Like maybe one in Notting Hill across from the park?"

Bronwyn smiled. "I think I know just the one."

The twins walked up to the table just then and looked at Bronwyn, who took Zahaar's hand and gently pulled him over to switch places with his brother. They both looked at her expectantly, their big brown eyes reflecting the candle on the table until Bronwyn smiled and nodded.

Azran extended his hand to Jaq, revealing a crumpled piece of paper.

Jaq picked it up and smoothed it out, noticing their mother peering out from the kitchen door, smiling. It was just three words, in Bronwyn's handwriting.

It's a girl.

Jaq held the paper in her hand and closed her eyes, not noticing the tear that slipped onto her cheek when she finally opened them.

"Really?"

Bronwyn smiled, nodding at Zahaar. He held his arm straight out toward Jaq and opened his hand to reveal an identical crumpled note. Jaq took it, looking over at Bronwyn as she smoothed it out enough to read.

This time, anyway.

The boys ran away giggling toward their mother, and Jaq took Bronwyn's hand and held it to her heart. Her voice was soft.

"You'd have more children with me, Bella?"

"In a heartbeat."

Jaq saw those children reflected in her eyes, the eyes like the forest floor, as she took Bronwyn's face in her hands and kissed her.

About the Author

Patricia Evans Jordan has been slinging ink and falling in love with her characters since her boarding school days and continues to write in her hometown of Eureka Springs, surrounded by the forest that inspires her.

Patricia has lived in Ireland and England and returns there frequently to write, as well as to a much loved tiny island off the coast of Glasgow, where the owner of the local pub saves her the red velvet chair by the fire. More of her writing can be seen at her website, www.tomboyinkslinger.com, or her Instagram at www.instagram.com/tomboyinkslinger.

Books Available From Bold Strokes Books

Accidentally in Love by Kimberly Cooper Griffin. Nic and Lee have good reasons for keeping their distance. So why does their growing attraction seem more like a love-hate relationship? (978-1-63679-759-5)

Frosted by the Girl Next Door by Aurora Rey and Jaime Clevenger. When heartbroken Casey Stevens opens a sex shop next door to uptight cupcake baker Tara McCoy, things get a little frosty. (978-1-63679-723-6)

Ghost of the Heart by Catherine Friend. Being possessed by a ghost was not on Gwen's bucket list, but she must admit that ghosts might be real, and one is obviously trying to send her a message. (978-1-63555-112-9)

Hot Honey Love by Nan Campbell. When chef Stef Lombardozzi puts her cooking career into the hands of filmmaker Mallory Radowski—the pickiest eater alive—she doesn't anticipate how hard she'll fall for her. (978-1-63679-743-4)

London by Patricia Evans. Jaq's and Bronwyn's lives become entwined as dangerous secrets emerge and Bronwyn's seemingly perfect life starts to unravel. (978-1-63679-778-6)

This Christmas by Georgia Beers. When Sam's grandmother rigs the Christmas parade to make Sam and Keegan queen and queen, sparks fly, but they can't forget the Big Embarrassing Thing that makes romance a total nope. (978-1-63679-729-8)

Unwrapped by D. Jackson Leigh. Asia du Muir is not going to let some party-girl actress ruin her best chance to get noticed by a Broadway critic. Everyone knows you should never mix business and pleasure. (978-1-63679-667-3)

The First Kiss by Patricia Evans. As the intrigue surrounding her latest case spins dangerously out of control, military police detective Parker

Haven must choose between her career and the woman she's falling in love with. (978-1-63679-775-5)

Language Lessons by Sage Donnell. Grace and Lenka never expected to fall in love. Is home really where the heart is if it means giving up your dreams? (978-1-63679-725-0)

New Horizons by Shia Woods. When Quinn Collins meets Alex Anders, Horizon Theater's enigmatic managing director, a passionate connection ignites, but amidst the complex backdrop of theater politics, their budding romance faces a formidable challenge. (978-1-63679-683-3)

Scrambled: A Tuesday Night Book Club Mystery by Jaime Maddox. Avery Hutchins makes a discovery about her father's death that will force her to face an impossible choice between doing what is right and finally finding a way to regain a part of herself she had lost. (978-1-63679-703-8)

Stolen Hearts by Michele Castleman. Finding the thief who stole a precious heirloom will become Ella's first move in a dangerous game of wits that exposes family secrets and could lead to her family's financial ruin. (978-1-63679-733-5)

Synchronicity by J.J. Hale. Dance, destiny, and undeniable passion collide at a summer camp as Haley and Cal navigate a love story that intertwines past scars with present desires. (978-1-63679-677-2)

Wild Fire by Radclyffe & Julie Cannon. When Olivia returns to the Red Sky Ranch, Riley's carefully crafted safe world goes up in flames. Can they take a risk and cross the fire line to find love? (978-1-63679-727-4)

Writ of Love by Cassidy Crane. Kelly and Jillian struggle to navigate the ruthless battleground of Big Law, grappling with desire, ambition, and the thin line between success and surrender. (978-1-63679-738-0)

BOLDSTROKESBOOKS.COM

Looking for your next great read?

Visit **BOLDSTROKESBOOKS.COM**
to browse our entire catalog of paperbacks, ebooks,
and audiobooks.

Want the first word on what's new?
Visit our website for event info,
author interviews, and blogs.

Subscribe to our free newsletter for sneak peeks,
new releases, plus first notice of promos
and daily bargains.

SIGN UP AT
BOLDSTROKESBOOKS.COM/signup

Bold Strokes Books
Quality and Diversity in LGBTQ Literature

*Bold Strokes Books is an award-winning publisher
committed to quality and diversity in LGBTQ fiction.*

Printed in the USA
CPSIA information can be obtained
at www.ICGtesting.com
CBHW020718081024
15421CB00001B/22

9 781636 797786